GW00370637

'It is often rash to predict the evidence of a first novel . . . bu Stuart Evers does not prove to be the real thing. This first novel is a fine achievement, something to savour. When I had finished it, I went back and read it again, and it seemed even better second time round.' Allan Massie, *Scotsman*

'Evers knocks out enviably beautiful prose, and the humming, affled, air-conditioned neverland of Las Vegas is conjured p with a captivating and woozy effect . . . A compelling book' *The Times*

'A ghost story, a murder mystery, a voyage of self-discovery . . . Wilkinson is such a familiar character, someone who follows his dreams only to find that life doesn't turn out the way it does in the movies. A quiet triumph' *Observer*

'Sparky, edgy and bursting with energy . . . an incredibly entertaining read' *Stylist*

'Clean and elegant; his sentences are unadorned, downbeat and honest . . . Evers is a talent for the future – of that, I think, there's little doubt' *Sunday Telegraph*

'A deft, affecting piece of work about possibility and identity. It heralds a fresh, new voice' *Irish Times*

'This is a hugely original, unforgettable debut that we've been telling all our friends to read . . . Both gut-churning and beautifully written, this is a must read.' *Easy Living*

'Evers is exceptionally good at dialogue: the cascading monologues of a taxi driver, hairdresser and bitter photographer made me simultaneously wince in recognition and smile'

Independent on Sunday

'The novel picks up a thriller-like pace, weaving in the odd, sometimes devastating twist, and marking Evers as an author with storytelling substance' *Timeout*

'Evers lights upon numerous themes, from the long-lasting effects of trauma to the reliability of memory' *Sunday Times*

'Evers manages to land every dramatic punch, with a final twist that has devastating implications . . . this is a fresh and eccentric novel that isn't afraid of attending to the broader pleasures.' *Spectator*

'Evers captures the frustration of adolescence and the lingering pain of careless destruction with sharp, flowing prose and a propulsive structure' *Metro*

'Don Draper style northern chancer flees to Vegas to escape his past . . . troubling and hypnotic.' *Elle*

'A sophisticated debut.' *Big Issue in the North*

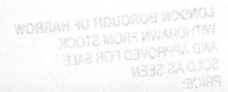

IF THIS IS HOME

Stuart Evers' debut, *Ten Stories About Smoking*, won the 2011 London Book Award and was longlisted for the Frank O'Connor Prize. *If This Is Home* is his first novel.

Also by Stuart Evers

Ten Stories About Smoking

STUART EVERS

IF THIS IS HOME

PICADOR

First published 2012 by Picador

First published in paperback 2013 by Picador
an imprint of Pan Macmillan, a division of Macmillan Publishers Limited
Pan Macmillan, 20 New Wharf Road, London N1 9RR
Basingstoke and Oxford
Associated companies throughout the world
www.panmacmillan.com

ISBN 978-1-4472-0763-4

1 3 5 7 9 8 6 4 2

A CIP catalogue record for this book is available from the British Library.

Printed and bound by CPI Group (UK) Ltd, Croydon, CR0 4YY

Visit **www.picador.com** to read more about all our books
and to buy them. You will also find features, author interviews and
news of any author events, and you can sign up for e-newsletters
so that you're always first to hear about our new releases.

L.I.B.

ONE

From the fifth floor of the Valhalla, I looked down onto the small courtyard. The slow dazzle of the sun on the pool, the palm fronds and sunloungers, the absolute stillness of the desert. I had been there for some time, waiting. I was sweating, shirtless. My running shoes were unlaced and the men were late. Without them, I couldn't leave. They arrived and then I went. It was the way it worked.

Eventually, they pushed through the double doors, talking and jostling. Some passed out beers from a coolbox, others opened buckets of fried chicken, many took their places on loungers by the pool. Their work finished for the week, money in the pockets of their overalls, the men formed loose groups: the younger ones in the sunshine, bills of caps and Ray-Bans shading their eyes; the older ones, bellies lolling over belt buckles, under the wooden awning. Cigarettes were produced from rolled-up sleeves, balls were tossed lazily over the water, card games were played with the mildest of intensity. Every week the same.

I'd given some of them names: Stevedore, the foreman; Moustache, one of the plasterers; Skinny, who wore the tightest of jeans; and Baggy, whose underwear was constantly on show. Sometimes I'd wave at them, even though they could not see me, but I was too tired to wave then. Instead I put my hand on the glass and looked for Stevedore. He was not in his usual place, but standing in close communion with another of the older guys. His arms were expressive; his companion nodding slowly along with him. It looked like conspiracy, or paranoia. Stevedore became increasingly animated, his hands making fists, then relaxing. He stopped talking and shook his head.

Over by the lazy palms, Moustache had emerged, a ghetto-blaster mounted on his sloping shoulder. The music must have been loud. All I could hear was the usual gymnasium noises: the machines, the air conditioning, the silent televisions. But down there, some of the older men were putting fingers in their ears and Moustache was nodding his head in time to the music. He nodded and then began to dance.

Moustache danced towards Stevedore, swaying his hips left and right. Some of the old men got up from their loungers, but they didn't try to stop him. He moved provocatively, like he was trying to impress a girl after drinking too much. Beside the pool, the younger men started clapping and Moustache rewarded them with a shake of his behind.

Stevedore could have been a football player once, the shape he was in. When he wasn't wearing protective head-gear he always wore a cowboy hat. O'Neil and I were a little afraid of him; Moustache didn't seem to care, though.

Moustache shimmied until he was right in front of Stevedore, then grabbed at his own crotch and began pumping his hips. The younger crowd continued to applaud. They clapped until the first beer can was thrown.

Moustache fielded missiles from both sides; laughing, one hand on his crotch, the other covering his eyes. He was still laughing when he took a can of Bud Lite to the face. There was no blood when he touched his hand to his head. Another can hit him on the arm, but he didn't seem to notice. The men stayed still, paused. Moustache kept touching his head. Stevedore looked at the ground, his wide smile slowly diminishing.

Momentarily the sun reflected off the pool, shining directly into my eyes. I looked the other way and buried my head into a towel. When I finally looked back the men were gone. The only sign they'd been there at all was the cans and long-necked bottles spilling out from the litter bin. I looked left and right, but couldn't see a baseball cap or ghetto-blaster anywhere. The pool was still, the palms splayed. There was just the courtyard and the desert, dimmed by the smoked glass of the Valhalla.

'Makes you want to jump right in, doesn't it?' Edith said. I saw her pale reflection in the glass, her head cocked to one side. I looked down. My shorts were wet at the crotch and at the seat.

'There were . . .' I said, turning to Edith. 'I don't know, but there was just . . .' But I didn't know what to say about the men. Perhaps there was nothing to say.

'Am I late?' I looked at where my watch should have been.

'Later than usual,' Edith said. She pushed herself away from me and walked across the floorboards. 'I went up to your room and no one was home. Figured you'd be here.' She paused by the treadmill and picked up my T-shirt. She balled it up and threw it at me.

'Come on,' she said, 'time's a-ticking.'

*

Edith never spoke to fill a silence. She was always careful with her words, as though they were precious commodities, niggardly rationed. Usually I was comfortable with that. As we took the lift up to my apartment the atmosphere was thin enough to split. As usual she was dressed impeccably. But she wore her slim black trousers, white blouse and pale blue necktie somewhat stiffly, like they

4

were borrowed clothes. Her hair was loosely tied back and I could smell tobacco beneath the perfume she'd used to disguise it. When the doors opened, Edith looked up as if to say something, then thought better of it. Instead she hummed a tune. She was still humming as we walked down the corridor towards my apartment.

The tune sounded familiar and I hummed along with her, following her lead. She looked at me with irritation and I fell silent. She started again, this time on her own. I shook my head and opened the door.

'You could have tidied up,' she said, 'you live like a pig.'

She thought this was funny: my rooms were always neat to the point of fastidiousness. The apartment was cool from the air conditioning and darkened by Venetian blinds. It was a vast octagonal space scented with pine cones and wax polish. On one wall were two Rothko prints, their colours complementing the scarlet rugs and pitch-pine floorboards; on the other a large television. The other rooms, all vast, were similarly clinical.

Edith settled herself on the far end of the sofa and removed a series of files from her tote bag. I went to the kitchen area to make coffee. As I opened the cupboard she continued to hum her ten-note tune.

'What *is* that?' I said, heaping coffee grounds into the filter paper. She looked up. Her eyes were framed by thick-rimmed spectacles. There was a quick look of panic behind the lenses, then a tightening of the mouth.

'What's what?' Edith said.

'That tune you've been humming.' I hummed back the notes.

'I don't know,' she said and shrugged. 'Just a song I heard, I guess.' She picked up a file and placed it on the coffee table, as if to close the matter.

'Oh come on, Edie,' – she scowled – 'you've been humming it all morning. You must have some idea.'

Edith shook her head.

'Please try to remember,' I said, joining her on the sofa. 'I know that I know it. It's going to drive me crazy otherwise.'

'I told you I don't know,' Edith said. She handed me a file. 'Now shush. Time for work.'

*

My partner O'Neil took to calling these 'strategy and intelligence meetings'. It was a private joke from back when we worked in the over-ripe sales offices of Brooklyn. In those days every meeting had a fancy name. Strategy and intelligence. Research and implementation. Experience and expectation. The names changed, but the content remained broadly the same: lay down the targets; belittle the weak; talk about the money.

The Valhalla was different. O'Neil may have joked about their names, but all the meetings were taken with the utmost seriousness. Selling the concept of the Valhalla was all about the details. The minutiae. The added knowledge that could force through a sale. We were selling a dream, after all. The guy who owned it, Mac – a man we had never seen or met – had been a whale watcher before he made it big: a slave to the whims of the high rollers whom casinos were desperate to keep happy. According to Paul, back at head office, Mac had become frustrated at not being able to give his clients everything they desired, so he'd quit. The Valhalla was his answer. By 2003, he'd sold over three-quarters of the apartments. It had become the place where dreams really could become reality.

*

'This is Brooks,' Edith said, passing me a photograph. It was a black-and-white shot of an expensively styled man. He was in his late thirties and his white-toothed grin looked stolen from a magazine. I leafed through his file. The only missing information was his place and date of birth, his contact details and real name. Otherwise it was a disturbingly frank picture of a man's interior life.

Originally, or so Paul told me, Mac had made the clients fill out a long questionnaire. They'd checked boxes

– their interests, sexual preferences and other requirements – but the results had been mixed. There had been
no way of gauging whether buyers were getting what they
really wanted. Mac wanted them to be surprised by the
sophistication of their desires; needed them to think that
their fantasies could only come true at the Valhalla. For
the first months, sales were sluggish to the point of total
collapse. In the end, Paul hit upon an idea. Sex-line oper-
ators. One phone call from a breathy, coaxing voice was
enough to reveal even the darkest of customers' wishes.

Brooks was the primary lead for the sale. The rest of
the group were there to make up the numbers. They
would probably invest in one of the smaller properties
on the ninth or twelfth floors. After three nights at the
Valhalla, very few now opted against some form of invest-
ment. But Brooks was the key: he had the money and the
hubris to spare. We hoped he'd go for the one remaining
penthouse.

'And this is Boulder, Miller and Hooper,' Edith said
passing me three more portraits. They were nondescript,
bored-looking: white and wealthy. I returned to Brooks.
He was like a cross between the Hooded Claw and a
young Jimmy Stewart. His face belonged behind the curtain of a nightmare.

'Are you there, Joe?' Edith said.

'Was I humming?' I said.

Edith took off her glasses and kneaded her eyes.

'No, Joe. You just weren't paying attention.'

'I was,' I said, 'I was just . . . you know earlier on, when I was in the gym? I was looking out of the window and I saw these, well, workmen, down in the courtyard by the pool, and they were drinking and eating. And I just thought: how simple is that? Imagine that.'

It wasn't what I was thinking. I was still humming; humming and thinking about the picture of Brooks.

'What are you talking about, Joe?' she said. 'Workmen by the pool? You're picking these guys up in two hours.' She got up from the sofa and made for the kitchen. There were two loud bangs as she slammed down a pair of coffee mugs.

'I'm losing the will to live here, Joe,' she shouted from behind the breakfast bar. 'If you're testing me, you're winning, okay?'

Edith filled the mugs and brought them over to the table. She put them down but didn't sit. Instead she looked down on me. Her cheeks coloured a little and something went off in her eyes. She picked up the stack of files and threw them to the floor. The papers and photos and photocopies scattered everywhere.

'I've tried so hard with you,' she said. 'So help me God, Joe, if I haven't tried my best, but the way you treat me? The way you act . . . ?'

9

There was a portrait near to me – Boulder, I think – and I moved to pick it up.

'Don't touch it, okay? Just fucking leave it where it is, okay . . . And don't give me that look. It's like you think I'm a piece of shit, you know that?'

It was probably the first time Edith had sworn in my company. She picked up her mug, blew on her coffee. I looked at the television, then at the window, then the files on the floor. I thought that maybe she was cracking up. I'd never thought that she'd be the first one to freak.

'I can't keep on excusing you,' she said and started fishing in her purse. 'Excusing you and letting others excuse you too. I don't see why it is that you get a free ride when the rest of us—'

'Hold on, Edith,' I said. 'What am I supposed to have done?' She kept rummaging in her bag and then took out a packet of cigarettes.

'It's everything, Joe,' she said. 'Every week the same: you look at me as if I'm stupid. Like you're the only one that knows anything in the whole world. And no one says anything. No one! And I'm sick of it.'

She lit her cigarette with a book of Peppermill Restaurant and Bar matches and wandered off towards the windows. She coughed, then looked back over her shoulder, a look of anger and pity.

'You're not making any sense, Edith. I don't know what's wrong, but—'

She started picking up the photos and files with a conviction bordering on aggression.

'You want to know what's wrong?' she said, laughing, her head bowed and the paper scraping on the floor. She looked up. 'You want to know what's wrong, Joe? You really want to know? You go ask O'Neil, okay? You go ask him.'

'What the hell does that mean?' I said, but she ignored me and bundled up the papers in her arms and dumped them on the table. She rubbed her hands on her trousers like she was wiping off something unpleasant.

'You have work to do,' she said calmly. 'Maybe afterwards it'll all become clear.'

She crossed the room and slammed the door. I hummed the tune again and then I heard the words. *You won't know what you're missing.*

In moments of crisis, Bethany Wilder always thinks of America. Or more accurately, she thinks of New York City. It is just past midnight and she is lying in the bath, smoking a cigarette, imagining its streets and buildings, the sights and sidewalks. Open in her hand is a guidebook that lives permanently in the bathroom and has become bloated and warped from the damp. Whenever she turns a page, the spine cracks and crumples. She's read the book so many times she knows its words as surely as song lyrics.

The first sentence is her favourite: *New York City is a metropolis of unimaginable contrasts; a haphazard, beautiful, maddening construction that cannot help but entrance even the most jaded of travellers.* In her edition there is a pencil annotation alongside the words *haphazard, beautiful, maddening* that reads *Just like you.* Usually those smudgy letters give her a small kick of pleasure; but now she avoids even glancing at the looping script. She doesn't want to be reminded. Not tonight.

The bathroom is up on the top floor of the house, a dark space with peeling claret wallpaper and stained oak floorboards. The bath – a claw-footed tub with a complicated shower attachment – sits in the middle of the room. Bethany flicks ash from her cigarette and imagines that the room looks out onto an autumnal Central Park or perhaps a sun-bleached Washington Square. Unlike the rest of the house, the bathroom has not been renovated: it is easy, then, to persuade herself that it has been transported across the Atlantic and into an East Village brownstone or tenement.

Her cigarette is almost down to its filter, the orange paper sagging as she takes her last drag. The coal hisses as Bethany drops it into a coffee cup, closes her eyes and blows out a long, fading trail of smoke. She hears herself talking to Daniel, his eyes wide as she speaks, her chin leant on her fist, a cigarette almost to her lip. In the bath, she colours; shocked almost as much by her confidence as by the recollection of what she said. She shakes her head and opens her eyes. She reminds herself that she doesn't have to go through with it, and turns the page.

The water is cooler now, she has been in there for almost an hour, and her skin is puckered and lightly pink. No matter what happens, he will not see her naked. This she has decided. If he wants to imagine her body, Daniel will have to piece her together from touch, like a blind man. Assuming she lets him do anything to her after all.

Bethany knows three girls who have slept with Daniel. One afternoon, while they were outside school, smoking, Claire admitted that she'd been with him. She said that his cock was thick like a gym rope. Bethany had rolled her eyes, but she'd been intrigued enough to kiss him around the back of the Red Lion, intrigued enough to almost put her hand there. When she'd seen him again, he'd called her 'the one that got away'. He was the kind of boy who could say that; a boy then, a man now; twenty-something and no longer at home, twenty-something with his band and his unshakable belief in himself. The other night, he'd called her 'the one that got away' again and she'd looked him up and down and said, 'Good things come to those who wait.'

She turns the page to a street map of Manhattan. The lines look so crisp and defined. With a slender finger she traces a route across the island, from Port Authority down to the Bowery. Around mid-town, she pauses for a moment and forces herself to think about Mark.

*

Three nights before he smelled of refuse and garlic, his hands scrubbed raw from the restaurant kitchens. They were in her room. It was late and despite everything – not least the smell – they made love with some urgency. She started it, pushing him onto the bed and removing her top with a determined swishing movement. It was over quickly. They shared a cigarette looking up through the skylight, watching the stars and aeroplane tail lights as they flew over.

'How long now?' Bethany asked.

'Five days,' Mark said. 'Four once we get to midnight.'

'I still can't believe it,' she said. 'You dream about something for so long, and then . . .'

'Don't you ever worry?' he said. 'You know, that you'll be disappointed?'

She kissed him just below the ear.

'Sometimes. But then I think, hey, it's New York fucking City.'

They laughed and talked for the hundredth time about what they'd do, what they'd see; how they'd find a way to never come back, to never return. They kissed, fooled around a little more, then looked at the clock. He would have to leave soon. The thought made her light-headed.

*

Bethany is eighteen years old and this memory already feels like nostalgia. She has lived in the town all her life. She talks at length to anyone who will listen about why this place is the worst of all worlds, a penitentiary – she uses the American deliberately – for those with a lack of imagination. She can trace it back, this desire to escape, to idly listening to her father's record collection: Simon & Garfunkel first, then Dylan. She listened to *The Free-wheelin' Bob Dylan* over and over, the album sleeve in her hand, wishing she was the woman on Dylan's arm. As a lonely fourteen-year-old, her greatest friend, or so she liked to think, was the idea of New York City: neon-lit, coffee-scented, like a far-away lover with whom she had scant contact.

Downstairs the phone rings but she does not move to answer it. It will be Mark, she suspects. It keeps ringing while she dries her hair with a towel, then it stops. Wearing a bathrobe she pads across the narrow hallway and into her bedroom, trailing an ellipsis of water behind her.

Her room is cluttered with things: records and cassettes, books and shucked clothes. The wardrobe door is half off its hinges and more clothes spill out of the gap. On the wall there's a Ramones poster that Mark bought for her. She puts on the Velvet Underground and sits at her desk. She picks up a book then sets it back down.

There is a knock on the door, a pause, and then her father walks into her room. He is dressed in a salmon-pink polo shirt and grey slacks. He is red-faced from the wine at dinner.

'We're back,' he says, though there's only been him for some years. 'Everything okay?' he says.

'Fine,' she says. 'Just had a bath.'

He scratches at his stubble as she applies moisturizer to her face.

'How was dinner?' she says.

'Fine, thanks,' he says. 'Saw lover boy there.'

'Oh?'

He shook his head. 'I didn't say anything. He looked busy. I do like him, though, that Mark. He's a good egg.'

'I wish you wouldn't say that,' she says, shuddering. 'It makes you sound like an old man.'

Her father sits down on his daughter's bed. The sheets smell freshly laundered and he wonders at how he has managed to raise a child that changes her own bedclothes without having been told.

'I don't know how you listen to this,' he says pointing toward the hi-fi. 'It's like nails scraping on a blackboard. Proper slit your wrists stuff.'

'You always say that,' she says, her face oily with the cream. 'Don't you ever get bored of saying the same things over and over again?'

'I wish I had the time to be bored,' he says. 'Being bored is a luxury only afforded to the young.'

'You always say that, too,' she says.

'Well, I'm nothing if not predictable.'

Bethany shakes her head. 'And that.'

He stands and puts a hand in his pocket, feels the money there, the sharp edge of another business card. He puts his hands on Bethany's shoulders. They look at each other in the mirror. As the track changes there is a crackle from the vinyl.

'Would you like a glass of wine, love?' he says. 'I'm going to have one. We could watch telly for a bit. Or a video or something.'

'Oh, come on, Dad,' she says, looking at the clock on her dresser. 'It's after twelve and I've got to be up early for this bloody carnival that I'm only doing because—'

'I know, love, I know,' he says calmly, and begins to massage her shoulders. 'But I just wanted to know what's new with you. We don't get to speak so much these days.'

She could tell him, but doesn't.

'Well, I'm up the duff,' she says. 'And I still owe my dealer for the last of the skag.'

He laughs and kisses her on the top of her head. 'And you say I'm predictable.'

He looks over to the easy chair where a ballgown billows under cellophane wrapping. The dress is white with pastel-pink and blue petticoats. He can't recall the last time he saw her wear anything that wasn't black or grey, and can't quite imagine her frame clad in this puff-ball of fabric. He picks it up and feels the softness of the material. It reminds him of the satin slips that her mother wore in bed, of how he would stroke her as she slept.

'I do appreciate it,' he says. 'I really do.'

'You'd better,' she says with a smile. 'I still can't quite believe you talked me into it.'

She was not talked into it. It was the last thing she could do for him, the last thing that will pass between them before she leaves. He'll cope, she thinks. He can cope with anything.

'Anyway,' he says putting down the dress. 'What time do you want waking?'

'Seven,' she says. 'With a cup of coffee.'

'Done.' He kisses her again on the top of her head, squeezes her shoulders one last time.

'Night then,' he says.

'Night,' she says, as he leaves the room.

'And stop smoking in the bathroom,' he shouts as he walks down the stairs. 'It stinks like a bloody ashtray up here.'

*

Bethany Wilder looks out of the window, out onto the rooftops and chimney stacks. There isn't much to see from here: the Town Hall's clock tower, the spire of a church, in the distance the brown brick and long windows of the factory where she's worked since finishing her A-levels. She puts her last cigarette to her lips and thinks of Daniel. She imagines how it will feel to be under him, his unfamiliar body, his unknown breath in her ear.

Earlier that night, she and Daniel had found themselves alone in the back room of the Queen's. They were waiting for people to get back from the bar. Mark was at work. For a moment the two of them sat in silence, smoking and listening to the soft rattle of other people's conversations.

'So, I hear you're going to be carnival queen tomorrow,' he said eventually. She nodded and sucked on her cigarette, noticing for the first time the lines on his forehead, the creases at the corner of his eyes. He had a strong accent which made him sound a little slow. But she liked how deep his voice was, how thick.

'I'm only doing it as a favour for my dad,' she said. 'Last-minute stand-in. The real queen got in a fight on Thursday at the Fox and apparently the Rotarians take a dim view of carnival queens beating the shit out of people.'

Daniel laughed and toyed with his Zippo.

'Any road, I bet you'll look a right picture up there,' he said.

'Judging by the photos of last year's queen, I'll probably look like a whore,' she replied, enjoying the slight look of surprise on his face.

'That girl were a right boot, though, love,' he said. 'Captain fucked her once. Said she needed to put make-up on with a trowel just to get rid of all the zits.' He checked his watch and stubbed out his Embassy, then lit another.

'Are you going to the carnival?' she asked. 'I'm hoping no one I know'll be there.'

He shook his head and blew a couple of smoke rings.

'Don't you worry about that. I never make it up in time for the procession.' He'd leant into her then. 'But we always go, me and Captain and that. Drinks in town first, few cans at the fair and then . . .' He laughed and leant in even closer, as though to confess.

'Then what?' she said.

'Oh, I can't say,' he said, his face behind a wash of smoke. 'Can't be seen to be corrupting the carnival queen, can I?'

She took a long drag on her cigarette.

'I don't need much corrupting,' she said as she blew out the smoke. 'Well, maybe a little . . .'

She looked around for a moment and then told him to meet her on Saturday. To pick her up in his van at the far end of Greenliffe Field, close to where they were building the new community theatre.

*

Now, with the window open and the cigarette in her mouth, she realizes that this is the right thing to do. She will sleep with Daniel and then she and Mark will make good their escape. Fucking Daniel will mean neither of them can ever come back.

For a moment she considers phoning Mark and telling him that she loves him; instead she flicks the cigarette across the roofing tiles and watches it skitter into the guttering. Leaving the window ajar, she gets into bed. She is dressed in one of Mark's old T-shirts. She turns out the bedside light and thinks of America: of America and New York City.

THREE

You won't know what you're missing. There is only a finite number of ten-note progressions, and how Edith had managed to settle on a jingle for an obscure 1980s commercial for Batchelor's Super Noodles it was impossible to say. But that's clearly what it was. The words were lodged on repeat in my head. *You won't know what you're missing.* And with it a memory of my father. I saw the same scene, over and over, the tune playing softly in the background. I could not recall the last time I had thought of him.

My father takes the bowl of water from the microwave. He still keeps it inside because he's afraid one of us will accidentally turn it on. He puts the bowl of water on the side and places two potatoes wrapped in paper towels on the glass wheel. He turns the dial and watches the potatoes spin slowly around. He opens a can of McEwan's Export and pours it into a pewter tankard.

'Good day?' he says.

'Not bad,' I say. 'You?'

'I'm nadgered,' he says.

He sips his beer as the potatoes spin. I think about the baked potatoes we used to enjoy when Mum was around. They bear no relation to the grey-green shells he takes from the microwave.

'Good television tonight,' he says, sitting in his armchair. He is wearing a cardigan which makes him look older than his years and he needs a new pair of slippers.

'Yes, Hill Street Blues,*' I say.*

I turn back to the grey blush of the television. It is a Ferguson set with a wooden exterior. It is on its last legs. We watch the adverts in silence. The last one is for Batchelor's Super Noodles. Packets of noodles dance. Pigtails twirl. A bow tie spins around a boy's neck. And on the soundtrack, a group of female voices sing: 'You won't know what you're missing.'

'How's that Bethany of yours?' he says.

'Fine,' I say, 'Bethany's fine.'

It was a nothing recollection, but it was clear and precise. There were no smudges, no fuzzy edges to it. As it spooled, I examined it, looking for faults. There were none; the joins were invisible. *How's that Bethany of yours?*

*

24

There is no first-kiss moment for a friendship, no expectation that eventually you will cohabit, commit or marry. It does not seek recognition or status: instead it exists in an uneasy space between the private and the public. True friendship is the one relationship you do not analyse, pick apart or scrutinize. Until I met O'Neil I had never quite experienced it; without him, I don't know how I would have lived.

It was O'Neil who fixed me up with a job; O'Neil who found us an apartment; O'Neil who set me up with my fake papers. It was O'Neil who made it possible for me to leave Mark Wilkinson behind. To become Josef Novak.

We met in a mid-town bar one afternoon, soon after I'd arrived in New York. I was eighteen and he was wearing a suit that didn't fit properly. His tie was slouched and crooked, his hair wiry and long, his shoes surprisingly burnished. He fed the jukebox with quarters, putting on old country songs and rockabilly as well as some fading heavy-metal bands. He ordered a burger which he ate while nodding his head and dropping ketchup and mustard close to the pages of the book he was reading.

How we got to talking, I don't remember: I was pretty drunk by then. He asked me about England and I told him that all I'd ever wanted to do was leave.

'How long you been in the city?' he asked.

'Four, maybe five days. I'm not sure. Jet lag, you know?'

'What have you seen? All the usual tourist shit, I imagine.'

'I went to CBGBs last night. Went down to the Brooklyn Bridge and to Grand Central. Mostly I've just been walking, though.'

'Best way, man. Best way.'

He went back to his beer and ordered another one, and one for me.

'I got canned today,' he said and held his bottle up and chinked it against mine. 'Was there two years. Cutbacks or some such shit.'

'I'm sorry,' I said.

'Don't be. They're all fucking assholes. Glad to be shot of 'em. Especially Reilly. He always fucking hated me, the fucking louse. Hey, bud, get me two whiskies here, please.'

The bartender poured the shots and he passed one to me.

'Let's get fucked and hate the world,' he said.

We wandered from bar to bar, me in O'Neil's wake, him telling stories about every street we walked along, and every drinking place we entered. There was the street corner where Simone Garvin – an old girlfriend who'd stayed a friend – had passed out from taking too much coke and he'd had to revive her; the block where his father had been having his hair cut for over five decades; the last bar he'd drunk in with another ex-girlfriend who was now an air steward for United. 'You ever see a place like this?' he'd say every time we walked into another smoky room or underground space. 'No,' I'd say. 'Nothing like this at all.'

When the bars shut we took a taxi to his apartment; a small two-bedroom place he shared with a guy called Bill who was out of town on a training course. We drank whisky until the sun came up, taking it in turns to select records to play. At about five we threw open the windows and looked down from the ninth floor onto the street below, the grey pavements empty save for a man in over-sized headphones walking a butch dog and drinking from a Styrofoam cup. O'Neil slumped down into the sofa and I joined him. He poured me another drink and lit a cigarette.

'So what's the story?' he said eventually. 'There's a story, I know. I can smell people's stories like cheap cologne.'

'There's no story,' I said. 'Why does there have to be a story?'

'I don't believe that for one moment. Not one moment.'

'I don't want to talk about it.'

'Spill,' he said.

'I said I don't want to talk about it.'

'You don't have to tell me. I know already. Honestly. It's like it's written on your face in Magic Marker.'

This was a technique I would later recognize as the least sophisticated in O'Neil's arsenal; but at the time I was vulnerable to it. He said that people were essentially simple creatures. They were happy. They were sad. They were horny. They were disappointed. He said that's how clairvoyants and mystics worked: all they did was identify which of the humours you were dominated by and then hit you with what sounded like facts.

'You're here to escape, to run away from something,' he said, standing up. 'Something bad. Something traumatic. This ain't a row with mommy and daddy. This is something deep and bad. Kinda thing that changes your life.'

I took one of the cigarettes and lit it. He was smiling slightly as he got up to switch the record.

'I told you I don't want to talk about it.'

O'Neil just shrugged and smiled.

'You'll tell me eventually,' he said. 'You can bet on it.'

'Maybe, but not tonight,' I said.

'That's what all the girls say,' he said.

*

The first place O'Neil and I lived together was a small apartment in Fort Greene. We worked all week on the phones and would go out most nights. The weekend was for sleeping. On Sundays we sat on the brown corduroy sofa with the curtains drawn, watching videos. One of us would go and buy beer and the other would order pizza. O'Neil used to follow the same routine with his elder brother, Jay, years before.

When O'Neil was about sixteen Jay and his father had a huge fight. Jay took the beating of his life, then took his rucksack and moved out of the family home. The family never spoke of Jay again. O'Neil and Jay were close though, so it wasn't long before he was pretending to go to baseball practice but instead rode the subway to see his brother. That was all I knew about Jay; except that he'd died somehow, and that O'Neil's father had never really recovered.

One afternoon, in between *Heathers* and *Big Trouble in Little China*, we watched *Somewhere in Time* – a time-travel romance starring Christopher Reeve as a theatre director who falls in love with the portrait of a long-dead Jane Seymour. It was a handsome film, all stuffy elegance and furtive glances. And though we were bloated from the pizza and the beer, we both sat rapt as Reeve hypnotized himself back to 1912 and into Jane's initially standoffish arms.

As a method of time travel, however, self-hypnosis proves to be a flimsy vehicle. Early in the movie, Reeve is standing in an Edwardian drawing room and takes a coin from the pocket of his starched trousers. He holds it in his fingers, then flicks it up in the air. It glints in the light and settles on the back of his right hand. When he looks down he sees the face of John F. Kennedy, and the illusion is shattered. Reeve's eyes open, and he is seventy years away from the woman he loves. His expression is one of aching, crushing loss.

That same night, O'Neil snoring in the next room, I tried the same thing. I lay with my hands on my chest, closed my eyes and tried to picture Bethany in Brooklyn, in Manhattan, eating at the Empire Diner, undressing in my bedroom. But she wouldn't come. I must have tried it for a week before I gave up.

When I eventually took possession of my faked papers – passport, social-security number, birth certificate – I thought again about Reeve and his lost love. The toss of the coin. The sun's reflection. The eventual breaking of the spell. I held the documents in my hand. They were surprisingly light. I looked at my new name, my new date of birth. Had someone barged down the door and demanded ID, I wouldn't have known what to say. The papers and the photos matched. This was the truth. I was Josef Pietr Novak. I was born in New Jersey, November

20th 1972. I could never have known Mark Wilkinson. I could never have known Bethany Wilder.

With the papers stowed in my inside pocket, I took the subway to the East Village. The stationers smelled of toner cartridges and pencil shavings. It was library quiet. From a spinner by the door, I picked out a leather-bound notebook with an elasticated strap. At the counter I added a packet of pencils. The clerk smiled and bagged up the items. This was, I think, my first act as an American.

I headed for a bar and sat at a table under the jukebox. In the window seat there were two guys sharing a pitcher of beer, talking about baseball. I lit a cigarette, sipped my drink and took out the notebook and a pencil. In my hand the pencil gave off a simple, schoolroom smell. I was still stuck like that when the guys finished their pitcher of beer. They looked back at me as they left the bar. One of them belched as he went through the door.

The page was white and lined and I hovered over it. Eventually I wrote 'My name is Josef Pietr Novak'. Then I put down the pencil and finished my drink. The bartender brought me another. I'd added another sentence by the time he'd placed it next to me. Once I'd finished that drink I'd neatly filled five pages. When I felt I'd made a misstep, I would erase it using the rubber on the top of the pencil. With care I constructed new memories. I was determined to be more resolute, more steely than Reeve.

There would be no spinning coin, no dead presidents: I would not be nickel and dimed that way.

I gave Joe – oh honest Joe! – romantic, intelligent, nomadic parents. They moved from New Jersey to the UK two years after Josef's birth and travelled across mainland Europe. They became research fellows at a university in the north-west of England, where they stayed, and where their children developed slight Mancunian accents. Mine had stuck. The darkened curl of my hair, the nose too sharp and slightly beaky, pale skin, a high metabolism, burnt-sugar irises, English teeth: for these I thanked my father – Josef's father – who everyone thought was the mirror of my adult looks.

On the way to support the striking miners in 1984, Josef's parents died in a car accident. Joe and his younger sister Maria – I had always wanted a sister – were taken in by their great-aunt, whom I based loosely on Jane Marple. Maria, I decided, became a marine biologist and emigrated to Norway.

There were friends and lovers too. At sixteen Joe lost his virginity to Sally, a girl the image of a fifteen-year-old Deborah Harry. His close friends were his great-aunt's neighbours – a pair of students who were older, but still enjoyed his company. Sarah and Victoria taught him about art and books. They showed him the best way to cook lamb. They made him feel more comfortable around people. When eventually he went to college – it broke his great-aunt's heart – he met a guy called Philip, who was the first male friend he'd ever really had. His three years in Manchester were uneventful.

I realized, as I added to the information over the months, that the humdrum was what gave a life quality, what gave it the ring of authenticity. So Joe's first proper girlfriend, Katie, was a mousy girl who decided that their relationship could not survive the distance of university. He sometimes missed her, but there were no hard feelings. She had fallen pregnant in her final year of college and was married with a son. They did not speak any more.

Joe was present at no cataclysmic events. He had been close to the Wall when it fell, but no closer than a million others. He'd stood next to Joey Ramone in a pub toilet in West London. He had once randomly come face to face with President Clinton while jogging in Central Park. Small tales of almost and nearly. The kind of stories we tell each other all of the time. I read them back, these inventions, and slowly they began to persuade. It was the truth.

I annotated the notebook until it was perfect. In the evenings, as O'Neil chased women in bars and clubs, I would talk to their friends, watching their expressions for evidence of suspicion or doubt. O'Neil thought it was amusing at first – 'It's like some kind of witness-protection shit,' he said one night – but, back then, he didn't like calling me Joe when we were alone. He only called me that in public.

In early October I went to CBGBs. It was a dry and crisp afternoon, the sky a perfect spray-can blue. I sat at the bar and ordered Jack Daniel's and Coke and read the notebook from cover to cover, then read it again. I put it in my satchel and took out a paper bag. I put the contents on the bar. A letter from Bethany. Her sketch of our friend Hannah. The inlay from a BASF C-90 mix-tape. And finally, the only photo of her I'd ever owned.

It was an accident that I'd even got it. If she'd known, she would have taken it from me. It was out of focus, oddly composed. Her sharp features appeared softened. Her eyes were almost shut. She hated cameras so much that a photo of her was the most prized contraband. It quickly blistered under the flame of my lighter, as did the inlay, the letter and the portrait. I shovelled the ashy contents into a baggie and hailed a cab, rode it out to the Brooklyn Bridge. I stood there, the wind icy and burning my face. I opened the baggie and said goodbye. To Bethany Wilder. To Mark Wilkinson. To everything that had gone before. We floated on the breeze and settled on the East River. I cried for the last time. A few hours later,

O'Neil met me for a drink. He looked at me long and hard. We clinked glasses.

'Welcome to America, Joe,' he said.

*

A dozen years later, over steaks at a restaurant just off Bleecker, O'Neil wore that same look as he told me about the Valhalla job: serious, proud almost. And though I refused immediately – I wasn't leaving New York for nothing or nobody – I knew I'd say yes by the time the coffee came.

'You know your problem, Joe?' O'Neil said. 'You don't dream the big dreams. Your dreams are small. Pygmy dreams. Old-fashioned dreams. You need someone like me to give you the widescreen, you know? Push you from the shadows into the light.'

I nodded and sipped at my drink.

'Worst thing in the world is small dreams not coming true,' he'd said tapping me on the arm and smiling. 'I'm serious. Worse than AIDS and taxes combined.'

The big dream he had was property. An old apartment building two blocks from our own place. His family were builders and labourers and so he knew about houses, what made them homes. His uncle had properties in Queens and in the Bronx. O'Neil had wanted the same in Brooklyn. Over the years it became more plausible, he had traded up here and there, saved his money where he could. O'Neil thought we'd probably make a million dollars from Vegas. When I laughed he looked at me as if I were crazy. He kept talking until the idea of the cash became infectious. A million dollars. I couldn't give a shit about the money. But I wanted him to look that way for ever.

*

How's that Bethany of yours? I heard it over and over, my father's voice repeating as I scattered my possessions over the bedroom floor, trying to find the notebook. Eventually, I found it tucked inside the fold of my overnight case, presumably for safe keeping. In my hand it felt somehow lighter than I remembered, less substantial. I hesitated before unfastening the elastic strap. I opened it and saw that every page was exactly as it had been left, filled with my pencil handwriting. I flicked through the pages, the edges thin against my thumbnail.

I read it from beginning to end, straight-backed at the small kitchen table. Then started again. The clock ticked. About halfway through the second reading, the ten-note refrain and my father's voice began to fade.

I saw myself walking back to our house from the bus stop. The darkening afternoon. The fields slowly becoming housing estates. Our home, a red-brick terrace with purple curtains in the bottom windows. A three up, two down. Inside, the dark hallway. The staircase punctuated with watercolours of the local countryside. Fussily patterned carpets. An electric fire that always seemed to burn. A glass-fronted sideboard housing Doulton figurines. I could see the cooling house, walk through its rooms. I could touch its walls. I knew that it existed.

I put back the notebook and opened the client files. I made notes, studied the photographs, went over the itineraries, but kept the photo of Brooks face down on the table. I was looking at its blank whiteness when there was a knock at the door. I didn't move. O'Neil was soon standing in front of me.

He was wearing a dark suit which flattered his bulk. His shirt was ash-grey and his tie coal-black. His hair had been swept into a slick ponytail and in his hand he carried a six-pack of Brooklyn lager.

'You okay?' he said. 'I just saw Edith.'

He sat down opposite me at the table, opened two bottles and passed one to me.

'I'm fine,' I said. 'Just nadgered, that's all.'

'You're what?' he said.

'Nothing,' I said. 'Just tired . . . what did Edith say?'

O'Neil took his cigarettes from his pocket and lit one. He took a pull on his beer. Until recently, he'd come round a little earlier, before showering and changing. But now he was always dressed up and edging into character. I'd much preferred it when he wore his shorts and over-sized T-shirts, the grey fronds wiring through his long curls. He'd started dying his hair too. Said that the grey was holding up the sales.

'Nothing. Just that she's worried about you is all.'

'Edith's always worrying. I've never known anyone worry so much. I'm fine. Honestly.'

O'Neil put up his hands – don't shoot – and cracked his long smile. He looked hot and somehow relieved. There was sweat on his top lip. I lit a cigarette and then took a sip from my beer.

'So,' he said. 'You reckon you've got a good bunch? One of mine looks good for the pent.'

'I don't want to jinx it,' I said.

O'Neil told me about his primary lead, a man called Hardy: his job, his weakness for coke and overweight hookers. He talked quickly and precisely, but I couldn't concentrate. I looked at the cigarette burning in my hand, the beer bottle on the table top next to the pho-tographs. O'Neil said something about derivatives, about the Grand Canyon, about helicopter pilots, but all I could see was Edith.

Edith and him together. The hidden smoke on Edith's breath, the concern on O'Neil's face, the hair dye and lateness for drinks. The images spun like a reel and then fell perfectly into place. I saw him with his face between Edith's legs, the splay of limbs as they embraced. I put the cigarette to my lips and shook my head. But the image was lodged: a jerky, shrouded, uncensored sight.

'Hello?' O'Neil said, snapping his fingers. 'Anyone home?'

'So you're fucking,' I said. 'I take it that's what this all means. You and Edith. That's what I was supposed to ask you about, right? '

O'Neil stuttered. I smoked my cigarette and closed one of my eyes. There was silence and then his phone rang. He clicked it off and shook his head.

O'Neil looked at his hands. He had big hands, like a goalkeeper or concert pianist. For a while he stayed that way, looking at his hands and almost speaking. I watched him loosen his hair, then tie it back into a tighter pony-tail. The light glowed behind the blinded windows, and still neither of us spoke.

I expected him to say that it just happened. I could hear him explaining: 'We didn't mean for anything to happen, but one thing just led to another . . .' And then: 'We were going to tell you, but it never seemed the right time.' And then: 'We know this is weird and sudden, but we love each other.'

But he said none of those things; instead there was only an insistent quiet. After a minute or so he drained his bottle and rubbed his hand across his mouth.

'We're going to stay here,' he said. 'Both of us.'

*

'You'll like this one,' I say, handing her the book. Bethany is on the bed wearing a T-shirt and jeans. She looks up, curious as to what's inside the paper bag. She opens it and it's the Adventure New York Guide, written by the improbably named John M. Fakes. It's a gaudy yellow volume with a photograph of the Manhattan skyline on the front. It claims to contain all you need to know and more. It is woefully out of date, written at the fag end of the seventies, and its advice is very much of its time.

'Turn to page seventy-three,' I say. Bethany reads out M. Fakes' enthusiastic descriptions of New York's 'swingers scene'.

'Sounds to me like old Fakes is a bit of perv,' Bethany says turning back to the front cover, then throwing the book to the floor.

'Don't you like it?' I say.

'Of course,' she says. 'But can't we talk about something else?'

'Like what?' I say.

'I don't know, anything. Nothing about New York. Tell me why you love me.'

I look down and run my hand through her hair.

'I love you because you share the same dreams. Because when I'm with you, I feel like a different person.' I say this ironically, though it's the truth.

'You'll have to do better than that,' she says. 'Not exactly imaginative, is it?'

'It's the best I can do.'

'It's selfish is what it is.'

'Selfish?'

'You love me because I make you feel good? I'd call that pretty selfish.'

'I love you because you're the most beautiful woman I've ever seen.'

'Better,' she said. 'But still only four out of ten.'

'So why do you love me, then?' I say. Her father calls up the stairs. The phone is for her.

*

That first day you arrive in Las Vegas you see the fat asses of the clients, their thighs chafing, bleeding maybe, sitting with their supersize cups of quarters and silver dollars, playing three slots at once, their grins slapped on, wearing their leisure suits loose, sucking on long drinks, some smoking cigarettes, some talking but mostly just pressing

41

the buttons, pulling the levers, and hoping. Hoping most of all. Las Vegas, you realize, runs not on money, but on the perniciousness of hope.

After a week, you no longer feel sorry for these people, their buffet dinners, their occasional wins, their banter with the croupiers. They are happy despite their losses; happy because there is always hope. If there's a difference between the people on the Strip and the people who live in its shadows, it's one of haves and have-nots. Those who have hope and those who do not. It's this hope that ultimately will leave you ripped, hollow-shelled, bow-headed. Watching hope, and those that have it, destroys you.

'You're thinking too much,' O'Neil said when I once shared this with him. 'You think about things like that here and you really will go crazy. It's like blackjack: you start thinking about odds and shit like that you're gonna start to lose. Don't think about it. Let's just do our jobs and get the fuck out of here, okay? We'll be loaded. Properly loaded.'

He laughed then and I smiled and raised a drink to him. To his laughter. I'd stopped thinking about all that stuff, just, perhaps, as O'Neil was beginning to think too much himself.

*

He was still talking.

'. . . Why not stay? What's in New York that's so great anyways? Here we can make real money. Make it and spend it. We could get a place in the old town, drive Cadillacs, have Olympic-sized swimming pools. We can't do any of that in New York, Joe. But here' – he came over to me with the face he'd worn back at the steak restaurant; the imploring love of money – 'we could go into business together. The three of us. Edith's got this great idea for a place over the other side of town—'

'The three of us, O'Neil? The fucking three of us?'

O'Neil nodded, looked at the floor, held his hands behind him.

'I know you're upset, but . . .'

But it was his upset that was palpable. He wiped his hand against his mouth and nose.

'I must've been crazy even thinking you'd understand. I said to Edith, "He'll just go fucking nuclear when we tell him." And she just kept saying that you'd understand. I knew you wouldn't.'

He rocked slightly. It was like old times, late at night, drink-fuelled nightmares.

'Of course I understand, O'Neil.' I put my hands on his biceps. 'I'm happy for you. I really am.'

His face shifted into a smile, his hands touching my cheeks.

'But do we have to stay here?' I said. 'Can't you both just come home?'

O'Neil shook his head. 'I love you, Joe,' he said. 'Love you like a brother, love you like my own brother. But things change. People change. You should stay. I want you to stay. It'll be good for you, for us, don't you think?'

'So you're all wise now?' I said. 'Fucking Edie's given you all the answers, has it?'

He pushed me away, a brief flash in his eyes suggesting he could send me sprawling over the floor without the smallest effort.

'Don't even start on insulting Edith. There's no need, okay? She just made me see things different, is all. About my brother, about you—'

'You told her about your brother? Fucking hell, O'Neil, you didn't even—'

O'Neil banged his fist on the table.

'I can't do this any longer. Not while you're like this.' He moved towards the door and then stopped.

'I'm sorry, okay?' I said.

'We'll talk later,' he said. 'And for fuck's sake try to relax before the sit, otherwise you're going to freak everyone out.'

He nodded towards me and I nodded back.

'You remember when we went to get tattoos,' I said as

he opened the door. He turned and there was the merest hint of a smile.

'You know, when we went to that place in the Village and—'

'Don't,' O'Neil said. 'Not now, okay? Later. We'll talk later.'

'I'm sorry,' I said. 'I didn't mean to be . . . I am happy for you, you know.'

'We'll speak later.' O'Neil said, and walked out into the corridor. I heard the door click shut. The two empty beer bottles were on the table, the cigarette butts in the ashtray.

In the bedroom, I dressed in a dark suit, white shirt, black tie. I sat on the edge of the huge bed and wanted so much to get inside it, kick down the sheets and sleep through until Sunday. The phone rang though and I rose stiffly to answer it. Carlo was not happy that I'd kept him waiting. I apologized and told him I was on my way. He put the phone down without another word.

The car park was underground. The cars were covered in plastic wrapping, but under the subdued lighting their shapes were distinguishable – Cadillac, Hummer, Ferrari. They had been delivered the day before from the leasing company, ten automobiles with a combined value of more than a million dollars. Brooks and Hooper were aficionados and wanted to drive these cars fast through the desert, perhaps even race them. Carlo was looking at a red, squat machine with a spoiler as big as a hydrofoil. He'd pulled back the plastic and had his hands on the leather of the seat.

'Hey, Polish,' he said. 'Sometimes, man, you see beauty and then you *see* beauty. She's just too much. Even touching the leather feels like getting laid. Touch it. Feel it.'

'I'll pass,' I said. 'Sorry I'm late, got caught up with studying.' I pointed at the files in my hand and he sniffed. He pulled the sheeting back over the car, unlocked the limousine and got in the driver's side.

Carlo worked out in the gym when he wasn't driving: didn't smoke or drink, wore his serge-coloured uniform with pride. Under his cap his head was shaved bald, which made the long tracing scar at the base of his skull twice as noticeable. He almost died from the blood loss, an incident that prompted him to move from security to logistics. 'Best thing that ever happened to me,' he told me once. 'Would never have met Elvis and Frankie and Howard Hughes on the doors. The guy who knifed me did me a favour.' O'Neil and I smiled. Every driver of a certain age had ferried Elvis and Frankie and Howard Hughes. It was the first thing they ever told you. There were only about six decent stories in Las Vegas, but Carlo always told them best.

We took the ramp out of the parking lot into the afternoon heat. I looked out through the smoked glass back at the Valhalla. The building was a shaft of dark metal and mirrored glass, like it was wearing shades for the sake of anonymity.

'Have you heard about Edith and O'Neil?' I said to Carlo.

He shot me a look over his shoulder.

'What about them, Polish?'

'They're sort of an item, or something. They've got it together.'

'No shit,' Carlo said. 'Really?'

He smiled and touched his finger to his nose.

'You knew, of course.'

'There ain't nothing I don't know, you hear me? Drivers always know the secrets, where the bodies are buried, right? That's why you guys pay us so much. Stops us mouths from wagging.'

He laughed and his eyes returned to the road. We were getting closer to the strip and the desert stretched out in umber and gold, rocks and hardy plants scurrying down into the earth. I kept my eyes on the window, a hand against the pane.

'You okay back there?' Carlo said. 'Not going to up-chuck, are you?'

'You ever feel like things are just falling apart,' I said. 'Just unpicking at the seams?'

'Every motherfucking day of my sixty-three years, Polish. Every motherfucking day.'

He shot me a look in the rear-view mirror and smiled.

'It's like that for everyone, Polish. You think you invented it? One time I was driving for Sammy Davis Jnr. Musta been seventy-four, maybe seventy-five. And Sammy's all happy and joking and talking in that way that he did, like he was going to run out of time and needed to tell you something real important. So we're listening to the radio and suddenly he just stops talking. Bam. Just like that. And after a while I realize what it is: he can hear himself singing on the radio. "Candy Man", you know that song, right? Then he tells me to pull over, and I do and we're sitting on the highway, Sammy listening to himself singing about fixing it with love and making the world taste good. He starts crying, Sammy. Crying like a baby. Eventually I ask him what's the matter. And he looks up at me, his glass eye all dry, and he says, "I believe it, you know. When I sing it I actually believe it." '

Carlo scratched at his chin and placed his hands back in a quarter-to-three formation.

'It takes nothing for things to turn to shit. A song can do it. The wrong look at the wrong dude at the wrong time. All's you've got to do is accept it and move on. It might not be fucking philosophy, but me? I take every day as it comes, one day at a time. If it all comes crashing down tomorrow, at least I've got today, right?'

I'd heard the Sammy Davis Jnr story before from other drivers – sometimes with Elvis or Sinatra as the passenger who breaks down at the sound of his own voice, but Carlo gave everything a better sheen. We drove on in silence. I took one last look at the files and then put them in the car's safe. We turned on to the Strip and went slowly past the Luxor hotel and casino. Opposite, the airfield was hazy and the private jet we usually chartered was alone in its landing bay. Its four passengers would be drinking champagne now, making small talk, waiting for their host and for us to deliver on our promises.

We turned into the airport car park, the long asphalt road steaming slightly.

'Time to take care of business, right?' Carlo said as he parked the car by the arrivals hall. I nodded and put on my sunglasses.

'This is the bit I hate the most,' he said.

Bethany Wilder wakes much earlier than she expected, even before her alarm clock sounds. It is already warm and sunlight streams through the sash windows. She props herself up and is immediately greeted by the dress, which in the shaded glow looks both cumbersome and fussy; something a doll might wear. Alongside it are the other components of the outfit – a crown, a sash, a lightweight sceptre – and to her, lying in bed, it feels like an awful lot to go through. But it is the only thing she can do for her father now; she understands that. He was probably as surprised as her when she agreed. It is, for Bethany, a gesture he can cling to; a reminder of her love. And it will be good for him, she thinks, he will be able to have a life again. She has thought this often.

The clock display blinks 7:32. She needs to be at the hairdresser's for nine, so she can probably afford another half-hour. She tries to sleep some more but eventually admits defeat, gets out of bed, puts on her dressing gown and goes to the bathroom. She runs a bath and reads her library book as she soaks. The house is still, but she struggles to concentrate. Her sleep was dreamless and she much prefers mornings where images linger from the night. She shaves her legs and thinks of Mark, then, sinking lower in the water, of Daniel.

*

Everything has been arranged. She will make her own way to the hairdressing salon, where the beautician will work her dubious magic, then a chauffeur will drive her to the cricket club, where the carnival floats are to congregate. She will wait inside the pavilion, where tea and light refreshments will be served. Photographs will be taken – lots of them, she has been warned – then, on the stroke of midday, the procession will leave; Bethany at its head, in a coach drawn by the fringed hoofs of shire horses. Following her, a brass band will make its deep masculine sound along Jackson Street, down Harrington Street, then along the Manchester Way. At the town's greasy spoon, they'll take a right towards the town centre. They'll march along Amhurst Street and past the Town Hall, where the mayor will salute Bethany, then back down Manchester Way and on to Cairo Street, where the procession will end at Greenliffe Field. From the coach, Bethany will wave as the retinue passes her by and scatters across the grass. To her right, a funfair's lights will already be spinning; to her left the military tattoo will be open, soldiers and reservists showing children and their fathers around helicopters, tanks and aeroplanes. After lunch, Bethany will get changed into her normal clothes in the leisure centre.

She will have a couple of hours to herself before she is due to meet her father, the mayor and a few other dignitaries for an early dinner. It leaves her plenty of time. At around four, she'll pass the church, take several rights and lefts until she comes to a secluded car park. There Daniel will be waiting. In the back of his van they'll fuck. Then she'll make her way home. She'll shower, change and later – at the restaurant, the most expensive in the town – she'll kiss the mayor, his wife and the dignitaries. And then they'll eat.

At the end of the meal, she'll go to the pay phone, light a cigarette and call Mark. She'll tell him she loves him, and he'll say the same. They'll make arrangements for Sunday. Shopping perhaps, a drink in the Queen's, a final check whether they have everything they need for New York. Everything back to normal.

*

Her father knocks on the bathroom door and tells Bethany that there's a cup of coffee waiting for her just outside. His footfalls are soft on the stairway and when she can no longer hear them, she fetches the coffee. She drinks it wishing she could have a cigarette, but the last one was smoked hours before.

Wrapped in a towel, she sits on the edge of the bath, her eyes trained on her feet. She has a blister from the shoes she's been breaking in. They have a steep heel that hurts her toes, bunching them up tightly like something oriental. It's the first pair of shoes she's worn in years and she imagines that they make her Dr Martens jealous. How she would love to wear *them* with the carnival queen dress! She can see herself standing up on the float, waving madly, then swishing up her skirts to reveal a pair of striped, laddered tights and the boots' air-cushioned soles, their eighteen eyelets reflecting the crowd's disapproval. And she would flick the Vs at them all, at the whole town. 'Fuck you,' she'd say. 'Fuck the lot of you. Fuck you all!'

Mum would have loved that, Bethany thinks, and imagines her sitting on the rattan chair where her underwear is scattered. What would she have made of all this anyway: the carnival, Mark, all their plans? Her mother was a fiery woman, yet given to moments of exquisite, bemusing silence. She often simply dropped out of what was going on around her and retreated into her book or whatever she was writing. Bethany would marvel at that. 'It's how I cope with this town,' she told Bethany once. 'It's how I cope with all these bloody people.'

'These bloody people' were behind everything that was wrong – and implicitly she included her husband with them. She would have preferred to be further towards Derbyshire, closer to the real plague towns, but she had been happy enough with the history of the town and its environs. She was endlessly fascinated by its dead residents, the Civil War, the industries, but hopelessly down on those who now populated it.

'People in this town,' she once said, 'would welcome a plague with open arms! They'd bloody love it, being hermetically sealed from outsiders. Protected from the unknown.' She held her arms across her chest. 'Mice! That's what they are. Shrews!'

The plague was Sue's thing; an unusual obsession that had drawn her to the North as an undergraduate. She'd spent her weekends and spare time reading and walking in the countryside, drinking pints of Tartan with the locals at pubs. At university she studied archaeology and history, the aftershocks of which subjected the house to a plague of its own; books that were supposed to stay in the small study had spread like a pandemic across every room. They were almost all gone now, along with the cheap bookcases. Her father had kept his wife's dissertation, though. It was shelved alongside the encyclopaedias, the David Attenborough hardbacks and an old book-club edition of the life of Tutankhamun.

After the cancer finished with Sue, Bethany and her father scattered her ashes on the grounds of an old plague burial site deep in the Derbyshire countryside; releasing them onto a breeze that smelled of burnt peat and leaf mulch, the ground damp and claggy beneath their booted feet. In unison, Bethany and her father shook the urn but it was too dark to see the grey dust take to the air. Years later Bethany told Mark that she'd felt the ash in her mouth and the grit catch at the back of her throat; but it wasn't true. Of all her lies this is the one of which she is the most ashamed.

The bath makes a loud sucking noise as the last of the water empties. For a moment Bethany misses her mother in a way that makes her draw breath. And with the missing comes the regret that she spent her early adolescence wishing her mother were someone else. Someone normal: well-dressed, skilfully made up, lightly scented with perfume and hairspray – in short, exactly like Hannah's mother.

After school, Mrs Nicholson would make them both Earl Grey tea in a proper pot and arrange a selection of biscuits on a plate. She'd ask them about their day as she prepared the evening meal and half-listened to *Steve Wright in the Afternoon*. The recipes she cooked came from *Cosmopolitan* or one of the other glossy women's magazines. Bethany would watch her slick through their pages, her nails translucent, finished in the French style. Mrs Nicholson, or Patricia as she insisted on being called, was a decade older than Sue, but somehow looked no age at all. Sue thought Pat a vacuous bimbo; Patricia suspected Sue a lesbian; Bethany loved Patricia like her schoolmates loved Madonna.

After Sue was diagnosed, Bethany's ardour towards Mrs Nicholson cooled. She noticed that she wore too much make-up, really, for a woman of her years; wondered why she seemed happiest talking about her school days and the boyfriends she'd had when she was younger. Bethany realized that Patricia's figure was sustained through taking no pleasure from any kind of food, and that the most contented she ever looked was at the stroke of six o'clock when she lit a Berkeley menthol – her first of the day – and poured herself a gin and tonic. Bethany wondered whether Patricia ever really escaped the kitchen, whether she felt safe only when she was a few feet from the cooker and the refrigerator.

The first time Bethany saw her after her mother's death, Patricia gathered her up into her arms and held her tightly in an embrace that was both theatrical and distinctly uncomfortable. Bethany could feel the woman's bones through the thin material of her blouse. The next week, Bethany insisted Hannah come to her house after school. Instead of Earl Grey, Hob-Nobs and the radio, they sat in Beth's room drinking coffee, listening to the tapes that Hannah's elder brother had posted from his university flat in Coventry, and talking in low, conspiratorial voices.

They began to dress in black, cut their long hair short and started sneaking cigarettes from Patricia's purse. They hated their schoolmates and whatever good marks they got were achieved without really trying. They dreamt of leaving, of escape. And then Bethany met Mark.

Back in her bedroom, Bethany picks up her mother's photograph, slightly blurry on its textured paper, a shot taken long before Bethany was born. Sue is looking directly at the camera as if to say 'don't you dare', her hair long and straggly, a cigarette burning between her fingers. She is dressed in a blue V-necked T-shirt and tight black denims, and behind her a young man and woman kiss against a red-painted pillar.

Bethany looks again at the dress on the chair. Mum would be proud, she thinks, she'd laugh and take the piss and probably give an impromptu lecture about the ancient traditions and origins of carnivals, but she'd still be proud. She puts down the photograph and reminds herself to take it with her when she goes away. There is a knock at her door which makes her jump. She hears her father's voice, still thick and muddled with morning.

'It's the phone, love,' he says. 'Mark.'

'Be down in a sec,' she says, pulling on some underwear and a T-shirt.

'Don't keep the poor lad waiting,' he says. 'He must spend a fortune waiting for you to answer that phone.'

FIVE

Edith was waiting by the entrance to the lounge, her manner cool as she talked quietly into her clamshell telephone. When she saw me, her eyebrows twitched and she ended the call. The smoked glass looked out over the airfield. There was a faint drone and a smell of engine fuel mixing with the scent of sandalwood and deep-pile carpets. The colour scheme was light fawns and beiges; there was pampas grass in huge terracotta bowls, geometric paintings in similar tones. Behind the door I could hear deep male laughter, the practised giggles of the hostesses following soon after at a higher, airier pitch.

'What are they like?' I said before Edith had a chance to say anything.

'Have you spoken to O'Neil?' she said.

'Yes,' I said. 'I'm very happy for you both. How are they?'

'And you're okay?'

'Why wouldn't I be? What are they like?'

'Assholes,' she said. 'Total assholes.'

I paused, my knuckles whitening around the door handle. Through the narrowest of cracks I could see shapes moving around, some towards the windows, others sitting on the couches, the floating grace of the hostesses with their champagne flutes and trays of blinis. I wanted to stay there, just observing these people through the tiny slit. Opening the door would bring the rushing sounds of their lives into mine; there would be no excuse for not knowing where they wanted to go, or what they wanted to do. This was what was expected. Edith put her arm on my shoulder.

'I'm fine,' I said. 'Honestly.'

'You've got to go in now. We're running late as it is.'

'I've read their files. They don't seem so bad. Not like Gardner's party. You remember them?'

'It's late,' she said, patting me on my arm. 'Time to go to work, Joe.' Her eyes were imploring. I opened the door and closed it quietly behind me.

The four men formed a horseshoe in the centre of the room, talking, sipping at their champagne, staring without apology at the ruffled behinds of the waitresses whose heels tapped across the black-tiled flooring.

Boulder nodded towards me and the conversations stopped. Three of the men moved closer to one another just as Brooks took four quick steps in the opposite direction. I looked straight at him and it was like looking down from the top of a cliff. My vision blurred. The waitresses smudgily made their way to the back of the room, past the bar and along the carpeted stretch which led to the kitchens. I closed my eyes for a beat and opened them again. I picked up a champagne flute that Louisa had left for me by the door. Standing next to one of the ornate pillars, I raised the glass.

'Gentlemen. Welcome.'

*

Edith's duplex looked like a small and highly specialized library. I had been there only once, some months after we'd arrived, and had been unsurprised at its prim practicality. There were no photographs and just one framed print on the wall – a Monet – otherwise it was books and folders and files. That evening she had given me and O'Neil a glass of wine each and promptly retreated to the kitchen to prepare the rest of dinner. O'Neil sat straight down in an armchair and looked for an ashtray; I ran my fingers along the spines of her books, noting their alphabetical organization and general good condition.

Most of the books were on group theory, or group dynamics. Titles by Bion and Tuckman, Lewin, and Schultz took up two long shelves, and each volume was bloated by just-visible yellow Post-it notes. I took one out at random – *Experiences in Groups* – and moved from marker to marker, making neither head nor tail of the academic language of science and psychology. When Edith returned, red-cheeked and wiping her hands on an apron, she looked at me with wounded scepticism.

'I studied it for my Ph.D.,' she said. 'I find them fascinating. Groups, I mean.'

'Tuckman's four stages,' O'Neil said, getting up from the sofa, clutching an empty glass. 'Well, five actually, if you count the breakdown, right?' He looked at Edith. 'Dude, I used to work with a guy who swore by that shit. Good salesman too. Fucking great salesman, actually.'

They talked about that a little bit that night. Maybe that's when they knew. Maybe they'd been fucking since then; how long ago, a year, eighteen months?

Before that meal, O'Neil and I had been perplexed by Edith's involvement with the Valhalla, but over shrimp linguini she explained the attraction. To her, it had become a continuing experiment, a living test lab for male group dynamics. She put them together, testing theories and ideas, then noted down the results: evidence gleaned from her own observations and those from O'Neil and me, from bartenders and hookers. The financial imperative was the only thing holding her back: she would love, she said as she served a Key lime pie, to observe a group designed spectacularly to fail just to see what happened.

A control, she called it, but the giddy look in her eyes suggested she just wanted to see some real mayhem.

As a salesman, you're always afraid of losing your edge. Things like group theory are a bit like whetstones or steels in that regard: they keep you keen. Following O'Neil's lead, I borrowed a few books from Edith and tried to get some basics down. There was little point, however: Edith was good enough at her job to be able to construct a group dynamic that was easy enough to manipulate, but interesting enough for those concerned. There had been some incidents – Gardner's being a case in point – but for the most part, she always seemed to get the boys feeling like brothers, rather than rivals.

*

Three men stood to my right; Brooks to my left. The three were clinking glasses and whooping; Brooks was stone silent and took a very small mouthful of his champagne. His positioning had given him a distinct edge over the others; he could observe them, but they needed to turn in his direction to see him.

'Gentlemen. Thank you for coming to sample the wonders of the Valhalla. We'll be on the move soon enough, but before we do, I'd just like to quickly re-iterate the rules. These are for your own safety and to ensure that you have the most relaxing time possible while you are with us. First, please do not use real names and please refrain from discussing specific businesses. No cell phones, pagers or other contact with work, home or family is allowed. There is to be no photography of the interior or exterior of the Valhalla.' Each one nodded at every stipulation, even Brooks.

The rules were one of O'Neil's better ideas. The restraint of a code gave the Valhalla the clubby whiff of a Masonic lodge or a fraternity house. 'All men need rules,' O'Neil said once. 'Without them we're just beasts. Give men rules and they know where they're at. Especially these rich assholes.' The rules were, however, without sanction, and had probably been broken a hundred times or more, not that we cared either way. The only rule that ultimately mattered was getting them to sign.

I finished the list of other rules and looked to the three men on my right, then, to my left, at Brooks. I watched him put down his glass and take a pair of spectacles from his inside breast pocket. He looked at them for a moment then polished the lenses with a thin cloth. He smiled flatly, put them on his nose, and the room went suddenly hot and white.

*

'I'm not sure I like the idea, if I'm honest, Mark.'
   Bethany is getting ready upstairs and her father and I

are sitting in the lounge, the television switched to mute. Mike is rubbing his glasses and avoiding looking at me. Since I arrived he has been withdrawn, has not cracked a single joke, nor offered me a drink or asked after my father. He is dressed to go out himself; he smells of expensive aftershave and is in his best V-neck sweater.

'I don't like it at all. I know you two are eighteen and all that, but still . . .'

'There's nothing to worry about,' I say. 'It's a big city, but it's no more dangerous than going out on a Friday night. More chance of getting your head kicked in here than—'

'It's not that so much, Mark. And I don't want to sound like a killjoy, but I'm just not happy about it. Can't you wait until next year? When you've both got a bit of life experience? A bit more, I don't know, street smarts? Isn't that what they call it?'

'We've been saving for a year, Mike. We just want to go and have some fun.'

He shakes his head. 'I know, Mark, I know. But still . . .'

Mike stands and goes to the drinks trolley and pours me and him a whisky. He passes the glass to me like a peace offering. I thank him and he sits back down in his armchair.

He looks wounded and disappointed; this has not gone

the way he expected. I wonder whether he really wants to tell me that he is keeping Bethany home. That he forbids us to leave. Perhaps he has already seen what will happen, that she will not return, that he can no longer control her life. We stay like that, in furious silence, drinking, the television still muted, until Bethany enters the room.

She looks more beautiful than I have ever seen her. Her hair has been cut especially for New York and her dress is short, revealing leggings and her boots.

She looks at me, then her father. 'Shall we go?' she says.

I down the whisky and thank Mike. He takes off his spectacles and rubs them again. Bethany kisses him goodbye.

*

'. . . is just a short limousine ride from the airport. Your bags have already been taken there, unpacked, and your rooms equipped with all the comforts one would expect from the very finest hotel. If there is anything at all you require, simply call zero from the telephone in your room. We will endeavour to supply it within one hour. Your pleasure here is the only thing that is important to us. If we can help in any way, we will do so. We have planned and tailored your stay to the very last detail. You have all experienced the rigour with which we interview our clients, so you will also understand how seriously we take your happiness. We're here to ensure that you have the best time of your life.'

'That's quite a promise, Mr Jones,' Brooks said. 'I look forward to seeing how well you can deliver on it.'

The men laughed and Brooks downed the rest of his drink.

'I think we're about ready now,' Brooks said. The other three loudly agreed – perhaps just as Edith had intended them to – but I raised my hand for silence.

'But of course. However, I just wish it to be clear that the rules are binding. Anyone found breaking them will be asked to leave. I do hope you gentlemen understand.'

They nodded, the four of them.

'Then we shall begin. Please follow me.'

Carlo was waiting by the elevator, stiff in his polished shoes. He pressed a button and the doors opened, smoked-glass windows looking out over the south side of the Strip.

'This is Carlo, he will be our driver for the weekend,' I said. 'He used to be Elvis's chauffeur. And Frank Sinatra's.'

'I love Sinatra,' Boulder said.

'The stories I could tell you about Frankie,' Carlo said, shaking his head. 'The stories.'

But Carlo didn't say another word. We rode down to

the basement in silence and were soon in a cool, darkened garage, a single stretch car, its doors open, welcoming us. I took the seat to the right behind the privacy screen. Brooks sat beside me; Boulder, Miller and Hooper arranged themselves on the banquette as though they were being interviewed. I rapped on the screen and the limousine pulled away. As we drove, I fixed the men their drinks.

They talked amongst themselves. Brooks was the only one who had been to Las Vegas before and he began to tell a story about how he had attended a business conference when in the first flush of youth. He had won over $5,000 at blackjack, then lost it all on the turn of a card. He shook his head at the memory and accepted the gin and tonic he had ordered. He stirred it clockwise then counter-clockwise.

'I learned a very important lesson that day,' he said, holding the glass up and looking through it. He sucked on the straw and nodded slightly. 'Yes. I learned that losing is a game for losers.'

The men laughed, all of them, and I laughed and drank down a vodka shot. I couldn't look at Brooks, instead I kept my eyes on Boulder, Miller and Hooper: men who had made money because it was easier to do so than to not; men of high expectations, moderate intelligence and inherited morals. They fell over themselves now to admit to tales of youthful folly. Hooper told a story of a lost file that had cost his company a large contract; Boulder about the time he'd given the wrong set of results to his boss, who had to retract his statement to investors some thirty minutes after announcing bullish profits; and Miller briefly outlined how he had come to after a corporate event to find himself missing an eyebrow. Each story was greeted with the exaggerated laughter of strangers. I could feel Brooks sitting back and simply smiling.

'And how about you, Mr Jones?' Brooks said. 'How about your youthful indiscretions?'

My mind stalled, blackened, emptied. I could think of nothing but taking the aeroplane to New York. The more I tried to dredge something back, the more the details flooded in: the coppery hair of the air stewardess, the small bag of peanuts I opened but did not eat, the red wine I drank until I could sleep. The cloudy sky that afforded no view of Liberty or Ellis Island. The movie flickering on a pulled-down canvas screen, an action film that even with my headphones on I could not follow. An old man hanging on to the edge of my seat *just stretching my legs, young man* and the cold bread roll – the only food I managed to keep down – accompanied by a dense pat of butter.

I closed my eyes, then I opened them again. '1992. September. A run on sterling. Need I say more?'

They laughed, all of them, and I looked out of the window to see the Valhalla in the distance. The three men were each unable to see what they had already given up to Brooks. His misdemeanour was still covered by his own glory; theirs were just the usual fuck-ups of young men given too much money and responsibility too quickly.

You can't hate a client. That's the golden rule: hate a client and you're jeopardizing the sale. Because it's not about them, it's about the dollars. They can be the worst bastards on earth: what do you care? It's about the money. But I still couldn't look at Brooks, his face behind those spectacles. Finally, he inclined his glass to me. I nodded towards him as we swung off strip and down towards the Valhalla.

*

The large wrought-iron gates opened inwardly and we drove up a winding gravel driveway. The men halted their conversations and looked out of the windows, the gardens radiant with sprays of colour and rolling lawns, rockeries, waterways and tall trees swaying in the slight breeze, all tinged sepia through the glass. We turned again and the Valhalla presented itself: a V-shaped building of windows and brick.

'The Valhalla,' I said, 'is not built to make a statement, gentlemen. It is, as I'm sure you'll agree, a functional building from the outside. This is deliberate and essential to our commitment to the utmost anonymity of our guests and residents. You will not be disappointed, however, by the interiors.'

'It's very . . . brown,' Miller said.

'I think it's really rather elegant,' Brooks said. 'I like its understatement. Like it doesn't need to try.'

'It is elegant, yes,' Hooper said.

'Yes, elegantly brown,' Boulder said.

'As I said, gentlemen: anonymity.'

The car stopped at a fountain, behind which stood a smart line of people dressed in blue Chinese-worker-style pyjamas. Two of them opened the car doors and then ran back into line. It was hot and the air was scented with jasmine and lavender and before we could break into a sweat I ushered the group past the water feature and into the huge atrium.

I paused in the centre of the room, the light spilling down onto the ornate mosaic, the fountain gurgling, the size of the space still surprising after all this time. The room had been modelled on the set design for a film about Atlantis that had never been shot, and the feeling remained other-worldly. Boulder and Miller craned their necks, looking up into the flawless sky through domed glass panels. Hooper walked to the east wall to examine the under-floor pond that ran around the perimeter, the koi, emperor angelfish, gobies and tangs oblivious to his feet above them. Brooks simply nodded and took off his spectacles.

'Welcome to the Valhalla, gentlemen.'

*

We took a break in O'Neil's kitchen, the evening plans for my and his groups set out on the table. We had a half-hour before I would rejoin Brooks, Hooper, Miller and Boulder in the East Wing Bar, and the two of us were half-heartedly exchanging notes. This was a time I had once looked forward to; before the tiredness set in, before the company of clients began to grate. It had been a half-hour of laughter and invective, of imagining how much we were going to sell, and how much we would make this time. Most of all, however, O'Neil's company was a reminder that this was temporary; that this wasn't really our life. Over the months though it had become less pleasurable, more about work. As I sat leafing through booking references and Edith's notes, I wondered whether the change had come when she and O'Neil had got together. Maybe it was a coincidence; maybe it was nothing at all.

'You think Brooks will go for it, then?' O'Neil said.

'What's that?'

'Brooks. You think he'll go for it?'

I took a sip of coffee and looked at the clock.

'Maybe. Who knows? He's got the cash, he seemed pretty impressed with the atrium. So yeah, I guess.'

O'Neil looked down at his sheet of paper, then up at me.

'And you're sure you're okay? We can always get someone else in to cover if you're not feeling it today.'

He stood and ruffled my hair as he passed to get some more coffee.

'I'm worried about you, son. Seriously,' he said.

'I'm fine.'

'You always say that, but you look pretty far from fucking okay from where I'm standing. You're all over the place. If this has anything to do with—'

'It's not. It hasn't, okay. Fuck's sake, O'Neil, not everything is about you.'

He came back to the table with the coffee jug and poured some more for me and some for him.

'You've not been yourself for ages,' he said. 'Months, even. It's like I'm watching you have a breakdown. I miss you, man. I mean how many sales have you made in the last month? I've never known you have such a barren run at anything. And you say you're fine? Fuck you, you're fine.'

'You sounded like Alec Baldwin when you said that,' I said.

'Fuck you, Joe. This is serious.'

I was somehow in his arms, my tears dampening his Agnès B jacket. I could not recall the last time I had wept at anything: it was violent and without warning, a kind of declaration of war. O'Neil held me, rubbed my back in the way that a loving parent might. He shushed me, told me it was okay, that everything would be all right. His grip was so tight I almost believed him.

Eventually I calmed, and he gave me a cigarette. I lit it and watched my hands tremble.

'Everywhere I go I see things from before,' I said. 'I can't explain it. It's just like everything's flooding through. You understand?'

He shook his head. 'I want to, Joe. I really do, but none of this is making any sense to me. You're not making any sense. Last week you were just vacant, like you'd been erased or something. We'd be talking and you'd just lose the thread. Lose it completely. And Edith said you just zoned out earlier on. No one home.'

I smoked the cigarette and drank some more of the coffee. We had about ten minutes left before I was due in the East Wing Bar for final preparations.

'It's probably nothing,' I said. 'Just tired maybe, or freaked out by this place. I mean I can't even begin to understand why you'd want to stay here—'

'I'm just worried, Joe. I'm worried you'll do something stupid and—'

'What, and jeopardize your cosy little life with Edith?'

'I don't know you any more, Joe,' he said and stood. 'You're like a stranger and it's breaking my fucking heart.'

He sat back down and I crushed out my cigarette, drained my coffee.

'I've got work to do. And so have you,' I said and stood up. I walked to the door without looking back.

'Don't leave like this, we have time,' O'Neil said. I stopped. He looked angry and sad and I wanted to take that look away from him. So I closed the door.

*

The East Wing Bar was on the fifty-first floor; wide windows looking down over the strip and over the desert. Searchlights scissored and neon bloomed and the sun went down in a smoky, pollution-pretty skyline. It was a bright room: red-plush sofas, black-leather booths, a brushed-steel bar with stools. Music was playing softly. I walked in and nodded at the two barmen. Apparently they were amongst the best cocktail-makers on the west coast. Each weekend they invented a drink based on the favourite ingredients of the guests. Their skill was often astonishing; their ability to mix incongruous flavours into something swooningly delicious a gift approaching alchemy. They were also arrogant, dislikable and fiercely unpleasant to one another.

Without speaking, Thomas, the elder of the two, poured me a club soda with ice and lime. He nodded as he set down the drink, then went back to his position, leaning against the bar, and back to the card game he was playing with Grayson. Judging by the stacks, he was losing comfortably.

To my left, three waitresses were reading magazines, drinking Diet Cokes and finishing their last cigarettes. They spoke quietly to one another, their faces bored, their features delicate. I knew most of their names but had not spoken more than a few dozen words to any of them; like us all, they kept themselves to themselves and only became animated when the clients were around.

Grayson looked at his watch and called time on the card game, scooping up his chips and putting them away in a drawer. Turning around I saw Brooks enter the room, accompanied by his assistant for the weekend. How he had managed to persuade her to allow him down to the bar before time, I never knew. It must have been a lot of money; or maybe the promise of something more precious.

'Hello, Mr Jones,' he said, sitting next to me at the bar. 'I do apologize for my early arrival, but I became rather bored.' He hailed Grayson and asked for a brand of whisky we had ordered in especially. He was not surprised at its availability, despite its price and scarcity. 'I do so hate being bored,' he said. 'It's the one thing I can't stand. Which is why I like Las Vegas so much. So very little time to be bored.'

'It must have made quite an impression upon you,' I said. 'As a young man, I mean.'

He swirled the whisky in his glass and looked at me with mild surprise.

'I've been coming to Las Vegas at least three times a year for the last decade. There are few of its secrets to which I am not privy. Which is why this place' – he moved his arms around – 'so intrigues me. Perhaps I don't know all the secrets, after all.' He winked and sipped at his drink, then removed a cigar from the inside pocket of his jacket.

'I'm sorry, Mr Brooks,' I said. 'I had the impression from your earlier conversation that this was only the second time you'd visited.'

Quickly, he clipped his cigar and lit it with a heavy silver lighter. He nodded his head.

'So you did, Mr Jones. So you did. But did you really think I'd tell the truth to these . . . I don't know what you'd call them? Anyway, let's just say I like being someone else for the weekend. That's what you promised, was it not: a holiday from oneself?'

He blew smoke in my direction and I picked up my club soda. I held the drink aloft.

'You must do whatever will give you the maximum amount of pleasure, Mr Brooks. That's what we are here for. We do not judge. Especially not where half-truths or obfuscations are concerned.'

The light caught his hair giving it a kind of auburn lustre; the hairdresser had cut and styled it to a rich kind of perfection. He kept looking at me as he smoked, his thin smile only broken to accept the thickness of the cigar.

Eventually he set it down in the too-small glass ashtray and laid his hand on my arm.

'I shall remind you of that, Mr Jones,' he said clinking my soda glass with his whisky glass. 'In my experience, no one is incapable of judgement. It's as inevitable and as pernicious as boredom itself.'

She winds the telephone cord around her wrist as she listens to Mark tell her a story from the restaurant; something about a local politician and a comment overheard by one of the waitresses. Usually she loves this kind of conversation; his dryness, the acuteness of his observations, his joyfully scathing descriptions of the customers, but instead she distracts herself by looking at the clock on the cooker. Just at the right moment she manages a laugh, and unwinds the telephone cord from her wrist, then sits down at the kitchen table.

'Anyway,' he says. 'How's the carnival queen looking forward to her big day?'

'The carnival queen wishes she could abdicate,' she says and smooths her hand over the crumb-gritted tablecloth. There are small dots of cheese, remnants from her father's late-night snacking.

'You could do a runner,' Mark says. 'You could dress up as a Russian peasant or something. Your own Flight to Varennes.'

'Oh no. I could never desert my subjects, darling. Whatever would they do without me?' She's smiling, despite herself, and soon they are both laughing, reminded of their history revision, names and dates read out loud as they lay in bed, variously dressed or undressed, sometimes still sticky from sex. He is saying something about Debbie, the restaurant owner, but Bethany is troubled by the precise date of the Flight to Varennes. She knows it is 1791, but despite all those hours of study cannot remember the month: June or July, she's not sure which.

'It's good news, isn't it?' he says.

'Yes, of course it is,' she says automatically, then pauses and scratches the back of her head. 'I'm sorry, what did you say? I was thinking . . . it doesn't matter. What did you say?'

'I managed to get out of the first hour of prep so I'll be able to come and see you fulfil your queenly duties. See what they make you look like.'

'Oh,' she says.

'Oh?' he says. 'Is there a problem? I thought you wanted me there. Support and all that.'

She wants to say yes, there is a problem, but doesn't. She scratches at her head again and then her left leg, leaving red track marks on her pale skin.

'I'd just got used to you not being there, that's all,' she says eventually. 'And I really don't want you to see me in that dress. I look like I live with a houseful of dwarves.'

'I bet you look gorgeous.'

'Please. I wish you wouldn't. For me.'

'I don't understand. Last week—'

'Last week was last week,' she says, thinking how trite that sounds, the kind of thing her father might say. She listens to him silent on the end of the line and realizes that he has a slight cold; his breathing is snuffled.

'You really don't want me watching you? Seriously?' he says.

'I don't know,' she says. 'I just wish this was all over and we were at the airport. I'm sick of wishing my fucking life away.'

'If you don't want me there—'

'Do what you like, Mark. Honestly, do whatever you want. Come and watch me, don't come and watch me. I really don't care either way any more.'

In the silence that follows, she feels suddenly naked, fragile and vulnerable: too much on show. The crowds, she imagines, are baying for her, laughing, pointing and staring at her, while he says nothing, or is oblivious, kitchen-bound and occupied by the cutting of carrots and the heading of lettuce. She feels like smashing down the receiver.

'I'm going to have to go,' she says. 'I've got to be at the salon soon.'

'I hope she goes easy on you. Last year they made that poor girl look like a townie skank.'

'I've got to go.'

'I'll see you later, though, right?'

'Course. Look, I've really got to go.'

'Good luck, honey,' Mark says. 'I love you.'

'You too,' she says and puts down the phone.

*

With the dress folded over her arm and a canvas bag bulging with the crown, sceptre and sash, Bethany walks down George Street and turns right onto the High Street. The bunting is already hanging in red, white and blue flags from the streetlamps, lines of it fluttering in the breeze. There are only a few cars on the road, perhaps other members of the carnival and the tattoo, and it's still too early for the shops to be open.

Approaching her on the other side of the road, a pinched man runs smartly along the pavement, his shorts far too short, his trainers a shocking neon blue. He is a maths teacher at one of the local schools and is always pictured in the local paper for coming sixth or seventh in national fell-running competitions. He checks the road and heads off down the High Street, kicking on quickly, his calf muscles clenched like fists. Bethany's PE teacher had said that she had the perfect body for long-distance running – so tall and lithe – and so to spite her, Bethany had made her father write excuse letters whenever a cross-country run was planned. Running, she's always thought, is pointless: you can never get far enough away.

She crosses over the road and passes Palace Walk, a new red-brick and glass arcade of knickknack shops with a cafe in its pyramid-shaped roof. The opening was a grand affair, a brass band played, there were clowns for some reason and the ribbon was cut by a local comedian who made the assembled shoppers shout out his catch-phrase before allowing them in. Palace Walk was supposed to usher a new kind of consumer to the High Street, to suck them from the bigger towns in the area, and though there are still empty units, its appearance has changed things.

A local schoolgirl had written a letter to McDonald's head office begging them to open an outlet, and apparently they were taking it seriously. Sainsbury's had been eyeing up land to the west of the town; Next, so the rumours went, was interested in coming too. The town is growing up: it is losing its inhibitions.

By the Queen's Head there is a half-full pint pot set down on the pavement, the beer flat and dark. Bethany looks at it intently as she passes, wondering what it would sound like if she kicked it against the stout door of the pub. The road is so quiet she can imagine the noise exploding, echoing around the streets, waking the whole town. *You should do it*, she thinks. *You won't get the chance again.* She ignores the impulse though and leaves the glass exactly where its drinker left it.

When she gets there, the salon is in darkness. She looks at her watch and lets out a sigh, then sits on the bench by the war memorial. There are always flowers here, though fewer and fewer in number over the years. She remembers the parade after the Falklands, but that all seems to belong to an outgrown time now. She can't imagine another war; not one, at least, for which there would be a parade.

*

Eventually a white VW Golf, its roof peeled back, pulls up alongside the salon and a woman gets out. Bethany crosses over as Emma fumbles with the locks, swearing each time she tries the wrong key. When she finds the right one, she looks up to see Bethany standing next to her.

Emma is hot-cheeked, yet well dressed; she has a bony, awkward face that betrays the old woman she will become, though she can be little more than thirty. Her blonde hair is dyed, ironed flat and has a brutal fringe. Bethany recognizes her from the Queen's and has seen her on several occasions crying in the toilets after rowing with her boyfriend. She mentions nothing of this as Emma switches on the lights and inadvertently sends a mug of tea crashing to the floor.

'Sugar!' she says. 'Oh, I am sorry, love. Late, and now this. I'm so bloody clumsy, me. Darren. That's my boyfriend Darren. He says I'm the clumsiest woman he's ever met. And he's not wrong neither. I'm always walking into doors or falling down stairs. Or at least that's what we tell people, right?'

Emma's laugh is loud and shrill and continues all the way to the back of the salon where she finds a dustpan and brush.

'Anyway, that useless girl should be here by now. What time is it, love?'

'Just gone ten past,' Bethany says.

'Told you. Useless,' Emma says and flicks on more lights. The salon is uncomfortably warm already and just watching Emma's nervous energy wears Bethany out.

'Sit down, love. Take the weight off and I'll pop the kettle on. We've got a bit of time, haven't we?'

Sitting down on the leather seat, Bethany begins to feel somewhat nauseous, angry too. Angry at her father for asking her to do this, at Mark for watching her, at herself for ever agreeing to do this. Every now and again Emma darts her head towards her and says, 'You know?' and

Bethany nods while imagining punching her once, as hard as she can, right in the face. When she puts the mug of tea down in front of Bethany, Emma suddenly stops talking, as though her power supply has just been severed. She puts her hand on her hip and takes a long look at Bethany.

'You've got great skin, you know,' she says. 'Not like last year's. Poor love was like a join-the-dots puzzle. Now you come and sit here' – she pats the chair in front of her – 'and we'll really make you look like a princess.'

Emma's is a face of deep concentration and Bethany tries to ignore her pinched precision and the reflection in the mirror. She gets her book from her bag. In the background the radio is tuned to Signal FM. There are adverts for local businesses and then the DJ plays the new Elton John record.

'I love this song,' Emma says. 'Isn't it beautiful?'

Bethany looks up and tries not to laugh. The soft, chocolate-box sentiment of the song, the passionlessness of it all, makes her want to puke. It's a physical thing: she can feel it as sure as the pull at the nape of her neck as Emma winds her hair around a brush. She thinks of her mother for a second and is surprised that a memory of her has surfaced twice in a matter of hours. Her father suffers far worse than her; he still sees her all the time. 'Supermarket moments' he calls them – fleeting glances of his wife looking at breakfast cereals or ordering ham at the delicatessen as he pushes a shopping trolley up and down the aisles.

'You okay there, love?' Emma says. 'You'll crack mirror with that face.'

'Sorry,' Bethany says. 'I was just thinking about something, that's all.'

'Don't want you letting me down,' Emma says as she applies rollers to the hair at Bethany's crown. 'Last year was a disaster and I'm hoping this one'll be different. I don't just do this for the good of the community, you know.' She laughs without humour. Then she stops and puts her hands back on her hips.

'You know, I've been trying to place you, but I just can't. Do you go to the Queen's sometimes?'

'Sometimes,' Bethany says.

'That'll probably be it, then,' she says and pauses.

'Were you there when that black lad let off that air rifle?'

Bethany has heard this story so many times she almost feels she was there. So many claim to have seen the kid brandish the weapon that the Queen's would have had to be the size of the Town Hall to house them all.

'No,' she says. 'I was at my boyfriend's that night.'

'Never been so scared,' Emma says. 'A gun. Like Moss Side or something.'

That's what they all say: like Moss Side or something.

Bethany looks at her watch, thinking to herself that it's just a matter of hours and then everything will be sorted out and level. For a moment she thinks of her father again, but there is nothing to consider, not really. She is leaving, he will get over it: be better for it eventually. He can come and visit and she will show him around, a new woman on his arm and a spring in his step.

'Time for the blow-dryer,' Emma says and takes Bethany by the hand. This is the part that she has secretly been looking forward to: being placed under the dryer like an actress from a fifties movie. She smiles as the hot air circulates and she loses herself in her book, in American vice and squalor, leaving Elton John and Signal FM far behind her.

*

Under the dryer she falls asleep, the book open in her lap. There are dreams that she does not understand and then she is awake, Hannah's hand on her shoulder. Momentarily Bethany is confused and then she smiles. Hannah is dressed in a black shift dress and is wearing self-painted Dr Martens, her lips blood-red and her ears pierced in several places. Around her neck she wears her headphones and she has a small army knapsack which she has plastered with acrylic paint. The last time they were in a salon together was in Affleck's Palace in Manchester, where a man with a Mohican and a woman with pink dreadlocks had cut their youthfully long hair, the two of them suddenly, properly adults.

Bethany holds up her hand to say five minutes and Hannah nods. She goes outside to smoke a cigarette. It is just coming up to eight forty-five and there is more traffic on the streets, people walking down to get the papers. They are dressed in shorts, some of the men are already shirtless, fat tongues in their trainers flapping as they walk, their skin blushed from the sun. The dryer finishes. Bethany can hear Signal FM and Emma talking on the phone, telling her assistant that she's too late. Not to bother coming in. When the phone is replaced in its cradle, Emma smiles.

SEVEN

Though the cocktails Grayson had prepared – lychee and vodka and something else muddled with it, several things possibly – were not his best, the men drank them with appetite and appreciation. We were sitting in a booth to the right of the bar, the five of us closely together, our fingers on the stems of our glasses, the waitresses fussing over us, bringing us snacks, napkins and more drinks.

We had watched the sunset while drinking champagne. All four seemed impressed, standing with hands in pockets looking out of the window. Boulder asked questions about Las Vegas's history and architecture which I could answer with a degree of knowledge. Inevitably they compared the finest sunsets that they had ever witnessed: Hong Kong Bay, Lake Como, Leeward Islands. Brooks said he preferred the sunrise and they all agreed with him immediately. He looked at me with his flat smile; one of challenge and reproach.

It is a delicate balance to strike, being at once in control of the group, while also allowing the dominant member to feel that he is in charge. O'Neil and I had role-played this endlessly when we'd first arrived, night after night with Edith, working at strategy and systems. The best we found was a variance on the éminence grise: letting the dominant member rely upon you for information and insight, while appearing just as obsequious to the others. Brooks had already subverted this strategy and his meeting with me earlier had given him the upper hand.

He beat me by a matter of moments in suggesting that we sit, and, when seated, firmly, if subtly, began to lead the conversation. He was careful to involve everyone, letting anecdotes and stories meander before cutting them off at their natural downturn and besting his companions with his own tales.

On the prior occasions when I had lost control, I had found the Valhalla itself the best possible corrective. It didn't take much to silence a group when you could describe the East Wing as the pleasure centre: fifty-five floors of desires and dreams. But letting Brooks take control allowed me some welcome respite from hosting.

'Gentlemen,' he said, stubbing out his cigar and blowing a smoke ring. 'I would like to propose another toast. To success.' We clinked glasses again. 'Success is what, after all, has brought us to this most exclusive of places. I am often asked by people what is the secret of my success, as I'm sure you have been too, many times.'

Boulder nodded his head with a weariness that suggested he wished he'd been asked this even once.

'I never tell those people the truth. Not because I am secretive, but because it is so staringly obvious that anyone who asks must lack the critical acumen to *become* a success. America, and to a lesser extent Mr Jones's Britain, understands success. America understands success's DNA. America understands that to be successful you simply have not to fail. Or perhaps more pertinently, you have to give the impression of not having failed. Success is not built upon a strange kind of eugenics, or gene pool. Unless you're a black athlete, obviously. It is not down to luck or fate or karma or any other kind of quaint belief system. Success is simply the power to project success. It is believing in it even when the evidence suggests the contrary. Power and belief, that's all. Everything else is just noise.'

He put his arms on the table and leaned in closer.

'Forgive me, gentlemen, for an indulgence, a little potted autobiography. I grew up in a small milling town in Washington state. My father worked fourteen-hour shifts at the saw mill. Fourteen-hour shifts, six days a week. At night he would sit on the porch and smoke cigarettes and drink whisky. That was his life. He saw a purity and honesty in hard work, in physical toil. And when I was about nine, I asked him if he was good at his job. He scratched his beard and looked me up and down and then said: "I'm the best damned saw-mill operative in the county. Probably the best in the state. Probably the whole damned world. Doesn't matter a damn though, does it, boy?"

'That day changed me. I studied hard at school and watched him come home, the greatest saw-mill operative in the whole world. And all I saw was a loser. No one knew if they passed him on the street that he was the best saw-mill operative in the world.

'When I got to high school I dressed well and started selling dope. There was a guy just up the road who grew it for his hippy friends. I researched the market, looked out for competition and exploited the opportunity. Entrepreneurship 101, gentlemen. I used the money to start a stock portfolio using my father's name. I left for college in a Pontiac. My father never saw it; he unfortunately passed away before I had a chance to make the real money.

'My mother always said that my father would be disappointed at the way I turned out. I say bullshit, gentlemen. If he were alive, he'd be too busy buying hot tubs and Jaguars and drinking good Scotch to find a second to be disappointed. His ethics would just be so much sand falling through his fingers. Because he would be a success. It's a shame he missed out on that. It's a shame he never got to see what it's really like.'

*

My father looks uneasy. He has smoked more cigarettes than usual and is on to his sixth can. It is a Wednesday, which is not a night when he normally drinks. We are watching television and it is just before nine o'clock. The news is about to start and he looks at me then turns off the television set.

'We need to have a little chat, Mark,' he says.

He looks nervous, slightly pink at the cheeks.

'Dad, it's okay,' I say. 'I know all about all that.'

I smile, but he does not look as relieved as I had hoped, instead he hitches up his trousers and shakes his head.

'You know that I love you. I don't tell you much, but you know that, don't you, son?'

I nod. I want to say that I love him too, but I don't ever say that.

'The thing is, Mark. What I want to talk about. Well, it's difficult, really. It's complicated. It's about Bethany. Well, I suppose it's really about you, but it's just that I'm concerned about you both. You know. It's not that I don't like her, I do. She's a lovely girl, but . . .'

I look at him and his face says that he wishes he'd never started this.

'You're just so young. Both of you. I mean you're eighteen, but you're just babies really. Too young to be carrying on like this, anyway.'

'Carrying on like what, Dad? We're not carrying on at all,' I say and laugh. He slams his hand down hard on the arm of his chair.

'Just for once, will you shut up and listen to me? Just for once, can you at least pretend that you're listening?'

It wasn't like him to speak that way; we didn't do much in the way of conflict. Mum had said that's why she left: that a quiet life was one that wasn't living at all.

'Listen, Mark, when I met your mother I was twenty-one and she was nineteen. She was so pretty then; so clever, and we couldn't help falling in love. But even then I knew that we were . . . I don't know, kidding ourselves. It's not real, none of it is. The romance and all that. None of it. What you think you know, you don't know at all.'

He's angry, I notice. Perhaps a little drunk, and I shake my head at him, like I pity him. It is a cruel thing to do.

'You think you do, though, son, don't you? You think you know it all, don't you?' he says, laughing. 'You wait, my lad, you just wait. You think you know everything, but you know bugger all. Bugger all.'

The angrier Dad gets, the more Scouse he sounds, and now he sounds like he's never left Liverpool.

'I'm going out,' I say. 'I don't have to listen to this. It's not my fault she left.'

I get up and walk past him.

'And you're sure about that are you, son? You're sure?'

The door slams hard on his words and I walk down the driveway. It is warm still and a tear catches on the coal of my cigarette. In half an hour's time I am in Bethany Wilder's arms, looking at the poster of Grand Central Station. We are never coming back. Never.

*

If they noticed my zoning out, not one of them commented; by that point I had become selectively invisible. While they were happy, they wouldn't need me; when they wanted something new, then that would change.

Kimya set down fresh drinks with as much erotic charge as she could muster. Her breasts were hoisted, her mouth close to each man as she laid down the paper napkins, then the glasses. I lit a cigarette and looked over at the bar. The image of my father came again. His widow's peak, his wet lips and threadbare slippers. I felt sweat drip down the hollow of my back to the waistband of my underwear. I put the cigarette in an ashtray.

'Would you gentlemen please excuse me for a moment?'

They nodded and I headed for the bathrooms feeling like I was burning from the inside out.

I sat in the stall studying my notebook, repeating phrases, sentences. I had been gone for over five minutes and knew that there was no time left to hide. I turned to the last page, the last line which for so long had given me comfort: My name is Josef Pietr Novak.

I washed my face and hands, then dried myself with a soft towel. I spent a moment staring at my reflection in the low-lit mirror. I did not look different. There was no betrayal there; my face remained impassive, a little darker under the eyes perhaps, but nothing that anyone would attribute to anything other than a few too many late nights. I wondered whether my father might still recognize me; Hannah even: faces that just a few days before I would not have recognized myself.

'It seems a little anti-social, Mr Jones, to be visiting the bathroom for so long alone. Are you such an only child that you don't like to share?'

He smiled. I thought of my sister, Josef's sister, but could not see her face, not even quite remember her name. I threw the towel in the laundry basket.

'Some things that people do in bathrooms are simply not for sharing,' I said. 'I wouldn't use the second cubicle for a while, Mr Brooks, unless you want some compelling evidence to that effect. But if there are any other requirements you might have, I'm sure I can accommodate them.'

I took the baggie from my pocket and he nodded, still smiling, still enjoying himself. I cut out four plump lines and watched him take two. He urinated as I dusted the remaining cocaine to the floor.

'You are a strange man, Mr Jones,' he said as he urinated. 'Most people would ask how I knew you were an only child.'

'I don't much go in for parlour tricks, Mr Brooks. My sister, on the other hand, is very fond of them.'

He zipped himself up.

'Interesting,' he said. 'I felt sure you were an only child. The way you are in conversation suggests that you are more comfortable on your own, rather than in company. In my experience, this is the preserve of the only child.'

'I was simply listening to your story. It was very . . . convincing.'

He laughed. 'I've told that story many times. There are a few wrinkles in it. They will believe it because they want to. And why would I lie?'

The tiled floor shone as the door opened again. It was Miller, his face red and his shirt already unbuttoned. He went straight to the urinal and let out a long splashing piss.

'That cocktail waitress has the best tits in the world. No word of a fucking lie. The fucking best.'

He turned and saw the bag of cocaine on the side and his eyes widened.

'I'll see you in a moment,' I said clapping him on the back. 'And you might like to reserve judgement on the peerless stature of Kimya's breasts until later.' I opened the door. 'The night is yet young.'

*

The East Wing of the Valhalla was non-residential, and access to each of its fifty-five floors was restricted by codes, issued only upon request. Most of the floors were empty, however; plastic sacking and litter strewn across bare concrete expanses. No one had the imagination to populate such spaces: it was the impression that was important, the suggestion that only a closed, locked door can imply. The more the residents became comfortable with the place, the more we adapted. An architect, for example, had provided sketches of his old Chicago tenement, which had been reproduced on one of the floors to his exact specifications; on another a scaled-down version of a nightclub that had briefly been popular in Ibiza. For the most part, the residents were happy with the places we had created: the bars modelled on famous drinking establishments, the restaurants that aped haute cuisine or felt like a hometown diner. We even had McDonald's, Pizza Hut and KFC concessions in an approximation of a food court at a Los Angeles mall. It was a place you would never need to leave – everything to all men.

I looked at my watch. We were just about on time, the five of us still sitting at the same booth. I banged my hand on the table to get their attention. Miller jumped slightly, Hooper and Boulder looked alarmed. Brooks smiled.

'Gentlemen. We are about to explore the Valhalla. Our first stop will be dinner. The thirty-seventh-floor restaurant was the first of the twenty to be completed in the East Wing, and the one that remains the most popular with our residents.'

The three men looked at me, then turned to Brooks, who was already standing.

'I don't know about anyone else,' he said. 'But I am hungry like the wolf.'

We took the elevator down eighteen floors in silence. It took seconds. The doors opened into a small reception area, where a woman was sitting at a small kidney-shaped desk. The door behind her was solid black wood with the word OSCURO etched on it in diamanté. She stood and bowed, then pushed a button on her desk.

'Your server will be with you in one moment,' she said. 'Can I just confirm that everyone wishes for the mixed menu of both fish and meat?'

'That's correct,' I said. 'Unless anyone has suddenly become vegetarian since entering the elevator.'

The men laughed, even Brooks, and the woman nodded again.

'Your server tonight will be Miguel. Please listen to his instructions when he arrives. Enjoy your meal. And the experience.'

She sat back behind her desk and picked up her head-set. She talked quickly into it and began to type. I'd had the same conversation with her for over six months and still didn't know her name.

The door opened and Miguel stood in the half light. I went to shake his hand and he smiled.

'Mr Jones, it's been a while.'

'Miguel, I was beginning to wonder whether you'd left us.'

'Where would I go, Mr Jones? Where would I go?' he said. 'Are they all here?'

'Yes.'

He raised his arms and asked for silence. 'Gentlemen, would you please form a line and place your left hand on the left-hand shoulder of the gentleman in front of you?'

After some muted conversation I felt fingers on my shoulder; light and almost apologetic. Hooper was at the rear, Boulder in front of him, then Miller then, behind me, Brooks.

'Mr Jones, is it all done?'

'Yes, Miguel, we're all in.'

'Good. This evening, gentlemen,' Miguel said, not turning his head in our direction. 'I will be both your server and your eyes. Everyone you'll meet at OSCURO is blind, which is useful as they know their way around the restaurant. You, however, will not and as the dining area is pitch black, you will be thankful for their help. There is no light at all. You will not adjust to it, you will be as blind as I am. And please, I have heard the one about the blind leading the blind too many times, so please spare me.'

We laughed as we walked in a loose chain gang, careful foot after careful foot. There were red drapes on the walls and a thick red carpet; the corridor dimming into the distance, the yardage to the dining room difficult to gauge. With clients this was always the most enjoyable point of the evening; the darkness could not help but unsettle and humble even the most bullish of characters. And it was a chance to relax, to leave everything in Miguel's huge and reassuring hands.

'You will be served five courses,' Miguel continued, 'all of which can be eaten with your hands, though to gain the full experience, I recommend you attempt to use the cutlery provided. You will be asked at the end of each course if you can correctly identify what you have eaten. There is no prize, just the satisfaction that your taste buds are as sharp without visual stimuli as with.'

'Is this some kind of joke?' Boulder said.

'Blind men don't joke,' Miguel said. 'Well, at least not to your face.'

At the entrance it was almost totally dark and the men had become silent. We stood there for a moment, Miguel ever the showman – before the accident he had been a magician's assistant – tapping his foot quietly on the nap of the carpet.

'Gentlemen, there is a heavy-set door in front of me. I shall push it open and to ensure it stays open please extend your right arm as you pass through. When we are through we will soon be turning sharply to our right, so please be mindful of that. Are there any questions before we proceed?'

'Are the chefs blind too?' Miller said.

'No, sir,' Miguel said. 'That would be something of a fire hazard, don't you think?'

Everyone laughed and Miguel heaved open the door. I brushed my hand along its wood. Everything went a pale shade of grey.

*

It is a Saturday night and the door to the Queen's gives grudgingly, a group of women leaning against it, their attention diverted by two men who want to buy them drinks. The ceilings are low, the air late-night smoky, thick with perfume and body odour. The jukebox is playing something by Thin Lizzy and the bar is three deep. I almost knock a pint from someone's hand and he tells me to watch out, kidder, and I smile and apologize. The man has a crew-cut and an earring and he is talking to a couple of blokes with the same haircuts and the same kind of earrings and the same kind of clothes: a kind of town uniform. I push past them along the narrow passageway and through into the back room. It is a brown-tiled space with a pinball table and a fruit machine. Hannah waves at me from a small circular table by the women's toilets. She is sitting with two people I don't know.

'What kept you?' she says. 'Thought you weren't coming.'

'Sorry, I got held up,' I say, sitting down.

'This is Rob and Beth,' she says. 'Rob and Beth, this is Mark. He's on my German course up at Kelmscott.'

I say hi and they say hi back. Rob has thick hair, the texture of wire wool, and unfashionable glasses. He wears a long trench coat, a dark blue shirt and denims. Beth has a sleek black bob, red lipstick, dark kohlled eyes and a cigarette in her mouth. She's wearing a Cramps T-shirt and is drinking what I assume is Jack Daniel's and Coke. She looks at me with a vague, disinterested smile. I light a cigarette and ask if anyone wants a drink. No one does.

I pause for a moment, not sure where to look, then push myself up and move to the bar.

I don't immediately know what to order. With my father I'd have a pint of Pedigree, but in the presence of the girl with the Cramps T-shirt it looks a bit common: a bit townie. I try to think what would be acceptable, but I am at a loss. The older barman points at me and I ask for a pint anyway. He pours it and lets it foam on a Foster's beer mat. I hand him some coins and he wanders off. I look at the pint and know I've made the wrong decision.

Back at the table the three of them are talking about someone at their school, a teacher whose son was arrested the night before: he'd been found naked and passed out in the park. They try to explain to me why this is significant, but I don't really understand what's so funny or so sad.

The conversation ebbs. Hannah asks me what I got up to in the day and, for once, I have a decent answer.

'Actually, I went to Manchester,' I say.

'I hate Manchester,' Beth says. 'It's so fucking up itself.'

She looks like no one I knew, and speaks without an accent. I glance down at my drink as she smiles.

'Well, yeah, I suppose. But the record shops are good, though,' I say. 'And they've got a Waterstone's. And everyone loves Affleck's Palace.'

'Full of over-priced bollocks, Affleck's Palace. Those fucking T-shirts with "On the Sixth Day God Created

Man-Chester"? The "I Like The Pope, The Pope Smokes Dope" posters? Fuck's sake. Save me from fucking Mancunians! Save me from baggy jeans and fucking skateboarders!'

'Where did you get that T-shirt?' I say.

She lights her cigarette. 'Manchester,' she says blowing out smoke. 'Affleck's Palace, if you must know.'

We laugh, all of us. Then she smiles at me behind a crosshatch of smoke.

*

'You okay back there?' Miguel said.

'Fine,' I said. 'Just stood on my shoelace, that's all.'

We righted ourselves in the small antechamber that linked the corridor and the dining space – a kind of decompression area between the darkness and the absolute black. Miguel pushed open the second door and the noise, the raging holler of it, greeted us. I had long since got used to the black pittedness of the darkness, but the insistence and surprise of that noise never failed to unnerve. I'd seen the room just once in the light and had been shocked at its size; lines upon lines of booths, a perfectly smooth and flat plastic floor, its capacity well over three hundred covers. Without that knowledge, however, I would never have guessed at its true size: there could have been hundreds crammed inside, thousands.

The thirty-seventh floor was the only part of the Valhalla's East Wing where guests were permitted. Non-residents were escorted up by a bell hop to meet their hosts, and escorted back down again at the end of their evening. It was the social heart of the building, with a conventional restaurant as well as three differently styled bars, all with modest views of the surroundings. Here in the blind dark there could be senators and rock stars, actors and financiers. It was the perfect expression of the Valhalla: anonymity for those who craved it most.

Once we were seated in the booth, our ears became accustomed to the noise in a way our eyes never would to the dark. Miguel explained how best to approach the place settings, our hands exploring bowls and glasses, plates and a quintet of cutlery on either side. Miguel put down glasses of iced water and then a glass of sherry next to each one. An *amuse bouche* would soon be served. I sipped at my drink, listening to the men talk of their new-found blindness, their excitement at the sensual abandon. Even Brooks sounded animated. 'It is a strange liberation,' he said. 'Don't you think, Miller?'

'Better than being deaf. Can't imagine anything worse than being deaf.'

'You ever meet my wife, you'd change your mind on that,' Boulder said.

'You ever meet mine, you'd understand what I mean,' Miller replied.

It was something of a script, this kind of exchange. In the company of strangers, we're compelled to joke, compelled, too, to laugh; anything to lighten the conversational burden. I read that in one of Edith's books. Better the thinness of jokes that no one finds amusing than sitting in a cloud of silence. Sometimes laughter can be the loneliest of sounds.

'Miguel, are you beside me,' Brooks said suddenly.

'Yes, sir. I'm just setting down your *amuse bouche*.'

'Stop it. It's fucking creepy. Like there's a ghost waiting on the table.'

'I'm sorry, sir, you will become accustomed to it, I assure you. It just takes a little time, is all.'

'Well, can you at least talk when you are serving? I would prefer to know when things are likely to end up in front of me.'

'If you wish, sir. But we are taught to be as unobtrusive as possible. That way it's more authentic. Waiters do not ordinarily talk as they serve. At least not good ones.'

Brooks coughed. He leaned into me: I could smell his drink-fudged breath and the cigar.

'Blind he may be; modest he certainly isn't,' Brooks said and I could imagine those lips twisting, the teeth slightly exposed, his tongue just visible. 'He calls him-

self a waiter, when he's no more than a blind man with
a tray.'

*

*It is after the last sitting in the restaurant. The chef is
next to me at the bar, too tired to speak, too drunk to
keep quiet. He is mumbling about the quality of the
meat, how when Drummond's was still in town, his steaks
were the envy of the whole of Cheshire. This is a familiar
story, yet unusual as he is the only person I know who
acknowledges Cheshire as a distinct entity. Everyone else
aligns themselves with nearby cities – Manchester, Stoke,
Crewe, Liverpool. Not him. To him, Cheshire is far from
a postcard-dull, field-strewn backwater, but a place of
which to be proud. He was once featured in* Cheshire
Life; *had his photograph taken with an actress from*
Coronation Street. *Perhaps there is more to it, and perhaps he is right. But now he is drunk and waiting for his
wife to collect him, a wife he is cheating on with the sister
of the restaurant owner: a secret that everyone knows but
will not acknowledge.*

*Behind the bar, the head waitress – Sonia, a ringlet-
haired flirt with a perky chest and a filthy line in innuendo
– is pouring herself a vodka and tonic. In a loud voice she
is talking to her underling, Laura, about the behaviour
of some of the customers, ignoring the two of us with the*

thoroughness she employs throughout her shifts. She has been with the restaurant since its brief glory days in the mid-eighties; her reputation is formidable and the list of her suitors extensive. She will not confirm or deny her relationships with George Best, Ian McShane or David Essex, all of whom at one time or another have dined at the restaurant.

There is a loud knock at the door, and Sonia gives a long, theatrical sigh.

'I wish they wouldn't do this. I hate them to see me after a shift.'

She pulls back the curtain and opens the door to find a young woman with her jacket up over her head. The rain is bouncing off the tarmacked street and umbrellas are hurrying by. Sonia is about to say something but the woman is past her already. It is Bethany Wilder and she heads straight for me; the look on her face one of hopeful complicity.

'Hi, Beth,' I say. The chef looks up from his drink, Laura and Sonia are motionless. 'This is my friend Beth,' I say to everyone and they nod. Her face says thank you and she removes her jacket, hanging it on the empty coat-stand.

'It's pissing down outside,' she says in explanation. 'Came down out of nowhere.' She passes by and sits next to me at the bar. The chef grunts, downs his beer and

wanders off towards the kitchen. Beth takes one of my cigarettes and lights it, her hands dampening the paper. 'Thanks,' she says in a whisper. 'I owe you.' I get up from my seat and make my way behind the bar.

'What would you like?' I say.

'Whisky, straight,' she says. 'Need to warm up after that soaking.'

I nod and pour the drink; Sonia stops staring and joins us.

'You're Mike Wilder's daughter, aren't you?' she says.

'Yes,' Bethany says, taking the whisky.

'Your dad's such a lovely man. Haven't seen him in a while.'

'He's been busy,' she says. 'He's a busy man.'

'He sure is that, love,' she says and picks up a tray of drinks. Beth shoots her a look of venom. Beth's mascara has run slightly and she has a spot on her chin only half hidden with diluted concealer. I sit next to her and she leans in closely.

'She thinks she's the bollocks,' Beth says. 'But she's just a pair of tits with a tray.'

*

The men were laughing and joking, speculating that they were about to be served monkey's brains or sparrow's hearts or insects dressed in vinaigrette. The first course arrived and I could only pick at it. A blackness swam in front of me. Bethany's face, her father's, the brass surrounds of the restaurant bar. Images came in stark projections, like cinema screens sparking into life then cutting out just as quickly.

I felt Miguel's comforting arm on my shoulder as he took away my plate. All four men guessed the dish was lobster bisque with caviar. I congratulated them on the precision of their palates. Miller almost knocked over his wine glass, but managed to steady it just in time. The men's voices were becoming more difficult to tell apart, their words forming an invisible chorus. I looked in their direction and saw the worn-out face of my father; Mike Wilder's raw eyes and stubbled jaw; O'Neil's increasing look of concern.

When the fork hit the floor, Miguel put his hand on my shoulder and a new fork onto the place setting. I thanked him and wondered how much longer this could possibly last.

She has never been in a limousine before and says so to Hannah as they clamber into the car.

'It's not a limousine, not really,' the driver says. 'Limousines are bigger than this. Bigger by a lot too. This is just an elongated car. For dignitaries, like.'

The driver is dressed in a gas-blue uniform with a peaked cap and white gloves. He also has a large black beard which has turned brown at the mouth from the pipe he smokes when not on duty. Hannah giggles; Bethany doesn't. When he turns the key, the car is flooded with music, which he immediately switches off. It is Dolly Parton, and he colours slightly. The car pulls away, the town distant and silent behind the glass.

'How bad do I look, Han? I mean, really?'

Hannah laughs. 'You remember that time Rachel Lowell went to that tanning salon?'

'Fuck off.'

'It's not as bad as I was expecting, to be honest. But my expectations were pretty low. Not as low as your neckline, but . . .'

'It's not that bad, is it?'

'For a prostitute, no.'

Hannah laughs and kicks her feet on the seat in front of her.

'You're fine, honestly, B. You should see your face, though. Even through the make-up you look horrified.'

'I have a crown and a sceptre. That means I can have you executed. Remember that.'

'Queen of all the Goths, yes,' she says as they pull up past Harrington Street and then onto Jackson Street. There's a white van parked outside the ironmonger's and the driver mutters something into his beard.

'He shouldn't park there,' he says. 'If I were the police I'd have him. I'd have him every time!' Hannah and Bethany look at each other. They're still giggling when they arrive at the cricket club.

*

The grass is shorn, yellowish and wheaty in the middle, greener at its edges. There is a rope-link barrier around the wicket and an older man by an advertising hoarding for Fusion hairdressers is busy with a roller. There are a few magpies and starlings tentatively pecking at the turf. The pavilion doors are wide open and behind the thin wooden columns, three men in linen suits are drinking from china cups. Women in aprons pass through the doors and back inside holding trays, removing things from the boots of cars. The men are oblivious and keep talking. They only pause their conversation when Bethany, flanked by Hannah and the driver, arrives.

She approaches them with her hands hitching up her dress. It makes her feel oddly feminine and weak, almost showy – as though she is preparing to mount a horse side-saddle. The men set down their teacups and the one in the middle holds out his arms in welcome; he is the mayor – once a friend of Bethany's father, now little more than an acquaintance. He is full faced, ruddy, with a silverfish moustache. He could be from any time in history almost: the kind of Little Napoleon her mother always loathed. It is, as her father often says, a small blessing that Bethany's mother never lived to meet the kind of people with whom he associates.

Alongside the mayor is George Fellows, the husband of the town's Conservative MP, and their usual golfing partner, David Waller, the head of the carnival committee. Both are wire-thin and clean-shaven and are applauding as Bethany walks across the gravel pathway. It makes her feel sick, the nakedness of their gaze. The dress is even worse than she realized; her breasts are exposed in a way that she would never ordinarily countenance.

At school she wore baggy shirts to hide them, and believed she'd succeeded, until she was fourteen and in a maths lesson a scatter-graph formed a rounded w shape. 'Look, it's Bethany Wilder!' Martin Bilton shouted and the whole class laughed. Bethany went quietly red behind her large spectacles, inwardly raging at them all.

The mayor kisses her first on the left cheek then the right, his skin smelling of strong aftershave and his breath of the bacon sandwich he has recently eaten. He holds her by the shoulders and looks at her with wide eyes.

'Bethany, you look sensational!' he says. 'Amazing!'

'I feel ridiculous. It's no wonder you couldn't get anyone else to do this.'

'You volunteered, my dear. You volunteered,' he says wagging his finger. The two men by his side laugh along with him. She puts her hand across her chest.

'The things a girl will do for the love of her father, eh?'

'We're very grateful, you know,' Waller says. 'After all that's happened.'

She smiles and looks back to Hannah, but can't get her attention. Bethany talks to the men a little longer and then explains that she and Hannah need to go to the toilets. Hannah flicks the Vs as soon as she's comfortably inside the pavilion. Neither of them laugh, though; something has passed behind a cloud. Bethany wonders whether she can tell Hannah about her plans. About Daniel and Mark and everything.

They steal out the back and immediately Hannah produces cigarettes. She has a Zippo lighter that Bethany bought her for her seventeenth birthday. They sit on a bench and look out over the crooked trees and bramble hedges, the litter thrown into them: the beer cans and crisp packets, the fag ends and chip wrappers. It is cool and quiet back there, just the sound of the occasional car in the still summer air.

Hannah talks but Bethany isn't really listening. Hannah is practical, scientific and ambitious: she does not see the point in travelling, in roughing it. 'Most people have never even been to Scotland,' she's fond of saying. 'When I've been to everywhere in this country I'll start on somewhere else.' It's an attitude Bethany finds both wrongheaded and curiously endearing.

'You okay, carnival queen? You were miles away,' Hannah says.

'I wish I was.'

'Oh, come on, every girl wants to be carnival queen.'

'So why don't you do it, then?'

'I'd never fill that dress, that's why.'

'You could stuff it with paper towels like you used to.'

They both laugh and the smoke spools between them; then there is just the sound of them sucking on the filter tips of their Marlboros.

'I saw Daniel Jerome last night,' Bethany says finally. 'He was coming out of the Carpenter's with Captain. The one with the hair.'

Hannah looks over the top of her cigarette.

'Daniel Jerome? I haven't seen him in ages, the fucking sleaze.'

Hannah always calls Daniel Jerome by his full name. Bethany is unsure why.

'He's been on tour, apparently, supporting the Telescopes.'

'Fuck off.'

'That what he said.'

'He's so full of shit.' Hannah throws her cigarette to the ground. 'But he is fit. You can't say he's not fit. You should have shagged him when you had the chance. I fucking would have done.'

'No you wouldn't,' Beth says.

She knows this and Hannah laughs. Hannah has not had sex with anyone; her sum total of sexual experience is long sloppy kisses, a groping of her breasts, and once, a rough hand twisting its way inside her knickers. She has had opportunities, she tells Beth often, but the men she desires are older and aloof, those she can drink with, flirt with, but always keep at arms' reach. She has decided this will change when she goes to university, she will reinvent herself: vampish, confident and in control. Most

of the blokes in the town think she's a dyke and sometimes Beth's happy to play along.

Behind them, the head of the carnival committee
emerges.

'We wondered where on earth you'd got to, Bethany.
It's time for photographs.'

'I'll be right there,' she says.

'Oh, do get a wriggle on,' he says. 'This is the fun part.'

*

The fun part lasts over half an hour. Bethany is primped
and placed, her face aching from the smiles and the fakery.
The photographer has Sonny Mann make-up and raised
veins on her hands. She is the local paper's only photographer and a lousy one at that. Bethany is uncomfortable
throughout, just the thought of doing this one last thing
for her father keeping her compliant – also the fact that
the dress and the layers of greasy make-up make her look
completely other. Not even Mark will be able to tell it is
her from these snaps.

Hannah watches from inside the pavilion, her headphones on and a book open in her lap. The sun shines
hard and Bethany wishes she was in the shade, or had
applied more deodorant in the morning. She is led from
one position to another, under the cascading baskets
that hang from the woodwork, then by the float that she

will ride into town. It has been carpeted with flowers and the name of the local garden centre is displayed on its back.

'Now with the sceptre,' the photographer says. 'And now without.' Bethany drops the sceptre and sees her father's car pull up. She stands a little straighter. When he makes it over to the float, Bethany is fingering the leaves of a flower and is being asked to blow a kiss.

'You're a miracle worker,' her father says to the photographer. 'Never known anyone as camera-shy as Beth.'

'She'd do well to listen better if she wants to do this again.'

Bethany laughs, as does her father. 'There's no danger of that,' he says.

'That's what they all say,' the photographer says. 'Then they get the taste for it. Anyway, we're done. If there's any that you like, you can buy them from the office in town.' She packs her equipment away, muttering to herself. Usually they take the lot, make an album out of it. Not this one, though. Got tickets on herself, the photographer thinks, and turns her back on Beth and her father. She once came third in a nature photography competition; a frog leaping from the waters by the river, caught fortuitously on her husband's Leica. It is the only one of her photographs on display at home, and over the years she has grown to resent it.

They watch her walk away, the bag smacking her tiny behind.

'How was Bitchy Beryl?' he says.

'She told me I was too tall for a carnival queen. And a bit on the scrawny side.'

Her father cocked his head. 'You got off lightly. Last year she called that poor girl a scrubber.'

'Nice.'

'Her father didn't think so. Or her brother. They had to take her into the pavilion for her own safety.'

'That true?' she says.

'Well, that's what I heard, at least. Time for a cuppa before the off?' He offers his arm and she takes it, feeling his misplaced pride as they walk. Her father waves at Hannah, who waves back and takes off her headphones.

'Does she go anywhere without those things on her ears?'

'Nope.'

'She'll be stone deaf by the time she's thirty, you mark my words,' he says.

'When did you get so old that you started to say stuff like that, Dad?'

He chuckles and pulls her closer to him. 'I don't know. I think it must be a genetic thing. You know, your hair starts falling out, you can't run about like you used to and suddenly you're talking like your dad. It's natural. Nothing I can do about it, love. Best just ignore it.'

'What was that?' she says and elbows him gently in the ribs.

'You're not funny, you know,' he says.

'I know,' she says. 'It's genetic.'

*

Inside, they drink tea as women flit around them, organizing trays of sandwiches, pies and slices of cake. Hannah is telling Bethany's father about the course she's going to be taking at Leeds University. They seem to have become closer since Hannah's work experience at the factory. It makes Bethany a little uncomfortable, but she doesn't pursue the thought. Hannah explains about the modules and her plans for a business empire that will rival Mike's own. He laughs politely and says that he doesn't doubt it for a moment. Bethany just nods, looking out across the room, the activity and her stillness within it.

Bethany had instigated the first time with Mark. She had it all planned; her father out for the evening, a bottle of wine bought from the off-licence that turned a blind eye, a vegetarian moussaka she'd made. Bethany and Mark had been going out for less than a month and she was in the first queasy blushes of love. He sat at the kitchen table drinking the thin red wine and talking about something or other as she made a salad and tapped her foot to the mix-tape he'd made for her. At that moment, on that evening, she liked the fact that he had slept with someone before, felt sure that he would quell any nerves she might have. In the end he had been the unsure one, the more hesitant. In her bedroom where they would later make love so many times, that first time was gentle and lasted longer than she expected.

They smoked cigarettes and listened to the Jesus & Mary Chain, their nakedness still a novelty. At half-past ten he dressed and they kissed for a long time before he left. When her father came home she felt sure that he would be able to sense it on her, her changed state. It's the same feeling she has now, a transparency through which she feels everyone can see the deception she is planning.

'It's time, Bethany,' the head of the carnival committee says, his hand needlessly on her shoulders. 'Your carriage awaits.'

NINE

Over an entrée of guinea fowl and braised fennel, which none of the men guessed correctly, the conversation became more serious. There was no argument, just a consensus on fiscal strategy and a slight disagreement on the merits of trickle-down economics. I offered little, sitting still, drinking wine, pointlessly closing my eyes. The darkness was choking. I saw Bethany naked; her breasts and buttocks, the slenderness of her thighs; and I felt her hand brush against my leg, the swish as she walked, the scrape of her heels on the floor.

After the men had finished, Miguel led us back through the restaurant, the space lightening as we walked the slightly inclining corridor. They were in high spirits, drunk now and loudly speculating on what was to happen next. We walked into the casino, its smell of cigars, the atmosphere heavy with the clipping of roulette tables and the shuffle of cards. A jazz band was playing in the corner, and we looked down on them from the top of the staircase. Women were serving the tables dressed as Playboy bunnies; there were cigar girls wandering the floors with trays of Cubans. Everything glittered, sparkled, seemed deeper coloured, more lush even than usual. I told the men we had a gaming table reserved and they followed me down the steps, perhaps relieved that the darkness had cleared.

'I have to confess to being quite impressed, Mr Jones,' Brooks said as we walked through the casino. 'The attention to detail is really something.' He smiled. 'It's like the Clermont, but a hundred times the size.'

'I'm glad you approve. We're rather proud of it ourselves.'

'Isn't that . . . ?' Boulder said, pointing towards a group of men playing backgammon.

'Please, sir, don't point,' I said and he held his hand down, momentarily shamed. 'If you think someone resembles someone you might be familiar with,' I said, 'the chances are that they are who you think they are. Which is why they come here: to escape the attention.'

'I'd love to party with him. I've always loved his stuff. And his style. You think—'

'I will see what can be arranged,' I said. 'But some things are beyond even my control.'

Boulder tried not to look too disappointed and shot a last furtive glance at the actor. He was one of the better of the lookalikes we employed, and enjoyed his role too much for O'Neil's liking. But it was undeniable that his presence leant a certain kind of glamour to the otherwise unprepossessing appearances of the residents and their guests. I hurried us along to our table, the men scouring the room for more famous faces.

*

Boulder made his excuses and headed for the adjacent roulette table, settling himself down next to a woman in an emerald ballgown with a flower in her hair. The croupier handed over his designated allotment of chips and Boulder heaped $3,000 on black. The rest of us sat at the card table, feeling the baize under our hands, waiting for poker.

I had become adept at maintaining a solid losing streak at cards. I was not playing to win, but neither was I playing to lose – an even riskier strategy. Instead I'd developed a series of tells and strategies that players of mid-level skill could soon decode. I would win the odd hand, but didn't go for grand gestures or pull random all-ins.

O'Neil had introduced me to poker not long after we'd moved in together. We played every Thursday with some of his old friends, six of us drinking beer and talking late into the night. It was an odd kind of education, an introduction to male American culture.

Before Joe, before my invention of him, I didn't really have male friends. There were boys that I hung around with but I was never part of a group, always somewhat on the fringes. At home, Dad's sadness excluded me. He was a quiet man, thoughtful, yet unsharing. He was easy not to love; a wary kind of thinness marked every interaction. When later, as Joe, I came to imagine my parents dead, it was the simplest part of the deception.

Brooks was, unsurprisingly, a canny and sharp player; neither a table bully nor a silent brooder. Miller kept us entertained with his ribald jokes and I settled into the routine demands of raising, calling and folding. The cards were falling in all the right places, but for the most part I just missed out on the pot. I drank a gin and tonic and watched the others count out their chips, smoothing them across the brushed green surface, the dealer flipping cards with rhythmic, soothing regularity from the shoe.

'I knew it was going to be seventeen,' we heard Boulder say from across the table. 'I could see it, see the little white ball hop into the seventeen and I just put it all on seventeen, and it came up. Fuck me, it came up.'

Brooks looked up from his cards and inclined his head towards me. I shook my head. It was not fixed. Whatever he thought, it wasn't. We took a break from the game and congratulated Boulder on his good fortune. He asked for champagne and it arrived with a wink and solid, satisfying pop. He tipped the waitress a thousand dollars, placing the chip in the cup of her brassiere. She bit her lip and curtsied. Boulder watched her bunny tail disappear into the bustle of the casino. He drained his champagne and another bunny girl refilled it. It was not fixed. He really had caught a lucky break.

The poker game resolved itself quickly after Boulder's interjection. Brooks won comfortably after fending off a late charge by one of our companions. He seemed satisfied by the outcome, but was modest in victory. He threw a tip to the dealer and stood.

'I think we need some proper excitement now, Mr Jones. Something to liven things up a little.'

I nodded and, once the men were gathered, escorted them towards the lifts. Boulder rubbed his hands as we walked.

*

In the basement, we were met by two men in top hats, their faces fleshy and moustachioed. Without speaking they parted heavy purple drapes exposing a thickly scented room, the flooring generously carpeted, the walls dressed in sumptuous velvets, the sound system playing old French music hall. We stepped through and were greeted by Rosalita, her tall cheeks rouged, her hair flowing, her breasts spilling out from her corsetry.

'Oh, gentlemen, you have arrived!' she said. 'Mr Jones, it is good to see you again!' She bowed to us all. 'Well now, sirs, why don't you make yourselves comfortable? There are some girls who are anxious to meet with you all.' She winked theatrically and as she turned women began to swarm in from the side entrances. Rosalita showed us to the centre table and the girls stroked our hair, smiled, sat on our laps. Boulder tried to touch one of the girls' breasts and she slapped him with mock annoyance.

Just off to our right was a small dais, a not-quite stage, and in turn, one by one, the women disappeared behind its curtains, until we were just men again. Boulder and Miller looked dismayed, Hooper and Brooks confused. A spotlight flickered and then held. There was a pole at the centre of the dais and Rosalita stood in front of it.

'Welcome to my house, gentlemen. Welcome. We have a little show for you now, something to get you in the mood. We do so hope you enjoy it.'

I had seen the show many times, and applauded as always, but with a sense of relief with every changeover of girl. I had a strong sense that I would blank out again. The apprehension grew as the floorshow continued. When it was over, I looked at the men in both relief and disappointment.

'And now, sirs,' Rosalita said, taking the dais once again. 'To the main event.' The music changed to a kind of bolero.

'In my humble house,' she continued softly, 'we have just one simple rule, and that is that everyone's pleasure should be serviced. Which is why we do things oh-so-slightly differently here. You will not be allowed to select the girl of your choosing tonight. No. Rather they will have free rein to make their own decisions. One by one they will come out, and one by one they will choose which one of you gentlemen they wish to give themselves to. Which one they wish to bestow all of their worldly charms on.'

Boulder whooped; everyone else was silent. Rosa shot me a little smile. 'But as madam of this house, I get first refusal. So, gentlemen, I wonder which one of you will be lucky enough to spend some time with me?'

She rustled her skirts as she walked over to our table. With a gloved hand she stroked Miller's face, then kissed Boulder lightly on the lips and pressed her bosom into a slightly surprised Brooks. She put her hand on the crotch of Hooper and widened her eyes, then sat on my lap.

'Sorry, gentlemen, but I think this evening is your lucky night, Mr Jones.'

'Oh, I don't think that's—'

'You reject me every time you come here, Mr Jones. Gentlemen, do you think that's fair?'

They roared no. No!

I shrugged and she laughed.

'Well, that's settled, then. Mr Jones, you're in for one wild night!'

She helped me up and I waved goodbye to the men.

'See you on the other side,' I said. 'Enjoy yourselves.'

We shut the door behind us and it was cool and silent in the corridor.

The routine was the same, everyone playing their own parts, whether consciously or not. Once Hooper's girl had made her long and agonizing decision, another girl would walk through the door dressed – who knew? – like a schoolgirl, or a streetwalker, or one of those girls who looked like both. And she would act out the same charade for Miller. The man would laugh and yelp, applaud the decision, and would look back to his comrades and raise his eyebrows – 'Hell, this might be just too much for me to handle, guys, know what I mean?' – and laugh again. But the laugh and the look would not be noticed: all the remaining men's thoughts would, by then, be on the next girl.

*

In the office it was dark and silent, the only illumination a computer terminal and a standard lamp emitting a queasy half-light. It was a large room, with two leather sofas, some bookshelves, a dresser at which Rosa immediately began pawing away her make-up, and a large map of the world above the computer desk. To its right was a coffee machine. I poured us a mug each, placed one beside her, then collapsed into a sofa.

I was too tired to speak, but the coffee was strong and good; Rosa got it imported from a town not far from where she was born in Puerto Rico. I lit a cigarette and placed the pack next to her, then moved to the old boom box by the computer. Rosa and I always listened to the same radio station, a dusty complication of consonants which only played records by old mariachi bands. Willie Dawson was the disc jockey, and he didn't talk too much. 'Trumpet sounds better than any voice, my flock,' he'd say, 'I believe in the word of the trumpet!'

'This bunch seems even worse than usual,' Rosa said, a cigarette dangling at the corner of her mouth. 'I told Harry to mind the guy in three.' She lit the cigarette with a box of matches.

'Why three?'

'I seen guys like him before.'

'He's just another asshole.'

'You don't see things the way I do. Remember that guy, what's his name?'

'Gardner.'

'I still have nightmares about him,' she said. Rosa sat down next to me on the leather cushions. She tapped my leg.

'You look tired.'

'You say that every week.'

'Because you're tired every week. You run, you drink, you run, you drink. There must be more, no?'

'There's always more,' I said and smiled. 'You know O'Neil and Edith are fucking, right?'

A beam of smoke emerged from each nostril; she stayed silent.

'Why didn't you say?' I said.

'Because it wasn't any of your business, Joey. And they look happy, no? Don't they?'

I looked at my coffee mug.

'I know I should be happy for them, but . . .'

'But you're an asshole, so you can't.'

She smiled and I smiled back. She kissed me on the cheek. 'You sure you're okay?'

'No, not really. It just feels like . . . like everything's coming to a head.'

'Things fall apart,' she said with a shrug. 'People, too. You're just going to have to deal with it when the time comes.'

She put her hand on mine and squeezed it. Her eyes were outlined in heavy silver, and her cheeks were still too rouged for the brightness of the room.

'Coffee's good,' I said.

'It's always good. The coffee is the one thing round

here I do recommend.' She wrapped both hands around her mug as though she was cold. She blew on it, then took a long sip.

'How long've you got left? Can't be long now.'

'I don't know. O'Neil says he's going to stay on here with Edith. Set up some company or something.'

'Will you stay too?' she said.

'I can't imagine for one moment staying here any longer than I have to. It's like . . .' I realized that I was going to say 'home' and paused. 'I love O'Neil. But he said—'

'He's in love, Joe. Things don't ever work out the way you plan them. You know that. And you must have known that this would come along some time, no?'

I shrugged. 'I don't want to talk about it any more.'

Willie mentioned a hoedown at a local bar then played another record.

'He's a good man, O'Neil.'

Her voice was serious. She'd always had a thing for big guys, she once told me, and O'Neil was just the kind of bear she'd love to be held by. The intercom buzzed.

'Room two ESL.' Harry's voice.

I looked at my watch. 'Quick one.'

'Never quick enough,' Rosa said.

'Who's in two?'

Rosa checked her notepad. It was Miller. I finished my

coffee and looked at the huge wall map. It had coloured markers pressed into different cities. There was a new one, a stub placed in the north-west of England. Rosa saw me look at it.

'There was a documentary on about the Beatles last night,' she said. 'And I thought I might go to Liverpool. It looks like a cool place.'

*

Liverpool is the only other city for which Bethany has ever claimed any affinity, though we go there infrequently. Tonight the Ramones are playing and we have had tickets for months. We're catching a lift with someone Bethany knows through a friend. He is known only as Captain, though neither of us have an idea why. We are to meet him outside the Town Hall and he is running late. Bethany is excited and a little drunk on the rum we've filched from her dad's drinks cabinet.

We stand, hugging each other by the gated doorway of the Town Hall, as people in summer dresses and chinos make their way to the Queen's and the Carpenter's. I look at my watch and try not to seem impatient.

'He'll be here soon, don't worry,' she says. 'They're not on till nine anyway.'

I nod and kiss her.

'Anyway,' I say. 'We'll be out of here soon. Out of here for good!'

I shout this so the whole town can hear, then a van – a battered blue Transit – lurches to a halt in front of us. Captain opens the door and doesn't say hello. We get in the cab and say thank you. He doesn't apologize for keeping us waiting for half an hour.

'I'm Mark,' I say, putting on my seat belt. He nods at me.

'You don't trust the Captain, eh?'

He is in his early twenties, his hair long and straggly, his face already careworn, though not unattractive. He puts the van into gear and accelerates to a great speed. The back of the van judders and crashes with things not fastened down properly.

'It's only Dan's drums,' he says. 'And he can't play them for shit anyway.'

I nod my head to the beat of the music. 'Fugazi, right?'

He nods again as we make our escape. He seems impressed.

Five hours later and we drive back through the rain-dirty streets. Captain has assured us that he is okay to drive, but neither one of us is convinced. I'm slowly cooling down from the heat of the gig, the new Ramones T-shirt itchy on my damp skin. Beth holds my hand tightly but seems *distant; not so much worried by Captain's driving but still somehow distracted. The music is loud and Captain chews Juicy Fruit incessantly. He is talking too, telling us both to relax, telling us that it's the best gig he's been to, that Joey Ramone is the coolest man alive. I keep my eyes on the road and say nothing, my ears still ringing from the drums and the guitar and Joey Ramone's voice.*

We are about four miles from home when he turns off the headlights. We are on a B-road and he is laughing; chewing and laughing and telling us that this is the best bit about night driving: the fear. He turns the wheel and we are in the middle of the road, the drums crashing in the back, Bethany's fingers are cold and laced in mine. We both tell him to stop, tell him to put on the lights and get back in the right lane. But Captain's just laughing at us.

'Just fucking stop it, Captain,' Beth says. 'Just stop it right now.'

I see the car coming towards us. Its headlights are not dipped and Captain is momentarily dazzled; he pulls the van left then right. I brace myself and pull Bethany towards me. We close our eyes and hunch our shoulders. We miss the car by inches and career off the road into a muddy ditch. The music is silenced and all we can hear is the ticking of the engine and the settling of the drums in the back. Beth is shaking; I am holding her and shaking too.

'You fucking idiot,' she shouts. 'What was that? What the fuck was that about?'

Captain starts to laugh again.

'We're only ever one step from death, Beth. Only one moment away from the oblivion.'

'You stupid bastard,' she says. 'You stupid fucking bastard.'

He puts the van in reverse and lights a cigarette. He nudges me.

'Admit it,' he says. 'That was the coolest thing ever, right?'

I want to punch him. I imagine how it would feel to knock him out, break one of his teeth, kick him in his throat. My right hand begins to shake. Bethany steadies it and says nothing at all. Ten minutes later, Captain drops us at a roundabout.

'Be seeing you,' he says and drives off. Mud and grass are stuck to the side of the van.

In the street we hold each other.

'I thought we were going to die,' she says. 'I honestly thought we were going to die.'

We walk to her house and make love. Afterwards we smoke a cigarette and suddenly she starts to laugh. We both get a severe attack of the giggles and kiss until they pass. I get dressed and remind her that there's just one more week to go. One more week before we escape. She *says nothing. I kiss her goodbye, almost like it's the last time.*

*

Rosa crooked a finger down my cheek.

'You were fast asleep,' she said. 'Out, just like that.' She snapped her fingers. 'You've got to look after yourself better. Take better care of yourself.'

I looked at my hands.

'How long have you known me, Rosa?'

She shrugged. 'Eight months nearly now, Joey.'

'And you know me? You know men? You feel like you know me?'

She was about to answer me when the intercom went again. Boulder had finished. She looked at the clock and then at the floor.

'Maybe we should get away? Head into the desert. Stay at a motel and get drunk and play cards. Maybe read a book,' she said.

It was hardly an improbable dream, but I couldn't picture it. I said nothing and looked at the map again; Rosa coughed.

'You sure know how to make a girl feel wanted.'

'I'm sorry, it's just I—'

'It's okay,' she said wearily and stood up. 'I just thought it'd do you good, is all.'

'Thank you.'

'Yeah, well, thank you very—'

The intercom went again in a shriek of static. Harry was shouting code blue code blue, and in the corridor we could hear raised voices, scuffling noises, bodies being bumped against the wall. Rosa and I ran for the door. In the corridor, two of the security guards were restraining Brooks. He was smiling, no longer struggling, his trousers unfastened. The men held him against the wall, his face still, his body loose. Rosa rushed past me and into the room.

I followed her in. Lydia was on the floor. Her face was covered in blood and semen. There was blood on the wall. Her nose looked broken and there were teeth on the floor; small, like milk teeth. She had bruises on her thighs, welts on her arms. She tried to wipe her face, but just smeared the mess over her hands and wrists. Lydia was the youngest girl we had; she didn't look older than sixteen. Rosa scooped her up and carried her down the corridor. As she passed, Brooks spat at her.

'Learn to suck dick properly, you useless cunt,' he said, then laughed.

I pushed him back into the room and closed the door. I had him by the lapels. The room smelled of shit and Brooks was still laughing.

'So what you going to do, Jones? I can do whatever the

fuck I want, right? I thought that was the point. You really think that was all I wanted to do to her? I had such plans for that bitch—'

I punched him first in the stomach, then went for his face. He dodged my fist and kicked the back of my legs. Everything was light for a moment and then I was flat on the floor. He stamped on my wrist and then jumped on my arms.

'I should fuck you like I fucked her,' he said. I had my hands over my face and he went to work on my torso. Left and right, right and left. The rhythm was soothing. The blows no longer hurt. I stole a look at him, the redness of his face, the sweat dripping down on mine.

*

The news report is read by Gordon Burns. The broadcast cuts to a picture of Bethany taken from the carnival; the production team must have rushed to develop the photos. It does not look like her. It could be anyone in that crown, in that dress, smiling and waving.

They cut to the crime scene, a roving reporter in shirt-sleeves reiterating the finer points of what can be disclosed. DI Simon Parks denies reports that the killing could be linked to others in the North-West. Then they show a picture of the man they have arrested. This is unusual, but they are appealing for people who know him to come

*forward. I do not recognize him. It is a mug shot and he
does not have the face of a killer. No one has the face of a
killer. On the floor in front of me is my suitcase, my small
army rucksack, my passport and my tickets. The funeral
will not take place for weeks while Bethany is sliced and
weighed and jointed. We still have the tickets; we are still
going to New York.*

*I see the man's face again and cannot feel anything. No
anger, no desire for revenge. I just think of the flight. How
much Bethany will enjoy it. The feel of her hand in mine
as we land.*

*

I had broken his nose somehow, an awkward punch that
caught him square on the bridge. I punched him again and
blood landed in my mouth. He clutched his face and I
kneed him in the stomach. He howled as I stood, howled
as I kicked his face, stamped on his head. I was grinding
my heels into his chest when they came in and stopped
me.

'You'd better get going,' Harry said, looking down at
Brooks, a pair of his teeth on the carpet. 'I'll sort this out.'

Rosa looked away from me and began to talk into her
cell phone. Harry pushed me through the door.

'Go,' he said. 'You really need to leave. Now.'

From the telephone in the office, I called O'Neil. He

answered after five rings, and for a long time I said nothing, listening to the sound of him move from the loudness of whichever place he was in, to somewhere he could speak.

'Talk to me,' he said. 'What's up?'

I couldn't speak.

'What is it?' he said.

'I'm sorry,' I said eventually. 'I'm so sorry.' I kept saying it, over and again.

'I'm coming over,' he said. 'Where are you?'

'I'm . . .' I said and looked around. 'I'm leaving. I'm sorry, but I've got to go. I can't stay here any longer.'

'Just wait, Joe. Just stay where you are. I'm coming, okay?'

I put the phone down. There was silence and stillness and then there was Bethany Wilder. Electric, living, her hand on one hip, her legs crossed, a cigarette tucked in the corner of her smile. I followed her up to my rooms. She watched me from the bed as I packed, wound her hair around her fingers as I checked my passport and credit cards. She said nothing. There was nothing to say. With a small bag over my shoulder, I headed out and followed her back through the corridor, down the elevator, through the atrium and then on to the airport.

There has been just one run-through, down at the scout hut on Higgins Lane, and all she was asked to do was stand on a series of boxes and wave. She was told to smile at all times, reminded to concentrate on the fact that this was all for charity. The previous carnival had been organized by another Rotarian, and David Waller was clear in his objective that more money would be made in 1990 than in 1989. He knew the exact figure and in any conversation he would mention the precise amount – £27,512 – as if it were a living person.

'Remember, smile and they'll put the money in the buckets,' he tells her before she gets on the float. 'But you've got to smile. You've got to look like you mean it. Poor girl last year, she was never convincing. But I know you'll do your best for your dad. And for the town. And for those little kiddies at the hospital.'

She is standing in the car park and the smell of the Impulse she has borrowed from Hannah is overwhelming. Around her kids are milling about, their faces painted like animals. They chatter incessantly, excited at the prospect of shaking the red buckets set out on a row of picnic tables, all of them pre-lined with one-penny pieces.

'I'll see you at the Queen's, then?' Hannah says. 'Just after six?'

Bethany looks at the children again, then at Hannah. 'I'll try. If I'm not there by half past, assume I'm not coming. Queenly duties and all that.'

'But you said—'

'I know, but you've seen what they're like. Waller'll have me selling kisses if he doesn't get more than Fordham did.'

'Just be there, okay? Bad enough that you're with all these old men in the evening, let alone not seeing you to celebrate your reign.'

'I'll try.'

'We haven't got too long together, you know,' Hannah says. 'What with work and all that.'

'I know, Han. I'll try my best.'

The lie doesn't hurt as much as she thinks it should.

*

Hannah was the first person Bethany told. Her head was full of the kiss and they sat on Hannah's sofa, watching videos, drinking tea and eating toast, while she was made to tell Bethany everything she knew about Mark, where he lived and where he drank and what he was like in general. Hannah confessed that there wasn't much. Except one thing she'd heard.

'You know I told you about Vikki Palmer?' she said.

'School bike, right?'

'Yeah. She says he cried after he shagged her.'

There was a moment of stillness, *The Lost Boys* playing on the television screen.

'She said that he wanted it to be special and they were on a school trip. She says he still denies it.'

'The crying?'

'The whole thing. Said it never happened. But why would Palmer lie about it? Boys don't like to admit they fancy her, but they do. Even someone like Mark.'

Bethany pulled her legs underneath her and blew on the top of her mug.

'So you think he did it, then?' Bethany said.

'Of course he did.' Hannah paused. 'But I wouldn't mention it if I were you.'

She didn't. And at first it didn't bother her. But afterwards, she often wondered whether he saw their first time together as the real first time. She could never be sure without asking – and he always clammed up when she skirted the issue.

*

The float is waiting in the shade of a stand of ash trees. A sweating youth dressed as a footman helps Bethany onto the float. She gives him a coy smile. Two of them will flank her as she moves through the streets, their buckets bigger and coloured gold. There is an x made from two strips of gaffer tape at the centre of the float, which is where she is supposed to stand, though there is precious little room to stand elsewhere. Above her is a wire arch, covered with flowers, and in front are two boys who will throw confetti to announce the arrival of the carnival queen, and they beam with the heat and their responsibility. There is a bullhorn at the back of the float which will play the soundtrack to Disney's *Fantasia*.

'You look wonderful,' one of the footmen says.

'Aren't you hot in that uniform?' Bethany says.

'Baking,' he says. 'But it's worth it, though, isn't it?'

She nods and the engine starts, a puny sound, like a scooter. They will be travelling at a speed just under three miles per hour for what Waller describes as 'donation maximization'. From the pavilion her father waves, Hannah waves and she waves back. The back gates to the cricket club open slowly. She can hear the drums and horns of the Boys' Brigade in the distance and tries to work out how long this can conceivably take. There is a drone, followed by heavy footfalls. Waller gestures and the float lurches forward, almost catapulting Bethany from her queenly bier. Everyone laughs except Bethany who is too busy adjusting her crown and ensuring that no more flesh is visible than is absolutely necessary. The force of the sun is shocking, the bonnets and windscreens of cars refracting the light and momentarily blinding her. The float makes a casual turn to its left and Waller waves maniacally.

'For Christ's sake, love, smile!'

*

The floats and people follow her; they fill the street, noise and clamour, costumes bright like the sun. In front, people are congregating and they whoop and holler as she makes her first tentative wave. Without thinking, she smiles too, her teeth on show, her arm tick-tocking as she comes up to the first of the spectators, loosely banded behind metal barriers. There are young girls in fairy outfits, their fathers holding on to their shoulders; boys in football kits – Liverpool, Everton, Manchester United, Stoke – and mothers holding bags and handing out coppers from their purses. Bethany smiles and waves and expects to see people she recognizes from the town, but these faces are unfamiliar and they are clapping as though seeing her for the first time. She feels like an actress taking the stage to collect her encore.

At Jackson Street there are even more people lining the

road. Some are waving flags, some blowing hooters, all are applauding; she has done nothing but wear a dress and yet they're all giving her their encouragement. There is a constant beat from the shaking of the buckets and the loud shouts of the kids and the footmen asking the crowds to dig deep. 'Look at how beautiful she is,' one of them says. 'She's worth more than that, surely!' Bethany doesn't catch what the man says back, but the look on his face suggests that it's probably just as well.

She keeps waving as they go past the Chinese place; the proprietors lean out of the window of the flat above. It is where she and her father used to buy their Friday night takeaway: spring rolls, vegetable chow mein, king prawn curry, prawn crackers. Before it had been a chippy, but the owner had been forced to sell after – at the height of the 'Don't Die of Ignorance' AIDS campaign – threatening a male customer with a hammer when he'd ordered a fishcake. 'That's a poof's order,' he'd shouted, running the man out of the shop.

Slowly now past the Gladstone, a pub that no one she knows has ever entered. They have flags hanging from every part of the building, two huge Union Jacks on the roof. Outside, she recognizes a group of lads formerly of her school. Three have their shirts off and are drinking cans of lager. She keeps her smile firmly set and keeps waving, alternating hands when it becomes painful.

'It's big tits, bad boots,' Kelvin, the tallest of the three, shouts. 'Oi, big tits, where's your boots?' The three crunch up in laughter, then start to sing 'Get your tits out for the lads'. Bethany colours and thinks about just getting off the float and walking home. She can't see why not – her father would understand – but she continues to wave and mouth thank you to the people who are throwing money into the buckets.

The lads become cruder, the three trying to outdo each other. She looks away from them, over to where the empty bookshop straddles Jackson and Harrington Streets. The stewards in their orange and blue vests do nothing; to tell the lads to be quiet would only make things worse.

She is long past the Taj Indian restaurant when she recalls that Mark first told her he loved her in there, drunkenly, food-flecked and lit by a low-wattage red bulb. What he said exactly she can't quite remember, but he used a song lyric of some kind, Dylan maybe, or Joni Mitchell. They were the only people in the place, in that lull between the early evening's middle-aged diners and the post-pub food fights. She knew already, knew also that she loved him. She took his hand and leant over to kiss him. 'You're stupid, but I love you too,' she said.

They went back to the restaurant just once more, on that occasion with her father. Mark was on his best behaviour, while her father acted the stentorian parent in a way Bethany found funny, but served to simply confuse Mark.

'You need to lighten up a bit, Mark,' he said over poppadoms, onion bhajis and vegetable samosas. 'If you take this world too seriously, it'll bite you on the arse, you mark my words.'

'Ignore him,' Bethany said to Mark. 'He thinks he's the funniest man in the North-West.'

'I *know* I'm the funniest man in the North-West,' he said. 'I'm just waiting for everyone else to realize it.' He put down his poppadom on his smeared plate. 'You know, they used to laugh when I said I'd be a comedian when I grew up. Well, they're not laughing now!'

Mark laughed along and put down his half-moon of poppadom.

'I'm not much of a fan of Bob Monkhouse, but that's a good one,' he said.

Bethany's father looked hurt for a moment and drank from his glass of wine.

'I always thought that was a Wilder original.'

Mark shook his head. 'Definitely Monkhouse. My dad loves him. Him and Tommy Cooper.'

The two of them spent the remainder of the evening quoting old gags, catchphrases from radio shows and comedians who had long since faded into obscurity. Bethany watched them; tracing the curious alchemy from indifference to something approaching respect. They drank more than they ate and wandered back to her house for a glass of wine before Mark had to head home. On the step they kissed and Mark whispered in her ear. 'I like your dad, but he's bloody mental.'

'You should have met my mother,' she said and squeezed his behind.

*

The footmen are sweating profusely and the beat of the change in the buckets has slowed. The procession is now by the roundabout on the approach to the bypass. The motorcycle shop has a big sign, illustrated with a ring of fire, reminding people to attend the formation bike display at the tattoo. Green's off-licence, the most difficult place to get served in town, has boarded up its exterior, presumably expecting violence of some kind.

Bethany looks out towards the roundabout. The town has won countless awards for them, and it has excelled itself with a centrepiece of a palm tree surrounded by red, white and blue flowers. Day trippers come from miles around to admire these displays, and then take a walk through the park's gardens, where the same horticultural-ists have been let loose.

Bethany smiles to herself. The palm looks so osten-tatious and strange, completely at odds with the town's otherwise militant functionality. One night, not long after they first met, she and Mark were walking to Hannah's and saw that the roundabout had changed once again. How it had managed to do so without either of them noticing was a mystery.

'It's the roundabout gnomes,' Bethany had said. 'Must be.'

'*Okay*,' Mark said. 'Gnomes?'

'You never heard about the roundabout gnomes?'

'New one on me.'

'Well,' she said, reminded of a story her father had once told her. 'Back a long time ago, just after the car was invented, there were three gnomes. And these three gnomes had no interest other than making beautiful gardens. They used the most unusual, most sensual, most vibrant flowers you could imagine, and some that you couldn't. They spent their lives travelling from town to town, from city to city, constructing gardens that would make princes, kings, peasants and knights weep with joy.' They sat down on a bench by the roundabout. Mark checked his watch.

'And then it came to pass that they found themselves just a few miles from here. The thing was, though, the town gardener was a powerful man, and one who had heard rumours of the gnomes' great skill. He knew that his standing would be destroyed if they came here, so before they could arrive he sent a witch to cast a spell over them and turn them to stone. But just as she was completing the spell, the last gnome pleaded for clemency. The witch cackled, but then saw the flower he had plucked from his pocket. It was exquisite. The kind of beauty not even a hoary old witch could resist. In exchange for the flower, she agreed to let all three of them come back to life just once every season. And now, four times a year, they decorate the roundabouts to let people know that they're still here, and that they remain cursed. No one remembers the old gardener and the gnomes, but everyone loves to look at the roundabouts and the little stone men who live on them.'

Mark lit a cigarette. 'I so wish that were true,' he said, as Bethnal's initial laughter melted into something sadder. 'But I've met the guy who does them. His name's Dave.'

She laughs now at the memory and feels for a moment that she might cry. Still waving. She is saying goodbye to everything; she feels that keenly, almost like a pain in the gut. She imagines her new friends in New York: thin, stylish people who will be entranced by her stories of growing up in such a place. And she'll say, thank God we found each other, and Mark will say, thank God we left while we still could.

They are by the banks of the river now, its water the colour of rust. Two huge factories overlook it, built just at the base of a large hill. They are red-brick and grimy, letters missing from their ageing signs. Smoke and steam pour from their vents and chimneys. Bethany's father manages the one on the right; a textiles company clinging to the last of the area's connection to the cotton trade. It is vast and ugly, a place her mother refused to enter for any reason. Bethany is glad she no longer has to work there, operating a machine that breaks down every couple of hours. She gives an animated wave at its windows as she passes by. As she does, she sees Daniel, alone, waving back.

*

The parade fades away. She no longer cares whether she is waving or drowning or just standing there like an automaton. She sees Daniel, smiling expectantly. And as Bethany nears the intersection by the leisure centre, part of her desperately wants to see Mark. She is reminded of the lecture he had from his father. The spitting rage Mark vented when he arrived at her house, the redness of his cheeks, the arousing nature of his indignation. And yet for all of her calming words, for all of her understanding, she also saw something in what his dad had said. Here they would always be children. Here they could never throw off what has gone before.

She keeps waving, or at least she believes she does,

and the beat of the buckets increases, the heat intensifies, the bugles and brass bands blow harder and harder. They are on the final stretch. The crowds are pressed willingly against the metal barricades and there are wolf-whistles and peals of laughter and the screams of young children. The foremen dance along, the sun melting the asphalt slightly, the light blinding from high windows and the air heavy with the smell of frying sausages and onions.

They are cheering her on; telling her that she is making the right decision. She looks left and right hoping, still, to catch sight of Mark. She waves and waves, smiles wider and brighter than she has all day. There is no more than a hundred yards until the parade's end, and for a moment it saddens her. She thinks of Mark, his careful hands, his late-night whispers. And then Bethany Wilder thinks of America. Of New York City.

ELEVEN

There was an empty seat next to me on the aeroplane, just as there had been the last time I'd crossed the Atlantic. I put the notebook there as soon as we reached cruising altitude. The economy cabin was not busy: a cluster of young men towards the back, couples dotted around talking quietly, the odd single person sitting silently alone. The engine drone was comforting, the red wine and aeroplane food numbing the ache in my chest. The beating I'd taken was suggested rather than broadcast: there had been no reaction from any of my fellow travellers or the airport staff. But I could still taste the blood, could still feel a sharp pain as I inhaled.

Bethany had once told me that she liked planes because they were magic: the kind of everyday magic we take for granted. She'd said that in my back garden, with my father standing beside us, turning sausages on the large barbecue he'd bought from the local garden centre.

'There's magic there all right,' he said. 'But a lot of hard work too. Did I ever tell you about the chickens? There's this hangar they've got on the shop floor—'

'You've told us about the chickens, Dad,' I said. 'You always tell us about the chickens.' It wasn't quite true. He had mentioned it once or twice, how they fired frozen chickens at aeroplanes to simulate birds hitting planes on take-off, and it was a story I loved as a child. But not then.

He made to say something but was distracted by another plane flying overhead. He did not call out its manufacturer or its model. He'd learned that much at least. It was one of the few times the three of us were together alone.

The video screen in front of me plotted our progress, the crude mapping as unconvincing as the video games O'Neil used to play: *Super Mario Bros.*, *Legend of Zelda*. I put my finger on the screen and traced the line all the way to our destination. Even with the perspective skewed so that you could believe you were almost home, England looked so small, so crooked: an island where battles and puzzles and big bosses would have to be challenged. I thought about O'Neil safe in the arms of Edith, his look of confusion slipping slowly into anger, as the tiny plane moved a pixel every minute. I kept my finger on it, half-remembered lines from Joni Mitchell's 'This Flight Tonight', one of Bethany's favourites, repeating over and over.

When I woke it was light outside. I opened the blind and looked out onto the clouds, ice fields waving into the distance. I got a cup of water from the stewardess and drank it down, stiff and uncomfortable, and picked up the notebook. I read it, but none of it rang true. Joe's memories were laboured; they wanted to retire. I turned to the last page and there was nothing there that gave me hope. It was a notebook, a life, written in optimism: it was not real.

It was only on the descent that I really thought about what I was doing. As we dropped incrementally – circling Manchester Airport, or Ringway as my father always called it – I saw the town, how it now was: how it should be. Risking the ire of the stewards, I got my bag down from the overhead locker and took a piece of paper ripped from the notes I'd made about Brooks and started to write.

I wrote about a town that still worshipped Bethany. That still mourned her. I imagined a place that had stayed black-clad and frozen in time, stopped just at the moment of my departure. I wrote until we taxied across the tarmac, and read it back as I waited to get off. It was the town to which I wanted to return. One that understood.

On the way out of the plane I said goodbye and thank you to the cabin crew. They said the same back. One of the men looked like someone I used to know, but I could not place him. He could have been from anywhere, any life I had cared to live. Outside, Manchester was bright and gleeful; no reservoir skies, just a perfect blue, as though refreshed from the night's dark.

The queue for immigration was mercifully short. I looked at the passport, the name on it, my face looking back. How had it got me this far? It was a fake and holding it then it felt exactly that: counterfeited and illegal. At Vegas airport I hadn't given it a thought, but in the quick-moving line in Manchester it seemed to lose all sense of authenticity. There would be conversations; I would be led to the white cubicles and asked awkward questions. Had that happened to the real Josef Novak? Had he even made it this far?

Uri, the fixer who'd organized my papers and everything else, had explained in a strangely formal, almost legalistic manner, that if I had any objections to the workmanship I should raise them there and then, because there were no refunds. At the time I didn't think I was ever leaving. What did I care?

I handed over the passport and landing card. The woman behind the counter looked up at me and down at the desk, then back at me. Perhaps on another day she'd have noticed the alarm on my face, the slight shudder as I'd handed over the passport. On another day it might have been different. Maybe that morning she was hung-over, or tired, or broken-hearted, or maybe she just hated her boss and didn't care. Whatever her reason, she waved me through, the security guards untroubled, the awkward questioning avoided. I put the passport in my pocket and walked quickly through security, looking at my watch as though late for something important and impending.

*

My father worked mainly on military aeroplanes but loved civilian aircraft. After Mum left he would drive us to the observation tower at Ringway and take photographs or look through his binoculars. I would sit on one of the hard seats and read a book or do my homework. He didn't seem to mind so long as I shared his enthusiasm when something unusual occurred. We did that regularly for about a year, then there were some problems. A boss, a project that failed, I can't remember. He was moved to the civil side of the business. He worked longer hours and saw enough tail fins and engine brackets to no longer care about those flying out from the airport. He asked me once if I missed it: the drive to the airport, the planes, the fast food on the way home, and I told him that I did. That I missed spending time with him. We were both satisfied with the lie and went back to watching the television, a mug of beer balanced on the armrest of his chair.

*

I was soon out into the cool morning air and in the taxi line. As I'd walked through the arrivals terminal I'd half hoped that someone would be waiting with a felt-tip written card with my name on it. No one knew that I was there, but I studied those cards for either one of my names anyway. I had perhaps got more used to my life in Las Vegas than I realized: there was no chauffeur, no limousine, just the taxi queue and the pull on the long-desired cigarette.

I got into a cab and told the driver where I was headed. He nodded and turned up the radio. Sunlight danced off advertising hoardings, the grass was muddy, the tarmac gummy with earlier rain. Out of the window, the landscape gave the lie to what I had written. No one was mourning Bethany. Nothing had stayed the same. Industrial parks had been replaced by shopping malls, American-styled and sprawling. The Little Chefs were Burger Kings; old pubs, McDonald's. The cars were smaller, less corroded. The only familiar detail was the signposts, their whiteness and blueness as we swept up the M56.

'Been on holiday?' the driver said as we mounted the slip road.

'What?' I said.

'I said, you been on holiday?'

'No,' I said. 'Well, yes. No. Business actually.'

He nodded, whether in agreement or in time to the music I couldn't say. He negotiated a roundabout and pulled into traffic. There was the sound of horns.

'I've always liked the airport run,' he said. 'Been doing it years now. Hours are shite, but you get to see what folk are really like, y'know? Folk are funny when they get off a plane. Can't explain it. True, though. There's some blokes that won't do it. Me, I like it. Tips are good and you always get to know about places. Makes you feel you don't have to go to 'em yourself, y'know?'

The man had a shaved head, like a bullet covered in milky skin. I could see his sunglasses in the rear-view mirror, they were sepia-lensed and made him look some-how ill.

'Been away long?'

'Long enough,' I said. 'Long enough for things to change.'

'Tell me about it,' he said and indicated right. He opened his window and rested his arm along the door.

'Got to say, though, I think it's for the best after all. I know what folk think of cabbies, but I'm optimistic, you know? I'm a glass-half-full kind of a bloke. Always looking on the bright side and all that. People forget too quickly, that's my point. People forget. Problem is that we think this is a new thing! That we all just invented it. Fact is it's always been this way. Always. But you know,

I believe in Blair. I do. Years from now they'll look back on him and they'll say he's the reincarnation of Churchill. Though he was a cunt, if you'll pardon my Français, ask any Irish.'

'You're Irish?'

'Second generation, but the hurt's the same, you know what I mean?'

A white van cut us up and the cab driver shouted out the window.

'Like I said, things don't change. Bastards still can't drive. Women still run off with your best friend, your kids still think you're fucking useless. But if you don't look on the bright side, what chance have you got? Take my kid, Stevie. Seventeen he is, fucking stupid haircut, looks a right state, but he's going go university. First of us lot to go. Both sides. You'd've told me old mum that one of us lot were going to university, she'd've laughed. Honestly. She'd've laughed until she'd wet her knickers.'

He took a very tight left bend and pointed to the dash-board.

'That's him there. Stevie. Back when he looked like a boy and answered to his father. I'm so proud of him. But I don't tell him that. Might fuck him up even more, right?'

He laughed and I laughed with him. He continued to talk but I'd stopped listening.

*

We were in Wilmslow and the cinema where Bethany and I saw *Beetlejuice* was closed down, plywood covering its art-deco exterior. Her father had been invited to a business function at a nearby restaurant, so we watched the film and went to the pub afterwards, drank whisky and ginger ale and were eventually joined by Mike. He looked tired but had another drink with us anyway. He told me a joke that he'd heard on the radio and I imagined my own father there, rather than snoozing on the sofa. He would have bristled, at least initially, and then the two men would have talked work or football, my father quickly assuming a position of deference.

The cabbie finished his long monologue just as we approached the outskirts of the town. To the left was what should have been the Duke of Wellington hotel, now a retirement home. In the distance and to the right was another retail park, a large sign advertising Tesco and Halfords and some other outlets I didn't recognize.

'I don't come here that often,' he said. 'But it seems a nice place. Kind of place you could retire in, you know?'

'You should have been born here,' I said. 'This place is a hole.'

'Where you're from is important,' he said. 'I keep telling my lad that.'

'He sounds like a good kid.'

We turned left, past what used to be a Chinese restaurant and was now a glass and aluminium fronted bar called Zeros.

'Good kid, yes,' he said. 'But he still couldn't put handle on a bucket.'

*

He dropped me at the Coach House Hotel. There was a small red sports car illegally parked outside. The barber's, John's, where you could get a haircut for under £3, was now a vintage sweet shoppe; the old video library an Italian restaurant with fishbowl windows, the travel agency a florist. The Coach House was the same, though. It was a renovated Tudor roadhouse, the white- and black-beamed exterior recently repainted. A chalkboard A-frame advertised a £10 lunch menu, and the steps were as steep as they always had been. I stood for a while, my bag at my feet. People walked past, but I did not recognize them, nor them me.

The Coach was where, ultimately, we spent most of our time, Hannah, Bethany and I. We had our usual seats by the jukebox and, for the most part, were left alone by the regulars. The hotel patrons rarely made it round to our side of the bar, which was angled into the corner of both rooms, the same staff pulling pints on one side and pouring wine and whisky on the other. We could see them, on the other side, but could not join them; at least not until last orders had been sounded and the barman – who had a long-standing and unreciprocated affection for Hannah – would usher us round and let us drink for as long as there were residents to serve.

I always wondered what it would be like to hire a room there, how decadent it would be to sleep with Bethany just ten minutes or so from our own beds. I always thought that if we ever came back from New York that was what we would do. One night in the Coach: the bridal suite with the four-poster bed, the stupidity of it all weighing against the defeat of return. One night, drunk and giggling, we'd stolen up the stairs trying to find an untaken room. A guest had heard us, opened his door and asked what the hell we were doing. Calmly Bethany explained that we were both so drunk we couldn't remember our room number. The man went back into his room and we laughed with relief and made our way back down to the bar. Hannah was furious, sitting alone, the barman looking mooningly at her.

*

I pushed open the door and entered the small lobby and open-plan bar area. The atmosphere was still clubby and genteel, retaining the faded kind of sixteenth-century chic that had been fashionable in the 1980s. It was empty.

On a small table there was an empty coffee cup. A copy of the *Daily Telegraph* was abandoned on the adjacent Chesterfield armchair. They were the only signs that anyone had been here recently. The reception desk had a service bell next to a display of flyers for local attractions. I rang it and waited, than rang it again. A woman in a burgundy waistcoat emerged from the back office, wiping her hands on a napkin. She was still holding a piece of toast as she approached the desk.

'Hello, sir,' she said. 'Can I help?'

'I hope so. I don't have a reservation, but I wondered if you had a room for a few nights?'

She typed something into the computer and clicked the mouse a few times.

'Well, I could squeeze you in. Single or double?'

'Double.'

'And is this for just yourself or—'

'Just me.'

'Thank you, sir. If you could fill this in for me.' She passed me a registration card and went back to the computer. It should have felt strange, all of it, but instead it seemed normal: a pen on a piece of paper, a key fob handed over, a hotel lobby shorn of its residents. The rush of images and memories did not come flooding back as they had at the Valhalla. Since landing it was as though I was just a slightly bored observer, someone dragged along at the last moment. I registered the changes but it was all flat, unengaging. I looked down at the registration card and saw my name: I had written it as Joe Novak without a moment's hesitation.

The receptionist gave me directions to my room and I wandered past the bar – a bored-looking man behind it, reading a magazine – then pushed open the double doors, where the olde worlde fixtures and fittings were replaced by the standard watercolour paintings and patterned carpets of a chain hotel. It smelled a little damp and some of the wallpaper peeled and flapped at the coving. At the top of the stairs, a chambermaid's cart was blocking the corridor, her plump behind leant against it as she spoke on her phone.

'I told him. I fucking told him last night. Put him on, Jermaine. Put him on now.'

I dodged the piles of towels and the miniature soaps and found room five. Inside it was tired, slightly grubby, the atmosphere fielding a battle between air freshener and cigarettes. The television was already on, welcoming me to the Coach House with classical music playing through its tinny speaker. The bathroom was small and plastered with health and safety notices, the bed surprisingly comfortable. I undressed and got under the sheets, then smoked a cigarette. I was glad that Bethany had never seen inside the rooms; she would have been bitterly disappointed.

At just before seven I woke and took a lukewarm shower. For a long time afterwards I sat on the bed, drip-drying. I had to see my father; this I knew. The place where Bethany had died; her father, too. Hannah. The thought of doing any of these things made doing nothing all the more attractive. I could sit there on the bed, simply sit and watch television, smoke cigarettes, order room service, drink a bottle of whisky and pass out. I looked at my bag, took out what I'd written on the plane and read the whole thing through, then threw it in the bin. I took out the notebook and tried to lose myself in Joe's life for a while and then threw that to the floor. It was after eight and I got dressed slowly, the clothes smelling of the Valhalla, of the fabric softener the maids used. Inside my jacket pocket was a business card. I flipped it over, wondered where I had got it. The name was unfamiliar.

*

The detective is in his mid-forties. He is flanked by a WPC. His mouth droops like it has never learned to smile and he flashes me his badge. He asks me if my name is Mark Wilkinson and I say yes and he asks if he can come in and comes in anyway. He smells strangely like my father, his tie crooked over a shirt that has sweat blooms down its back and front. I ask what this is all about and he tells me to sit down. I sit on the sofa, the WPC beside me, and he sits in Dad's armchair. I can't imagine what it is that I am supposed to have done. I ask him again what's up. The detective tells me his name is DI Simon Parks and that he has bad news, but that it is important that I am strong. He has a face that is some way between cruelty and kindness; a one man good-cop/bad-cop. Matter-of-factly, he tells me about Bethany. His voice is a steady monotone until he says that he is sorry. I see the WPC bite her lip. I want to tell them that they must be joking, that there must be some kind of mistake. But instead the WPC puts her arms around my shoulders. When I eventually look up, the detective is taking his glasses from his pocket. He wipes them on a thin piece of fabric. He does it absently, as though just marking time. Then he starts to ask me questions.

Bethany's father had told him that if anyone knew Bethany's mind, it was me. I answer as well as I can, but I can't tell them why she went down to the secluded park at the back of Greenliffe Field. He skates around the questions he wants to ask, those that decency precludes him from saying out loud. He sighs and polishes his spectacles once again.

'You will catch him,' I say.

'We've got him,' he says, surprised. 'It's just he's not talking. Anything we can do to understand what happened tonight might help.'

'You've got him?' I say.

He nods. 'We've got him. He's not going anywhere, don't you worry about that. It's just . . .' – he puts on his spectacles – 'I just wanted to make sense of it. Get it clear in my mind, you know? You've been most helpful at this difficult time, son. I appreciate it.'

He hands me his card; the first business card I've ever been given.

'If anything comes to you, anything at all, you call me, okay?'

I hold it in my hand and flip it between my fingers for the rest of the night. The sun rises and I remain sitting on the sofa, watching the deep orange light warm the windows.

*

There were only a few people in the residents' bar. I poked my head round the restaurant door, where a lone couple was eating soup. The menu was expensive and uninspiring, dotted with French words and heavy on cream and butter. A waiter paced the back wall, moving wine glasses and adjusting arrangements of cutlery. He looked at me and picked up a wine list and a menu. I turned quickly and headed towards the residents' bar.

Through the opening I could see the public side. It had been refurbished in an unconvincing style. There was a brown suede sofa and a glass table. An unattended cigarette was smoking in an ashtray. Where the jukebox used to be was another watercolour. The barman took my order, set down my drink and went to smoke the unattended cigarette. I picked up the bar menu, its faux-leather binding creaking as I opened it.

'If you're wanting to eat,' a voice to my right said, 'I can recommend the nuts.' The woman passed me the bowl from which she was eating. 'Everything else is foul. The restaurant's awful, the room service stinks and don't even think about the bar snacks. Seriously. Take it from me.'

She was in her late twenties or early thirties, blonde hair tied back, a nose too large for her face, a book open in front of her. She wore business clothes and little make-up, her throat slender and her chin prominent. Her voice was not local, probably southern. I put down the menu and took a couple of nuts from the bowl.

'I don't know,' she said, lighting a cigarette with a match. 'There may be worse hotels in the world, but if there are I've yet to find them.'

'It's not that bad,' I said. 'I've stayed in much worse.'

'I've been here for a month,' she said. 'I've probably lost all sense of proportion. Don't mind me. It's just been one of those days.' She laughed. 'Been one of those days since I got here. But the food? I feel like it's my civic duty to warn you.'

'Thank you,' I said. 'I'll take your word for it.'

She nodded and went back to her book, crunching nuts from the bowl every now and then. I smoked and thought about what it had been like before, sitting on the other side, looking in at the residents, wondering where they'd come from and what on earth they'd done to deserve a night in the town. Had I been looking out, years ago, at Hannah, Bethany and me, I'd have asked the same question: what the hell are *they* doing there? Wasn't there something, anything better that they could be doing?

'Is there anywhere you'd recommend, then?' I eventually said to her. 'I haven't eaten since the plane.'

She picked up her glass and looked thoughtful.

'Well, the Indian is all right. The Italian over the road is edible, just about, and the pub down the road is okay. Best place is the Thai up on the other side of town. But it's rammed on a Friday. Most nights I get a salad from the Tesco's. Can't go wrong.'

She put a beer mat inside the book to save her place and stubbed out her cigarette.

'You here on business too?'

'Sort of,' I said. 'No other reason to be here, is there?'

'People like it. I've met people who've come here to see the park. To see the roundabouts. You'd be surprised. I know I was.'

The barman came back and picked up her glass.

'Are you staying for another?' she said. 'It's on expenses so if you are, I can buy. Like I said, shitty day.'

'A drink would be good,' I said. 'I'm Joe, by the way.'

'Ferne,' she said. 'It's nice to meet someone else stuck here too.'

*

Ferne told me she worked for the architectural firm that was redeveloping the old mills, turning them into loft apartments for commuters. The hard hat she wore most days played havoc with her hair and the workmen were rude and sullen. She'd been staying at the hotel – with only short breaks back to her home in West London – for almost six weeks, and everything about the place made her mad. She knew no one and was tired of eating dinner alone. The days meshed into one another, weekends too.

'I've stopped going home, though. It only makes it worse, you know?' she said as we drank our wine. 'When you're here you sort of forget that other people's lives go on while yours just falters and stagnates. Two weeks I was supposed to be here. No longer than that. Now it's going to be two months, three probably.'

We ordered more peanuts and I let her speak. She talked about her ex, her best friend and her best friend's newborn child, about the men at the site who at first had taken her for a soft touch, but were now a little frightened of her. I could see why: there was something hard about her, flinty. It was not unattractive.

'You don't talk much,' she said after a pause.

'I like listening,' I said. 'I prefer it. People don't listen enough, I always think. Always jumping in at the end of a sentence, trying to sum up what you've been saying. My friend O'Neil says that one of the most important things to realize in conversation is that everyone's always thinking what they're going to say next. Which means if you're properly listening you'll understand what people are really saying, what they actually want you to know.'

'But if the person you're speaking to,' Ferne said smiling, 'is already preparing what they're saying in their own head, they're not listening to you and you can't get across what you want to say, right?'

'That's sort of the point. O'Neil explains it better, though. He's a better talker than me. Better at everything really. Apart from table tennis. I always kick his ass at that.'

Ferne laughed and lit another cigarette. There were a few people in the other bar now, though I recognized none of them. The three regulars, Stan, Tom and John Boxer, had probably moved on somewhere else, or perhaps were dead. Over those years I had got to know them slightly.

Tom was, almost improbably, a former jazz drummer who had fallen on hard times and was working at a garage. Stan always stayed for four pints of best before heading home to his invalid wife, while John Boxer talked as though everyone was listening and everyone was in agreement with his views. He'd once told me I would amount to nothing, that I would never be a man, not really. He'd also once been barred for getting his cock out in the bar, for pulling out his trouser pockets and showing everyone his impression of an elephant. The owner had personally escorted him from the premises, but a week later Boxer was back as if nothing had happened. Beth thought him the only good thing about the whole town.

'What're you laughing at?' Ferne said.

'I'm sorry?'

'You were laughing. Were you laughing at me?'

'No, it's not you . . . there was this guy I used to know, that's all. Haven't thought about him in years.'

She nodded and we both went silent, looking through the hatch at a group of women drinking cocktails on the sofa. They were loud, dressed in shiny fabrics, their hairdos fresh from the salon, their features smudged by make-up. They looked unaccountably happy; the way the same kind of girls looked when Bethany, Hannah and I lived there. 'Can't they see it?' Bethany said once to me. 'Can't they see that they're trapped?'

177

Watching these girls now, I saw that Beth, Hannah and I had seen nothing of life, just the town and the people within it, and the trap was one of our own making. One Thanksgiving at O'Neil's parents' house, his mother had ended a typical argument between O'Neil and his father by saying: 'You can no more escape where you're from than you can escape your shoe size or your age. So let it rest.' She'd put the pie on the table and the conversation had wilted. I wanted to tell her that escaping was exactly what I had done.

'They remind me of the girls from school,' Ferne said. 'It's like regressing being here. Makes me feel like a teenager.'

'I know people who'd like that.'

'I hated being a teenager. Who would ever want to go through all that again?'

'It's the possibility of it all, isn't it? A life still ready to be lived. I can see the attraction.'

'So you'd go through that again? Really?' she said.

I thought of lying in bed with Bethany, the aeroplane tail fins, the rickety bookshelf.

'Good God no. I was just saying I can understand it, that's all.'

Ferne nodded and looked at her watch. She had very thin wrists and downy arms.

'I think that's me done. Got to be up in the morning.'

'Would you like to eat with me?' I said quickly, knowing it was unfair. I just wanted company, someone to share the evening, someone to deflect from the crabbing sense of what I would have to do the following day. But I did not expect her to say no.

'I have a salad,' she said. 'And I do need to be up in the morning.' She drank down the last of her wine. 'Maybe I'll see you tomorrow.'

'Yes,' I said. 'Tomorrow. Maybe.'

'Your best bet is the Indian. Follow the road down and it's on the left.'

'Thanks. Goodnight, Ferne.'

'Thanks, Joe. See you later.'

She got up unsteadily and headed for the stairs to the rooms. I watched her leave and looked again at the menu. The women in the other bar screamed at something. The barman took my glass and asked if I wanted another. I shook my head.

*

There had been women after Bethany. New York was easy that way, and there had been adventures and brief affairs. Those that lasted over a month were few and far between, ending usually with an awkward conversation and on one occasion with the words: 'Just go ahead and fuck O'Neil.' But mostly it was just the hand on the arm, saying that I needed help, that no one could be that cold and survive. I did not think of Joe as unfeeling, but all the evidence pointed to the contrary. I had constructed a persona incapable of love in any meaningful sense; a man for whom true intimacy was locked off like a bank vault. Joe had always assumed everyone was the same way; or at least that O'Neil was. I thought of Edith and O'Neil, the two of them in bed and wearing their nightclothes, talking in hushed voices about the mess I'd left behind. I imagined the conversations they'd had over the last few months, how many times my name had been mentioned.

Saturday, 7th July 1990, 1.41 pm

Bethany's father has tears in his eyes and is applauding as the procession comes to an end. Over the PA, the assembled crowds are asked to give a big round of applause for the carnival queen. There are loud whistles and shouts. Bethany waves for the final time. 'I now declare the tattoo open!' the announcer says, and crowds surge forward through the gates and spill out onto the fields. There are two large spaces, busy clusters of local stands and booths in the first; in the second, military equipment and personnel, fighter planes to sit in, helicopters to queue for and a fun fair with dodgems and a waltzer. In both there are sellers of balloons and hot dogs and ice creams. There is little shade. A few lads kick around a football, a family searches for a spot to set down their picnic rugs and begin their lunch. A knot of teenagers smoke and laugh, drinking from an oversized bottle of cider. The change is seamless, and Bethany is almost forgotten, standing still on the float on the periphery, her crown slightly askew.

When she steps down from the platform, she is force-kissed by the footmen, who tell her how beautiful she looks. Marchers stream past, removing costumes if they can. A team wanders aimlessly towards the field, dressed as Egyptian slaves. 'If we don't win this year,' one of the men says, 'they can fucking forget it next time.'

Her father approaches along with Hannah. He is smiling; as is Hannah, but in a different way. Someone wolf-whistles and Bethany can't help but colour. It is a strange nothing space she's occupying: not quite queen, not quite commoner.

'You were amazing, love. Just amazing. You look incredible,' her father says.

'I look a mess,' Bethany says. 'I'm melting in all this stuff.' Her father hugs her tight and whispers, 'Thank you,' one more time. She holds him as tight as she can. She kisses him on the cheek and wishes she could tell him the truth. All he has ever said is that she will always be his baby. Always. He says it in a way that is at once proud, protective and resigned.

'I have to say that you looked okay up there. But I kept thinking you were going to freak out or something, or shout something to the crowd,' Hannah says. 'I'm sort of disappointed.'

'Can someone get me a drink,' Bethany says. 'A Diet Coke or something?'

Her father asks Hannah if she'd like something too. She asks for a Diet Coke and he sets off towards the queue for the ice-cream van.

'You okay?' Hannah says. 'You look kinda odd.'

'Fine,' she says. 'Just fucking knackered. You know how exhausting it is to look happy for that amount of time? Feels like my face is going to fall off.'

Somewhere a klaxon sounds and to their left some primary-school kids start country dancing, their parents surrounding the roped-off area, clapping along to the music.

'I fucking hate the carnival,' Bethany says.

'Ah, but the carnival loves *you*,' Hannah says. 'You're a celebrity now. You're world famous in the North-West.'

Bethany kicks off her shoes and feels the grass through the mesh of her tights. The thought of Daniel in the crowd makes her scan the area, hoping that he hasn't followed her, that no one will see them together before they are due to meet. She has no idea why this is important, but still she searches. The only person she recognizes is an old school teacher and the woman who sells the cigarettes at Gateway.

'Is this what happens when you become famous,' Hannah says, 'you start to ignore your friends?'

'What's that?' Bethany says.

Mike returns with the cans, freshly cold from the

fridge, and they pull the tabs and Bethany drinks half of hers in one long pull. It freezes her head, makes her stomach feel immediately chilled and bloated.

'Thanks, Dad,' she says as Hannah throws her cigarette to the ground and crushes it out.

'No,' her father says. 'Thank you. Thank you for everything.'

*

Bethany has two more queenly duties: the first a photocall with the soldiers and airmen in the second field. Waller is late and heavily sweating, his mind lost in the agenda he carries on a clipboard. His expression is fatigued, which suggests that he has not reached his stated target yet; but his voice is light enough to imply confidence that he will prevail. A young male assistant is with him, his ill-fitting suit looking peculiar in the heat. He carries a walkie-talkie, which only adds to the incongruity: it is big and cumbersome. It clicks and barks just like the old CB radio Hannah's father used to own.

'We're a very little under forecast,' Waller says as they pick their way past picnics and coconut shies, 'but overall, with a bit of a push later on both here and in the pubs, we should be okay. We might even make it to thirty thousand, which I never thought was even possible.'

'That would be quite an achievement, Mr Waller,' the boy says.

'Let's not count chickens, Olly. No chicken-counting here. Anyway, Bethany, I do apologize for your having to do this photocall. I did say that it was inappropriate, but they were insistent. Something of a tradition, apparently.'

At the recruitment stand for the army and air force, they are greeted with a stiff salute from the commanding officer for the day. His name is Peters and he has a neat, greying moustache which makes him look both military and clonishly homosexual. Peters accepts Waller's hand-shake in silence and turns his attentions to Bethany.

'This is what the men look forward to the most,' he says. 'It's the highlight of the carnival, these days.'

Waller rolls his eyes; a moment later, Olly does the same. The dealings with Peters over many months have been fraught. He had wanted there to be a bigger military presence than ever before, an assault course, a hand-to-hand-combat demonstration and a tug of war between the air force and the army. Waller had vetoed them all. At meeting after meeting, he had tried to impress upon Peters the changes in the world, the changes in the country at large.

Peters walks Bethany past a Harrier jump jet and then around a missile launcher. The men are lounging by a tank, waiting for them. They are dressed impeccably and the tank looks freshly cleaned, a shining olive green. Bethany wonders whether it has seen action, whether this is more for show than for real. In history, they'd studied the Great War and for a moment she is reminded of the paper tanks that had been used to fool the American public. The press photographer, the woman who took her picture earlier in the day, arrives just as Bethany is being introduced to the men. They are young, still coming to terms with their increased fitness and musculature. They shake her hand firmly and she tries not to wince. The one on the end of the line pauses before greeting her.

'Bethany? I don't know if you remember me. We were at school together. Graeme. Graeme Lee? I was a couple of years ahead of you.'

'Yes, of course,' she says, having no recollection of the boy this man had once been. 'So you ended up in the army, then?'

He is still shaking her hand.

'Chance to see the world. Learn a trade. Make a difference.'

'Nice to see you again,' she says. His smile never falters.

The airmen march across; there are a dozen of them, their serge uniforms smarter and more elegant than the fatigues of the soldiers. She shakes their hands too, the head airman introducing each man as though she is important. The photographer smells slightly of wine and tells the men where to stand. The head airman – Jeffers – suggests that they line up by the Harrier, but the photographer simply shakes her head. 'The tank's better,' she says. 'Besides, we did the Harrier last year.'

*

Her picture is taken with Graeme Lee's arm around her waist. He smells of an aftershave that she recognizes from the pub; a pungent sportswear-ish scent. It is over in a matter of moments, the photographer checking her watch and saying that she needs to be back in the other field for the judging of the floats. Bethany feels Graeme's hand on her and thinks of Daniel again. Graeme is smiling. He lets her go.

'Are you busy later?' he says. 'Perhaps we could go and have a drink?'

He seems somehow confident that she will say yes; it is a curious kind of arrogance. She thinks she remembers him now as a shy but thuggish boy, a boy who sat quietly at the back of the class, but whom everyone knew to avoid angering. He was suspended, she remembers, for beating up a classmate. He had used a piece of wood.

'I'm sorry,' she says. 'I'm busy later. But it was nice to meet you.'

'You too,' he says. 'Sometimes being in the army's lonely, you know. It's good to see a friendly face.'

'I have to go,' she says.

'You look wonderful,' he says. 'Like a princess.'

'I'm a queen,' she says, laughing. 'But thank you all the same.'

THIRTEEN

I picked up my cigarettes and walked out of the hotel. There were lamppost halos, a steady stream of cars making their way up the road. A short walk to my right would take me to the Queen's and the Red Lion; to my left my secondary school; to the north my father's house; somewhere to the south-west the place where they found Bethany. They all felt far away. It was slightly chill and I buttoned up my jacket as I descended the stone steps.

The Italian restaurant was half full, all wooden floors and bright lighting. I scanned the room through the glass, faces unfamiliar except for one table of four towards the front. Simon Beech and Ian Mawby were sitting eating pizza with two women I didn't recognize.

They drank their bottled beer and laughed; one of the women got up to go to the bathroom. It is possible that the two men remembered me; possible that they still had occasion to think of me passing them the football, shouting something random at them. If they'd seen me they might have paused, trying to place me. But I kept on walking.

The Barclays bank was now a pub, two men guarding its door, the swinging sign above – calligraphic writing announcing it as The Counting House – the only clue to its previous incarnation. The noise was audible outside, the banners describing promotions on wine and cider. I paused for a moment, wondering whether this might be the place where the Coach's regulars had decamped. But everyone I could see through the protected doors was young. Young and dressed for a night out. One of the bouncers looked at me and chewed gum. The other one spat on the floor. A group crossed the road from the High Street and a car sounded its horn. One of the kids flicked him the Vs as it sped past. No IDs were checked, despite how young they looked.

Ferne would be dressed in her nightclothes, her salad eaten, watching whatever was on the television. Though I had met her only briefly, it would have been nice to have her with me, sitting at the window seat in the Indian restaurant. The dining area wasn't bad, though it was overlit like all the new places I'd seen: as though people had become afraid of the dark. The table next to me was occupied by two younger women, but most of the patrons were my father's age: roughly middle-aged and softly packaged, their cheeks reddened from the heat of the food. They could be any one of many people's parents.

Some of them could have known Bethany, some may even have been at the funeral.

I ordered and passed back the menu, looked around at the diners. As I did, I realized the risk I had taken. I shifted my seat closer to the wall and closed my eyes, the way I had as a child, imagining that no one could see me.

The food arrived and I could think of nothing as I ate; just the curry and the bread, the beer and the rice. It was better than the Indian places where O'Neil and I used to eat in New York. O'Neil had never seen the attraction, but would humour me when I got a craving. He preferred chilli, his own a version that consisted mainly of beer and bourbon, and was dismissive of any of the curries I forced him to try. I only went when I could no longer face down the longing, full as the curry houses were with ex-pat Brits, or small canteens where the food was too authentic and the waiters' Gujarati delivered with ill-disguised sarcasm.

I drank my second Cobra and stared out of the window, at the young people walking up Mill Street. The styles had changed little, still sportswear and earrings and short skirts. Hair was iron-flat, skin tone an unnatural orange or blistering white. *They look happier than we ever did*, Bethany said. *You ever think about that?*

'Can I get you a dessert?' the waiter said. The plates

had gone and the table had been swept. A cooling twist of towel lay in a wicker basket.

'Just the bill, please,' I said and he nodded. The women on the next table were talking loudly.

'Looks real from where I'm sitting, Trish. I'd kill to have legs like that these days.'

'They look like scrubbers.'

'They're just having fun. Might as well while you can.'

'If that's fun, you can keep it.'

'You weren't ever young, were you?'

'With my life? With my old man?'

'Come on, let's go Queen's for a drink.'

The woman shifted in her seat, looked at her watch. 'Okay, but just one. Can't be back later than ten. Going fucking kill me anyway.'

'What's that thing about sheeps and lambs? Me dad used to say something like that.'

'Maybe I'll call him first,' the woman said, taking out her phone.

'Oh, just come for a drink. Say it took ages for a taxi.'

The waiter returned with their coats and I lost their thread. They couldn't have been too much older than me, if they were at all. *I knew them at school*, Bethany said.

The waiter had the bill, the waxy paper inside a leather wallet.

'They were always like that, always bickering,' he said with a smile. 'Funny how things don't change.'

I handed over some notes and then looked up at the waiter. For a moment I thought it was Abel Farah, captain of the school football team.

'Did you go to Kelmscott?' I said.

'No,' he said. 'Eaton Valley. They don't remember me, but I remember them. Bad girls. Bad girls both of them.' He laughed and headed back to the bar. On the pavement, the two women were continuing their argument. *If we'd stayed,* Bethany said, *that's what we'd have become.*

*

Where Mill Street meets Harrington Street you can see over the town. Green's Off-Licence was still there, as was the motorbike showroom. The Masonic Hall too, dark and smutty behind a row of new flats. Fully dark now, there were stars in the sky, and the hum of cars and the smell of dope from a bunch of skateboarders sitting on a bench by the entrance to the Safeway car park. *We bought our first joint from people like that. You remember? From a guy called Gillon, and you misheard and thought he said Dylan.*

I heard her laugh and saw her talking to one of the long-haired guys, him passing her a spliff and her running across the road. Seventeen years old and with her arm in mine, telling me that she loved me. *I must because I'd never have done that for anyone else.*

By the car park's chain-link fence I lit a cigarette and followed Bethany up the street, past the discounted home and beauty shop, the butcher's that had somehow survived, a betting shop with pictures of sporting legends unchanged since the late eighties, the same clusters of teenagers drinking on the benches, the same clack of shoes on the brickwork. *You used to call this the gauntlet, you remember?* she said. *You always thought you'd get beaten up.* I took a right up to the restaurant where I had worked; it was called something different now, candles visible through the window. The menu was sophisticated, but I couldn't imagine such cuisine being prepared in the tiny kitchen out back. *Things change*, Bethany said. *You can't be surprised at everything.*

We passed the Chinese take-away. *Sore finger?* she said laughing. *You remember that, right?* With Hannah we'd get chips on the way home, the Chinese woman asking if we wanted salt and vinegar and it always sounding like 'sore finger?' If there were a group of men there would be the inevitable joke and we would roll our eyes, even though we had found it funny many times before.

The passageway dipped down and on my left there were three small conjoined cottages, tucked away, the bust of a local philanthropist between them. It was said that in his direct eyeline a young boy's body had been found, drowned by the adjacent river. It was just a story, but we always walked quickly past the cottages and never saw anyone go in or come out. *Creepy fucking place,* Bethany said, *always was.*

At the top of the cut we reached her old house, the lights off, the gate in need of some attention. Bethany's bedroom window was at the back, the view extending over the untended fields. I sat down on the wall and smoked a cigarette, wondering if Mike really was still there, in bed now, dreaming of Bethany. *No time for that now*, she said. *We have places to see!*

We walked past the Woodman, the sound of karaoke coming from the doors. To the right was a church, the gravestones bent by age. A man was shouting into his phone and for a moment I thought it was John Boxer. *You're not looking,* Bethany said, *this is not the place you left, so just let it go, okay?*

The Carpenter's was the first pub Bethany and I went for a drink alone. I ordered a Jack Daniel's and Coke and stood to the side of the bar, Bethany laughing. *You don't change, do you?* she said. *Everything changes but you.*

In fact little had changed in the Carpenter's, though the music was less abrasive and there were fewer leather jackets. We had agreed to meet there as it was neutral territory: no one from either of our schools would know us. So we drank and smoked, talked about our absent mothers, but quickly, and moved on. When we kissed, drunkenly, I felt like the world had started anew. It was one of those kisses. I was young, full of hormones and full of everything else, but the power of that moment—

Had I lived, would you feel the same way? Bethany said. *Poor boy, you'll never know, will you?*

Bethany sat on the stool next to me, smoking a cigarette, drinking gin and tonic. She watched me with amusement. *You never cease to amaze me, Mark. Your capacity for delusion.* She finished her drink and walked out onto the High Street; I followed as she walked over to the Queen's, the record shop opposite now a mobile-phone store. *They shut down the Melody Maker too*, she said. *It was only a matter of time.*

The Queen's was stinking full, hard to negotiate and packed with people who had a glimmer of girls and boys I had once known about them. They did not look my way. The bar was three deep as it always had been, the same beers on, the same look of veiled dislike on the bar staff's faces. I ordered a pint of Pedigree and it foamed on the bar towel, thick and faintly smelling of sulphur. The barman took my money and I turned away, bumping into a belly. I looked up at the man it belonged to.

'Matthew,' I said. 'Matthew Cunningham?'

He looked down on me, his height cramped under the low roof.

'Yeah,' he said. 'Do I know you?'

'We went to school together. Kelmscott.'

'Oh. Okay. Yes, I remember. You well?'

'Good, yes.'

'Funny accent you got there. Sound like a Septic.'

'I moved there years back,' I said. 'Must have picked it up.'

He nodded. He had no idea who I was. He liked hip hop and had an attractive elder sister; he liked to draw and was funny without being a clown. He was always trying to make money, always had a scheme on the go. Now he looked, dressed as he was in smart jeans and a Ralph Lauren shirt, like he had made his money, was living as best he could. He got the barman's attention and ordered a round of drinks.

'Nice to see you again,' he said. 'See you around.'

Bethany laughed. *You think they remember you? What an ego you have!*

I stood in the room where the pool table used to be. I placed my pint pot on the mantelpiece of an unlit fire and watched Bethany drink a pint of Guinness. She kept a cigarette lit at all times. *You think this is bad,* she said, *you've got your father to see yet. Mine too. Imagine how that's going to play out! You just dropping by like this with no word for what, how long? And then you're back. What are you going to ask them? What are you going to say? Sorry? That isn't going to cut it, not by a long way. Sorry, Dad, I walked out on you. Sorry, Mike, that I never contacted you? You have no clue what you're doing, no idea of the wounds you're going to open up with your salty fingers. But so long as you're okay. So long as you feel like you're doing the right thing. Fuck everyone else, right? What exactly is it you want here? If you've come looking for answers you're a decade and a bit too late. Anyway, you're Josef now, right? You're a whole other person. Go back to New York. Go back to America. Just fuck off now, okay? Home is where real life happens, where we can't just hide behind stupid names and bought identities. There isn't anything for you here, Mark.*

I wept then, softly, unable to stop Bethany's questions, stop her smiling mouth from scything through me. I drank my pint quickly and headed through the bodies to the door. Bethany followed, a jacket covering her Cramps T-shirt. *You don't get away that easily, you fucking coward,* she said. *There's more to see. Much more to see than this!*

*

The war memorial had fresh flowers by it, soldiers fallen in Afghanistan. I sat on the bench and smoked a cigarette, Bethany, still holding her pint of Guinness, was standing in front of me. *You think I matter? All those people who die, they don't matter, so why should I? What makes me so fucking special? I was raped and murdered. Happens all over the world. Every single minute of every single day. But you had to take it personally.*

'I loved you. I still love you,' I said.

You love yourself.

Bethany drank the last of her Guinness and sat down next to me on the bench. *We need to keep moving*, she said.

*

Hannah's house was a long walk away. Her estate was typical of those that had sprung up in the seventies. Cars guarded garage doors like sentries. Bethany walked in silence until we arrived at her red front door, the crazy-paved driveway. There were lights on inside, the flicker of a television projecting onto drawn curtains. It was where the three of us used to meet before going out.

They probably fucked in there, Bethany said with a snort. Bethany marched off and I hurried in her wake. *Imagine it, the two of them!*

We came out at the east corner of the estate and met the Crewe Road. *Now this you're going to love*, she said. My school, the reason we had met in the first place, should have been up on the right, but as I approached, the road looked too wide and open. Cranes and diggers were chained together behind big wooden boards, the gaps in between showing the deep excavation of the ground. Where the science block had stood there was rubble, where the playing fields had been there were the first imaginings of a housing estate: scaffolding, breezeblocks and partly constructed roofs. Bethany stood with her hands on her hips. *I told you*, she said.

The Carpenter's meeting had been arranged in the school, a note given to me by Hannah. It was not long, written in Bethany's scratchy, elegant handwriting. *I remember that note, long and stupid it was. I think I quoted from some band you said you liked. I asked you if you'd meet me sometime, said that I'd had such a good time with you in the restaurant and that I owed you a drink for being so nice to me, taking me in out of the rain. The letter I got back was a disappointment, to be honest. Just half a side ripped from an A4 binder. Your handwriting was poor and it was hard to make out what you'd written. But it quickened my heart anyway.*

I put my hand to the boards and looked again over the building site. She sparked up another cigarette and laughed. *The thing is, if you go looking to destroy yourself, someone else will always do it better.*

Saturday, 7th July 1990, 2.33 pm

Lunch is held in a marquee, roped off from the general carnival crowd. The mayor is wearing his heavy gold chain, which bumps his perfectly round, pregnant-looking belly every time he moves. There is wine and tea and beer from a local brewery pumped from casks. A string quartet plays in the background and sandwiches and pastries are arranged on silver salvers. Since they arrived to a round of applause, Waller has not left her side, introducing her and himself to each group or couple they meet. They are the local businessmen and Rotarians, local councillors and their wives. They all dress in the same style: Gabicci shirts, Farah slacks, double-breasted suits with too wide lapels, everything bought from Waverley's in the town. They tell her how beautiful she looks, what a great job she's done. She smiles and shakes their hands, thanks them for their kind words. She no longer recognizes herself.

Her father is there, standing alone by the buffet, and she waits patiently to be with him. She can see him watch her as she is passed from one group to the next and she sees his pride again and reminds herself that this is for him. Only for him.

After her mother died, Bethany looked after her father. There was no one else to do it. The factory was left in the capable hands of his deputy and Mike made it in only when he felt well enough, which was not often. He didn't do much. He didn't cry, watch home videos, obsess over old photo albums; he just sat in his armchair, staring at the wall or the window. Bethany didn't interfere, but she coerced him into at least a semblance of a routine. She made him eat at the right times, shower and shave, change out of his dressing gown. Her grief she carried to her bedroom, her anger to school, her sadness to whenever she was alone. It took her father over a year to begin to function again; the slight hoods over his eyes now the only suggestion of his loss.

Bethany and Mark talked about those months often; the months of waiting on a heartbroken parent. Mark's father was angry and drunk and scared to leave the house; became paranoid that everyone was talking about him, about how he'd let his wife run off with another man. He went to work as usual, came home and, despite his apparent rage, sat watching television and drinking beer. He's pretty much the same these days.

Mark wouldn't talk about his mother much; something that Beth found difficult to understand. She'd asked him whether he missed her at all. He shook his head.

'My mother was . . . I should say is . . .' he said, never finishing the sentence.

Bethany is shaking another hand and accepting a kiss from the man's wife. She nods as Bob and Rita say how beautiful she looks, what a great job she has done. The marquee is stuffy and Hannah is nowhere to be seen. For that at least she is grateful.

'I was the carnival queen once,' Rita says. 'Nineteen fifty-five. It was the happiest day of my life. I can remember it like it was yesterday. You don't forget things like that I can tell you. I've still got the photographs somewhere.'

'She was a right stunner in them days,' Bob says. 'I don't know what she ever saw in me.'

'He had a motorcycle,' she says with a laugh. 'And he looked good in leathers.'

The image of the two of them, young and in love, riding a motorcycle out of town and over the hills towards Macclesfield and Leek, stays with Bethany as Waller steers her towards the next group of couples. They tell her how beautiful she looks and what a good job she has done.

'Last year, we called her the carnival scream,' one of the women says and they all laugh.

Could they be like that, Mark and Bethany: later,

older, still in love, still clinging to memories of excitement? It seems so improbable, to get to that age, to see the years slip by. She never wants to be like Rita, thinking back to when she was her happiest.

Eventually she reaches her father. He has heaped a plate with sandwiches, crisps and a couple of vol-au-vents; he has also poured her a glass of white wine. He hands the drink to her and she resists the temptation to drain it quickly.

'You know,' he says, 'it's times like this I miss your mum the most. What would she think of all this?' He sweeps his arm around the room. 'I mean, look at these people. Can you imagine her spending more than a minute with any of them?'

'She would have loved it, Dad,' she says. 'Imagine all these Tories to bait, the whole lot of them in one place. No escape!'

'And with Thatcher gone too,' he says. 'Imagine that!'

'She'd have been in her element.'

'And she'd have given me hell when I got home.'

'Both of us.'

Bethany finishes the tuna sandwich and the last of her wine. The string quartet pauses and there is a small flourish of applause. Her father goes to the bar and returns with wine for them both. He smiles but it's more for his benefit than hers.

'I think I'm going to head back,' he says. 'Have a bit of a snooze before this evening.'

'I'll see you at the restaurant for seven,' she says. 'Assuming I haven't killed Waller by then.'

'See you there, love,' he says.

*

She is guest of honour at the motorcycle stunt display and is seated on a raised plinth with half a dozen other dignitaries. The crowds are scrunched around the barricades and sawdust has been scattered in the arena: there are various obstacles lined up: ramps and jumps and hoops and pipes. She is under the full beam of the sun and can feel it tightening her skin. The woman to her right has a battery-powered fan that buzzes like a swarm.

Waller looks at his clipboard and checks his watch. On cue the motorcyclists pull out from their trailer. One is dressed all in red, one in white and one in blue. They pause, rev their engines and wave at the crowd, then they roar away, towards the three ramps, hit the planks together and take to the air, turning their front wheels in Bethany's direction. They lift their hands from their grips and join gloves, then break. They hit the ground just in control and the crowd goes wild. It is all lost on Bethany Wilder.

She spots Daniel. He is drinking from a can of lager

and talking to some men, none of whom are looking at the motorbikes. She imagines that they are talking about her, that he is describing what he will do to her later. They could be telling him that they'll come and watch, all of them hiding in the woods, their trousers round their ankles. Part of her is not as disgusted as she wants to be.

She watches Daniel drink, his mate draped over his shoulders, the men laughing together. She watches as they light cigarettes, as one pulls more beer from a rucksack. None of this is real, she reminds herself, none of it. She is rebalancing the past; there is nothing more to it than that.

Two men run into the display area and move three rings into its centre. They set them alight and there is a long oooh from the crowd. The riders rev their engines and the smoke billows. Bethany can smell diesel and something else, like the garage at Mark's house. She looks at Daniel and then at the riders. The crowd seem to want them to fail, even though they know they won't. The PA plays 'Ring of Fire' by Johnny Cash. Bam-badam-badam-bah-da-um; bam-badam-badam-bah-da-um. The riders take their jump, make it through, put their hands in the air, take off their helmets. They are all women and the crowd applauds.

'You didn't see that coming, did you?' Waller says.

'No,' Bethany says. 'No, I didn't.'

FIFTEEN

There were people in the hotel bar, a couple of men drinking brandy and smoking small cigars. I was damp from the rain. Bethany had stopped talking to me, disappearing as we made our way through the downpour back into town. I ordered a whisky and carried it to my room, turned on the television and smoked cigarettes one after another. I watched a rolling news channel, stories tumbling out, presented in strobing graphics and discussed by experts and the professionally concerned. I wondered if Bethany's death would have made it on to the news now, and knew that it would. A pretty white woman; a carnival queen, how could it not?

The next morning I found a pizza box and an empty bottle of wine outside Ferne's room. The maid was cleaning inside, piles of clothes on the floor and a mess of cosmetics on the dressing table. There was also a stack of cheap thrillers. She caught me looking, but was too wrapped up in her phone call.

'Can't you just for once sort this out yourself?' the

maid shouted into the mouthpiece. 'I'm supposed to be working here, aren't I?'

Outside it was bright again, the roads sludgy with traffic and the High Street surprisingly busy. I found the police station next to the library that Dad and I used to visit every Saturday when I was young. He liked to read military history, mostly about the air force, and he would deposit me in the children's section while he browsed the shelves. He liked the silence, I always thought, and there was precious little at home in those days. The building was looking seamy, like it had been left to fester, though there was a windowed atrium tacked on where people were using computers and drinking coffee. Bethany and I used to walk past on the way home some nights and see the books that people had posted through the letter box. There used to be a sign telling lenders not to. There was no sign there now.

After my interview with the detective and the WPC, there had been no follow-up. I was never required to attend the station and so now couldn't tell whether it had changed much. The desk sergeant was talking on the phone and taking notes. A woman waited on one of the brown sofas, her handbag close to her chest. In front of her was a plastic cup of coffee, steaming and ignored. A policeman punched the digits on the combination lock and she looked up.

'How much longer?' she said. 'I've got to be at work for twelve.'

'They're just processing him, Mrs Reynolds. Shouldn't be too long now.'

'He'll never learn, that boy. Maybe this time someone'll press charges. Might do him some good.'

The policeman smiled and disappeared into the back of the station. The desk sergeant put down the phone and looked up at me.

'Can I help?' he asked.

'I'm not sure,' I said. 'I hope so. I was wondering whether it might be possible to speak to DI Simon Parks.'

The man chewed his pencil and screwed up his eyes.

'And what is this concerning?'

'Well, I'd prefer not to say. It's just important I speak with him.'

'Really?' the sergeant said. He had deep-ringed eyes, a smirk to his face and hair protruding from his shirt collar and his jumper's rolled-up cuffs. 'I dare say it is important, but DI Parks retired about five year ago. So whatever it is, you'll be needing to speak to one of the other DIs. And I'll need to know what the "important" thing is before I can refer you.'

'It's sort of a personal matter. I really need to speak to DI Parks.'

'Well, I can't help you there, sir. I'm sorry.'

'Do you know where I might find him?' I asked. The desk sergeant shook his head and the heavy door opened. A youth came out accompanied by an officer; there was blood on his T-shirt and his jeans were ripped.

'Here you are, Mrs Reynolds. Be seeing you soon.' The officer turned to the lad. 'Lucky day again, Scotty. Let's hope they don't ever run out, yeah?'

'Fuck off,' he said.

'Be seeing you,' the officer said.

Mrs Reynolds pushed the boy out of the double doors. He was laughing and telling her to shut the fuck up as he lit a cigarette.

'They should give her her own parking space,' the sergeant said.

'I really need your help,' I said, leaning against the desk. 'It's important. Is there no way you can give me his contact details, or a phone number or something?'

'Do you really think that we give out that kind of information? We might be coppers but we're not stupid.'

'I need to talk to him about Bethany Wilder,' I said. 'I've come a long way and I need to speak with him.'

He cocked his head to one side.

'You journalists never give up, do you?' he said. 'That story's dead anyway. He said all he knew on that television programme they made. Just watch that and let the man alone.'

'I'm not a journalist. I just want to talk to him, that's all. Ask him a few questions.'

'Whatever you are,' he said. 'He won't speak to you.'

The telephone rang and he answered it politely, looking over at me with disdain. I remained standing, not to show resolve, but because there was nothing else to do. I watched him take down notes and reassure the caller that a squad car would be there as soon as possible. He put down the phone and put out the call to the cars on the street.

'You still here?' he said to me eventually. 'We've got work to do, you know.'

'I appreciate that, but look, I need to see him. It's . . . look, he interviewed me at the time. I was Bethany's boyfriend. Mark Wilkinson.'

It was the first time I'd said that name in well over a decade. It felt like a confession all of itself.

'You have any ID to prove that, sir?'

'Not on me, no. Look, you've got to trust me on this.'

'Trust is something I've kind of lost track of, sir?' he said, laughing. 'Now this might come as a shock to you, *sir*, but I tend not to believe everything I'm told. And even if you are who you say you are, why do you think he'd want to go back over all that?'

The sergeant stood up and placed a file in a wire-mesh

tray. He was taller than I expected with a colossal rear that shuddered as he walked.

'You'd think,' he said, 'that people would just forget about it. There's been enough murders since and no one comes round asking about them.'

'I just need to talk to him. It'll only take a moment.'

He settled back into his chair, rocked on its back legs and laced his fingers together.

'So why now?' he said.

Bethany laughed, sitting on the sofa that Mrs Reynolds had recently departed. *Yeah, why now. Why don't you tell him?*

'I don't know,' I said. 'Things have just kind of . . . I don't know, come to a head.'

He looked at me for a moment, rubbed his eyes, then looked at me again. The double doors swung open and a middle-aged man flanked by two uniforms came through. He was booked in for shoplifting meat from Tesco's. He looked as grey as his Farah slacks. The desk sergeant watched me throughout the procedure. Eventually he slammed down his pen and shook his head.

'When things come to a head,' he said to me as he filled out a form, 'I tend to go to the pub. The Crown mainly. You know it?'

I nodded.

'Well, they'll be open in a half-hour or so.'

'Thank you,' I said.

'Good luck,' he said and went straight back to his paperwork.

*

The Crown was over on the other side of town, a pub designed to serve the boxy housing estate in the hinterland between the town and its more expensive environs. I knew it only by its reputation for lock-ins and as the venue for Hannah's dad's fiftieth birthday, which we had attended under sufferance. There was a St George's flag on the roof, banners advertising *All Sports Shown Here* and inside screens everywhere: small ones inset behind the bar, large pull-downs and flat screens on the walls.

I ordered a drink and sat down, on some paper wrote down the detective's name and underlined it, looked at it for a time, then lit a cigarette. *You know what you want to ask him, right?* Bethany said. *You must know that, surely?* I shook my head. She laughed. *You're here, at least. That's something, I suppose.*

Someone ordered a pint of best and I felt a tap on my shoulder.

'I heard you want to speak to me,' the man said. 'Come on, I don't have long.' He picked up his pint and walked over to a raised area by the pool tables. DI Parks had aged rather better than I had expected, his body lean and his eyes still sharp. He held his back erect, but shook slightly as he drank. He hadn't shaved, his stubble greying at the corners of his mouth.

'If you're a journalist, I'm walking out of here right now,' he said. 'I've had it up to here with journalists.' He raised his hand to his face as in salute.

'I'm not a journalist. You know who I am,' I said. 'We've met before. You interviewed me. I was Bethany Wilder's boyfriend when she died.'

He leaned over the table. 'You're not writing a book, are you?'

'No,' I said. 'Nothing like that. I just want to talk, that's all. I need to talk.'

You don't know what to say, though, do you? You're looking at him and you don't have the first idea. Are you scared? You should be scared.

I looked at my notes and then back at him.

'So?' he said finally. 'You wanted to talk. So talk.' He shifted his weight on the stool and looked straight at me. It was perhaps something he had learned as a policeman, the right way to elicit a confession or to get a prisoner to open up.

So open up, honey. Talk to the man. Ask him what you really want to know.

*

I finally told O'Neil on a bright Sunday morning, as we drank coffee. It was Bethany's birthday and I hadn't slept. It came more simply than I could have imagined.

'My girlfriend was killed,' I said, hoping it would shock him. It did not. 'Murdered,' I went on. 'They found her body a few months back. He'd hurt her so badly that they wouldn't even let me see her.'

I told him everything: the first and last time I went through it with anyone. Maybe he looked like he'd opened something up that he wished he hadn't, I don't remember. What I do remember is what he asked when I'd finished.

'Did they ever think that you'd done it?'

*

I looked down at my notes, the empty space below his name. Parks had necked almost half of his pint already and was glancing at his watch. Bethany was sitting on the top of the fruit machine, her legs dangling over its display. *Go on*, she said. *You can trust him.*

'Did you ever think that I killed her?' I said eventually. Parks looked genuinely surprised and rapped his fingers on the table, then laughed.

'What a strange thing to ask, Mr Wilkinson,' he said. 'I wasn't expecting that. Not in a million years.'

215

He shook his head and laughed again. It was low and guttural.

'No, you were never a suspect. There *were* no suspects. If there'd been a sniff of anything wrong, we wouldn't have let you go abroad, would we? America somewhere, wasn't it?'

I nodded. 'New York.'

'Yes, I remember now,' he said, rubbing his head.

'Anyway, Mark. You mind if I call you Mark?' I waved my hand at him. 'Look, the only mystery about what happened was whether Bethany was the only one, or whether the sick bastard had done it before. That was the only question we had. All the reports were conclusive: he killed her. There wasn't any doubt. Like I said, the only doubt was whether she was the last or the first.'

'Did you ever find out?' I said. *You're not asking the right questions, honey. Ask him why. You want to know that, don't you? Don't you?*

'We never had the chance. He was arrested at the scene. He refused representation and didn't talk. We held him. We charged him and he went on remand. DNA came back with nothing. He couldn't be placed at any other sex crime or anything else. Then he hung himself.'

I had not thought of him as being alive or dead, only imagined him as he was in the photograph, blurry and undistinguished, that the local news had somehow found of him. *I wondered when you'd get to this*, Bethany said. *Why didn't you want to know anything about him?*

'We kept the case open for a while,' Parks continued, 'but there were no leads. I thought he was good for one or two murders but there was nothing we could prove.'

He spoke with an evenness that, despite the police-report staccato, betrayed a slight agitation. He chose his words with deliberation, almost reticence, as though worried about giving too much away. He coughed, sank the rest of his drink and pointed at mine, pushed himself up and went to the bar. He walked stiffly, as though he had just woken from a long sleep.

'You see,' Parks said when he returned, 'I'm looking at you now and you seem . . . what, disappointed? That's the problem. This isn't a satisfying story. I don't even tell it well. Journalists, they come and go, you know? They're always asking the same question, desperate to uncover some dark secret or something they can sell. They come here for the truth and when they find it, they don't like it. They always end up writing about how a sleepy town woke up into the modern world. They don't mention the murder the year before. They don't write about the three kids taken into care after their father was discovered interfering with the youngest daughter. None of it fits. Whenever that case is mentioned, it's like a fantasy land. None of it seems real, the way they put it.'

But there's something, Bethany said, *there's something he's not telling.* She was sitting on the pool table now, cross-legged, her cheeks flushed with revelation. *Something about it all that doesn't quite make sense. I can see it in his face. In his hands. Ask him. Ask him why he's really here.*

'I don't remember much about it,' I said. 'I remember you coming to the house with a woman police officer. I remember you saying that if I had anything to tell you, I should call you.'

He wiped his chin and started to fiddle with the ashtray. He was avoiding my eyes.

'Why did you do that?' I said. 'What were you thinking I'd remember?'

Parks looked up.

'Look, Mark, I'm not one of those people who obsess about things. You meet people who do in the force. They're the ones who end up alone and drunk and working as security guards. For a time I thought about it. Thought about it a lot. I mean, how can you forget something like that? But after a while, I had to let it go. I don't think about it now, I just don't. I'm just a normal bloke. It's not like I sit at home and go through the case files trying to find evidence of something else. The case is over. It's done, okay?'

He got up suddenly and I grabbed at his arm. He looked down on me with surprise.

'Please,' I said. 'Please tell me.'

He sank back down and shook his head.

'It's nothing. Not really. It's just . . . I always wondered why she was down there. That's what I couldn't ever get.'

I wish I could tell you, Bethany said.

'There was no struggle, you see, no tyre marks to speak of. There was no evidence that she was coerced down there. No suggestion that she had been moved. The time she was last seen outside the leisure centre suggests she walked straight to where she was killed. Not that it matters. The case was closed.'

If I could tell you, honey, I would. You know I would.

'And that's what you wanted me to remember.'

He let out a long breath.

'I don't know. What difference does it make now, anyway? Like I said, I don't sit at home and mope over it. Thing is that there's always crazies. Always those who'll want to kill and there's no reason why. Personally I'm amazed there aren't more. Murderers, I mean.'

He looked like he was about to launch into a long screed, a well-rehearsed monologue, but instead he put his head on his fist and gave me a long stare with his once-detective eyes.

219

'Can I ask you something, Mark?' he said. 'Why now? Why now, what is it now, twelve, thirteen years later? Why come find me now?'

Tell him, Bethany said. *Tell him I won't leave you alone.*

'I don't know,' I said. 'I've been away for so long . . . it's complicated.'

I could think of no more questions. The only one that mattered he couldn't answer. *Does it really matter, though, honey?* Bethany said. *Like the man says, what does it matter now?*

'Why did you agree to see me,' I said. 'If none of this matters.'

Parks chewed the inside of his lip and smiled sadly. He fumbled in his bag and took out his darts case and began affixing the flights.

'I didn't remember you when I first saw you, you know that?' he said. 'I thought I would, but I didn't. Funny isn't it, what you remember and what you don't? When they came to do that telly programme, the researcher kept asking me whether the case still kept me up at night; whether I was working on it now that I was retired. You could see the glint in her eyes. I told her the truth: I didn't really remember a whole lot about it. I can tell you what was in the police reports, but I don't actually remember all that much about it.'

He's lying, Bethany said, *he's good at it too. Watch him. He thinks about me all the time. The way I looked when I was found, the inquest and the post mortem, the days of trying to get the man to speak, to get to the bottom of it all. How can you let that just go? How do you just go back to your house and sleep at night?*

'So you don't think about it? Not at all?'

He laughed. It should have sounded cruel but it was oddly comforting. He stood up and started throwing his darts. He had a practised, fluid rhythm.

'Of course I do. I didn't work many murder cases, so it was a big deal. But that's it. Now I draw my pension, do some odd jobs on the side and come for a pint and a game of darts while the wife's round her mother's.'

Bethany smiled and shook her head. *He wants you to believe it. Perhaps he believes it himself.*

I nodded at both of them and looked at my watch. It was just gone one.

'Listen, son,' he said, the darts thudding into the board. 'I'm not going to pretend I know what it is you're going through. But my advice is just to leave it. You've got a whole lot of life to live, don't live it knee deep in the past.'

He's fighting it. He wants to ask you something. He wants to know if you were with me that evening, Bethany said, clambering down from the pool table and lighting a cigarette. *Look at the way he's throwing those darts, the precision of the anger.*

'I wasn't with her, you know,' I said, standing up. 'If that's what you were thinking.'

'Oh no,' Parks said. 'She couldn't have been with you. I knew that already.'

He stood, his dart stalled.

'Was she meeting someone?' he asked. 'Did you know that she was meeting someone?'

There was white skin on his knuckles and a colouring to his cheeks.

'I wish I knew,' I said. He stood like that for a moment, then threw the darts. He took them from the board and turned to me.

'If you do find out,' he said, 'don't come looking to tell me, okay? I don't want to know.' He weighed the darts in his hand. 'I'm serious. I don't want to know.'

I said goodbye and left the pub. It had rained while we were talking and the pavements smelled of playgrounds.

*

The last time Bethany and I were in the park was after someone from school died. He was killed instantly as he came off his motorcycle while negotiating a roundabout in Crewe. We knew him vaguely. It was a summer's evening and we didn't fancy the pubs or being at home. So we sat on the bench by the bowling green smoking spliffs and drinking from a bottle of red wine we'd pushed the cork into.

'I don't feel anything,' she said. 'I know I should, but I don't.'

'You didn't know him that well. He was just some guy from school.'

'I should feel something, though, shouldn't I?'

She passed me the spliff and took a long pull on the bottle of wine.

'Maybe it's the shock,' she said.

You didn't feel anything either, did you? Bethany said. *Not a single thing.*

There were still rugby posts up on Greenliffe Field, but now joined by a small skate park around the back of the leisure centre. The bandstand was still upright, still peeling paint and rotting wood; the aviary by the north gates too. I walked past the birds in the cages, so few of them now it seemed that they had been abandoned, left to fend for themselves. Beyond them were the old factories: cranes swaddling the brickwork, diggers at their foot, Portakabins and Portaloos in close proximity. I took a right and followed the path through the woods.

The area at the end of the path was clear, paved now with asphalt and with a bin for dog shit and one for re-cycling. Parking spaces were marked out in thick white lines. *They paved paradise . . .* Bethany sang. *Some fucking paradise. Some fucking parking lot.* There was a plaque on one of the benches dedicated to a woman called Susan. *She must have been a bit of a one, that Susan,* Bethany said. *Imagine wanting to be remembered here . . .*

I sat down, the wind troubling the trees, the bags in the bins flickering. It did not look like a place someone could die; a place where someone could just be erased. My expectation was of somewhere cold and unforgiving, icy even on that summer's afternoon. And of somewhere that was for ever hers. *What were you expecting? A memorial? A cross? Some flowers?* Bethany said.

I was expecting to feel something, Beth. I was expecting to feel something.

*

I slept for hours, without dreams. My notes were on the dresser, Simon Parks's name scrubbed out in biro. I kept hearing Bethany ask me: *What did you expect?* and having no answer for her. Not Parks' strained indifference. I should have been more rigorous in my questioning; but what would that have gained? There were the facts: a death, an arrest, another death. Would it have helped if he'd produced the case files, explained his theories, worn his obsession like a costume?

I wonder if I'd lived, whether I'd have come to pity

you the way I do now, Bethany said, lying on the bed in her underwear. 'You're not helping,' I said out loud. 'You're really not helping.'

I know, she said, *I could never help you. No matter how hard I tried.*

Ferne was sitting on the same stool at the bar. Her hair was down and she was winding it around her index finger as she read. I watched her for a moment, wondering whether I had upset her the night before. *You care about her feelings?* Bethany said. *Already? You sure about that?*

There was a clear way of exiting without alerting Ferne, but I decided against it. Instead I sat next to her and tried to catch the barman's attention. She looked up and folded down the corner of the page.

'Hi,' she said.

'Hi,' I said as the barman poured me a pint of bitter.

'Did you go to the Indian in the end?' she said. 'I hope it wasn't too awful.'

'It was okay. Didn't realize how hungry I was till I got there.'

'I'm glad it was okay,' she said.

She went back to her book and I took out my notes. I wrote Simon Parks' name, and underneath: *Gives the impression of knowing more than he lets on. But doesn't. Does not dwell on the past.* After a pause I added: *He is lucky.*

'What you writing?' Ferne said.

'Just notes. I had some meetings today.'

'They go well?'

'Sort of.'

She smiled. It was simple and beautiful in a fractured kind of way.

'I can't stand the thought of another night in this place,' she said. 'I could show you around if you'd like. Not that there's much to see.'

I didn't say anything and she wound her hair tightly in her fingers.

'You probably have plans, though, right? Saturday night and all that.'

'No plans,' I said. 'But no matter how drunk we get, promise we won't end up at Chaps.'

I smiled but Ferne looked confused. Chaps was the town nightclub, and the only place to get a late drink. Before going out, Hannah, Beth and I would promise we wouldn't be tempted.

'What's Chaps?' she said.

'I thought you told me about it,' I said. 'A nightclub or something? Upstairs on the High Street?'

'No. Not me,' she said. 'Must have been someone else.'

'My mistake,' I said. 'Must have been in one of my meetings.'

Very convincing, Bethany said, leaning against the

fridges behind the bar. *She must think you're a fucking weirdo already. She's pretty, though. Looks a bit like me, don't you think?*

'Well,' Ferne said, 'I promise not to take you to the place I've never been to. Guide's honour.'

Ferne did not look like Bethany; a little around the mouth, a similarity in the eyes, but that was it. It did not stop me from staring, though, keeping my eyes on her as she lit a cigarette. She blew out smoke like Bethany; held her cigarette in much the same way. She set her cigarette in an ashtray and put her book in her handbag.

'We don't have to, you know. I just thought it would be nice, that's all. Since we're both stuck here and all that.'

Bethany put her head on one side and filled up a drink from the optic, then shot down the whisky. *I think she likes you, honey. Maybe you should go and fuck her.*

'No,' I said. 'I'd like to go out. You can show me around.'

Ferne smiled and flicked her ash. 'I'll just get my coat and then we'll go and eat.'

She came back ten minutes later, her jacket furred at the collar and long over her trousers. She had done her eye make-up like Elizabeth Taylor in *Cleopatra* and had changed her handbag. As she approached I could smell her perfume: it was heady and surprisingly light.

'Where to first?' I said.

'The Counting House,' she said. 'I really fancy a cocktail.'

*

Over a Mai Tai and a gin and tonic, we traded stories about our friends, Ferne doing most of the talking. It was a strange sensation, standing in an unfamiliar place, talking about a past we did not share, and none of it scripted, no chance of my guessing whether everything was true, or what was embellished, no recourse to notes, no background intel. It was like being unmoored. Yet it was real and easy: just two people in need of company. Like me and O'Neil, once. It felt like a long time since I'd had such a conversation, a long time since I'd been able to relax and not worry about an endgame or resolution. We talked because that's what people do: they talk, they laugh and they find other reasons to keep on going.

'Right, time to make a move, I think,' Ferne said. 'The Falcon next.'

Perfect, Bethany said. *Twat central. I wonder if you're still barred?*

The Falcon had always looked like an Alpine ski lodge, had always been full of the people we sought to avoid and was always the most expensive place in town. Nothing had changed. Ferne bought a bottle of white wine and we sat by the window. I wanted to tell her that

I had once sat on the same table with Bethany and Hannah, the night we discussed whether Hannah should do anything about the mystery man in her life, and both Bethany and I tried to dissuade her, thinking this could only be about Bethany's father, but hoping it wasn't.

'I prefer this place,' I said. 'Less . . . gaudy.'

'And you've been here before, too,' she said with a smile. 'So what's the deal?'

'I don't understand,' I said.

'You've been here before. When we left the last place you knew that we were turning left, you knew the Falcon was the next pub along and you knew where the toilets were, even though they're not signposted. QED, Joe. QED.'

Tentatively, she put her hand on mine.

'Talk to me, Joe. Why don't you talk? All you seem to do is sit there and listen.'

Don't talk, Mark, Bethany said. *Just listen.*

Saturday, 7th July 1990, 3.41 pm

She sits in the changing room of the silent leisure centre, dressed only in her underwear. The gown is hanging from a peg, her shoes kicked out over the rough, slip-proof flooring. Her bag is open, her clothes lolling out of its open zip. She has showered and the ends of her hair are slightly damp. On the other side of town, Hannah and Mark will, she knows, be checking the pub clock and wondering where she has got to. Mark will be optimistic of her arrival; Hannah already swearing at her for letting them both down. They will get over it. All she has to say is that she was caught up and couldn't leave as planned. Hannah will sulk for a while, pull her face, then let it go. Mark will just be happy to see her whatever.

Though she is determined to go through with it, she has stalled at the point of dressing. When she was at school her class used to come to the swimming pool here and it was the real low point of the week, her talent for dressing quickly beneath a large towel only matched by her speed in the water. There was no way she would be

230

sitting around in just her underwear then. She has finally started to come around to her own body.

The T-shirt feels thin in her hand; it has Big Black on it, a band she only got into through Daniel. 'They sound like a fucking heart attack,' he'd said as he'd played her one of their records in the shop. 'They just fucking hate everything.' She pulls it over her head and then puts on her jeans. Her Dr Martens are polished to a high shine, something her father does in the mistaken belief it is an act of kindness. They look too new, too fresh from the box. She begins to lace them up, all images of her as queen now slipping away.

She had been distracted for so long after the motorcycle display that she expected Waller to shout at her afterwards, but instead he told her how well she'd done, what a fine effort she had made, and how she deserved a nice stiff drink. He looked hurt when she turned him down, explaining that she had to change out of her dress and meet friends before dining with him and the rest of the carnival committee later.

'Oh, just a quick glass of wine,' he'd said. 'You've earned it.'

Bethany laughed. 'Thanks, but I have plans. I'll see you later.' And she took off, picking up her bag from the boot of her father's car on the way to the changing rooms.

She is dressed now and she looks at herself in the

mirror. It is a moment she wants to record, to ensure that she remembers. The clock on the wall tells her she has twenty minutes to make her rendezvous. She checks her watch to be sure. Her bag shouldered, she pushes open the swing doors. A man in a blue polo shirt and tracksuit bottoms is mopping the hallway. He looks up and nods.

'Quite a transformation,' he says with a smile. 'I wouldn't have recognized you.'

'Thanks for letting me in,' she says. 'Another minute in that costume and I'd have . . .' She shakes her head as her voice trails off. The reception area is angel-bright and she takes out a pair of sunglasses and puts them on: the lenses soothe everything but the sun's heat. The car park is still full and families troop towards their vehicles, the kids holding balloons, their faces painted like animals, their parents keeping them well-drilled alongside their picnic baskets. She puts her bag in the back of her father's car, lights a cigarette, sucks in the smoke. A man taps her on her shoulder. He has an unlit cigarette in his hand.

'Got a light please, love?' he says and she nods and passes him a box of matches. He lights five before the cigarette catches, then passes back the box.

'Weren't you the carnival queen?' he says. Bethany nods and starts to walk away.

'You looked better in a dress. You know, you look like a tramp done up like that.'

She turns to stare at him. He is an older man in his thirties; cheap glasses, neat shirt, jeans and trainers. He is wearing thick spectacles. She vaguely recognizes him from the pubs.

'Fuck off, four-eyes,' she says.

'Very original,' he says.

She turns to walk up the bank and on to the main road. He says something she half hears behind the clotting of adrenaline. She's tempted to turn and look back at him, to see whether he is still there, shouting abuse in her direction. But she lets it go and at the top of the bank she sneaks a look down, but the man has gone. She is surprised to feel angry with herself for being so rude, for giving him a reason to say such a spiteful thing. Of course, she's heard worse, in the pubs, on the streets. Really there is nothing left to tolerate: these men deserve all they get.

There are groups standing outside the Grapes, plastic pints of beer in their hands. They do not recognize her, for which she is grateful. This part of town is unfamiliar to her, as much as any part of such a small town can be unfamiliar. It is less genteel, given over to the sprawl of the council estates. One of them is still known as Tin Town. Her mum explained about how the temporary roofing used immediately after the war had given it the nickname; how the bombed-out residents of Manchester and Liverpool and Stoke were shuttled here for a new life in the town's remaining mills and light industry; how this exodus had engendered the strange mixture of accents the town has co-opted as its own.

The further she walks, the quieter it becomes. There are no cars at the petrol station, no kids pumping up their tyres with pressurized air. The corner shop is open but looks dark inside. She checks her cigarettes and considers going in to buy some more, but the thought of speaking to anyone, even to ask for twenty Marlboro, is too much. She looks at her watch; she is supposed to be there in ten minutes and though she is no more than five away, she hurries her pace.

By the closed-up post office she smokes another cigarette and checks her watch again. Over the road is a telephone box. It doesn't help. She can't call the pub now; Mark and Hannah will probably have moved on. She imagines Mark trying to pacify Hannah, Hannah complaining that Beth always does this, and wondering how he puts up with it. Hannah has always had a disarming interest in her and Mark's relationship. Initially Bethany found it amusing, then intrusive, then somehow achingly sad. For a moment, she thinks again about her father and Hannah. We all have our secrets, she thinks, secrets are important things. Our secrets are the things that define us.

The lane is narrow and dusty, mud baked to dry and

brambles pricking her skin as she negotiates it. She scuffs her boots in an attempt to take off the shine: it is only partly successful, and it makes her feel self-conscious again. It's a stupid thing to feel, she thinks as she walks the last dog leg towards the clearing, all he wants is sex: nothing more. Just like her, just exactly the same as her.

The van is already there. He is sitting on its bonnet smoking a joint; she can smell it clearly over the woods and the water. Perhaps he is nervous too, she thinks, but reminds herself that this is not something that gives him nerves. This is what he does and this is why she is here.

She sits next to him and smiles. He takes a toke on the joint and passes it to her.

'My queen,' he says, laughing.

'Fuck off, Daniel. I've had about as many jokes as I can stomach today.'

'It were okay though?'

Beth nods. 'It could have been worse.' She thinks momentarily of the guy shouting at her, calling her a tramp. 'It could have been a lot worse.'

She has not imagined how they will get from there, from idle conversation into the back of the van, from strangers to lovers. She wishes she could be like Vikki Palmer, turn dirty mouthed and say: let's stop with all the talking and let's fuck. But that would be ridiculous, he would laugh and the moment would be ruined; there would just be his laughter and the feeling that she had shrunk back into girlhood. She passes him back the joint, and with it clamped in his mouth, he bends to pick up a stone and pitches it out to the river. The water looks like flattened metal, then breaks. He comes back and puts his arms around Beth's neck.

'You surprised me,' he says. 'I thought this ship had sailed a long time ago.'

'I was young then.'

'You're young now.'

'I was nervous then.'

'And you're not now?' he says and laughs again.

'No. No, I'm not.'

'You looked good all dolled up, you know. Barely recognized you.'

'Were you hoping I'd wear the dress?'

He laughs again, and so does she. For a moment she thinks that he has lost interest, that this was just a nice game to play. In the bright afternoon light he has lost some of his allure; he is better framed by wreaths of smoke and the hum of people, by the beat of music she wants to like and the smell of stale beer. He passes her the joint and she holds it, not smoking it, the two of them sharing a silence that has promise but still uncertainty. He will not turn her down, she is aware of that, but the idea of him suggesting that, after all, this is a bad idea is somehow appealing. He turns and they watch the stream return to battered metal. She thinks that it may be down to her to actually move things on. It is not something that sits well with her.

He places his arms around her again.

'You on the pill? Or do I need nodders?'

She can smell him, his aftershave and the beers he has drunk. There is a slight scent of cherry about him, the tobacco he uses for his roll-ups. They have not even kissed. Not even touched each other in any meaningful way, but it is his use of the word nodders that gets her. That he broached the subject is no bad thing, but that word! Almost anything else would have done, anything other than the kind of word a nine-year-old might say. It makes her feel slighted, unwanted.

She kisses him. He kisses her back, well. He puts a hand on her behind, then one on her breast. It is clumsy but arresting: she had expected nothing less. He pushes her against the bodywork of the van and she can feel the tensing in his shoulders, in his whole body. His legs are in between hers and his erection is against her thigh. He makes a slight humming noise as he kisses her below her ear. She unbuttons his fly, feels his cock through the fabric of his underwear then scoops her hand under the cloth. She tugs it once or twice, then suddenly feels repulsed.

She stops touching but for a moment Daniel seems not

to notice. His eyes are still closed, his mouth open. He looks vaguely simian, paused by the van, leaning against her. She wants to feel that this pause is because of Mark; that he has a bearing on all of this. But it is nothing to do with him, not in the way that she would like. In a way she can't quite fathom, she realizes that it is all about her mother, how she would react to seeing her there.

It is not about disapproval, but her mother's life-held acceptance that we all make mistakes in life; her understanding that people fuck up from time to time. She would have understood; she would have seen the situation for what it is. If her mother had been around, and had she spoken to her, she would not be here, a large, partially clothed cock pressed against her. She would be at the pub with her best friend and the boy she loves, dreaming of New York and counting down the days. None of this would have been important, the tit-for-tat, the need to get even. She would have seen it sooner for what it was: a tawdry bunk-up in the back of a Transit van.

He kisses her again. And pushes her towards the back of the van. His eyes are wolfish. He opens the sliding door to reveal a mattress and one pillow. She can see evidence of clearing up, but still an empty packet of Rizlas and the wrapper from a Mars bar. He grabs her, holds her close.

'Shall we go inside,' he says. He has her by the wrist. At another time, in another place, she would be excited.

SEVENTEEN

O'Neil loved Sundays. Back in New York, he would always wake earlier than me, listen to the radio as he cleaned up the apartment, go for a long morning walk, returning with breakfast and a newspaper. He'd make pancakes and sausage, brew proper coffee and call members of his family while flicking through the international news. If I was not woken by the slam of the door, or the sound of the music or the allure of the cooking smells, he would bash on my door and tell me I was wasting the day. He called it the safety of Sunday: a day when nothing bad could happen, when there was a bubble of hope. I told him that Pearl Harbor happened on a Sunday; Bloody Sunday too, hence its name. Exceptions, he'd say, that proved the rule.

In the hotel room, curtain open, looking out over the car park and listening to the pealing bells of the St John Church, I wondered whether he would see such possibility here. The sky was powder blue and the smell of bacon was coming up from the kitchens below, but this was no different to waking the previous day. Sunday here was indifferent: it didn't care either way.

There were sketchy puddles on the tarmac and my clothes were hanging damply from the coat hooks on the back of the door. Ferne and I had been caught in a storm leaving the Thai restaurant and had run with our coats over our heads back to the hotel, laughing drunkenly past other people similarly caught unawares. We were still laughing as we got to the bar, ordered drinks, and then went to our separate rooms to change into dry clothes. We drank a final bottle of wine sitting on bar stools, her dressed in sweatpants and jumper and me in another black suit.

'I didn't pack properly,' I said. 'It was all I had.'

'I feel underdressed,' she said. 'But I don't care. Is it wrong not to care?'

I assured her it wasn't.

As I began to talk to Ferne, Bethany shook her head. She'd been sitting there in disapproval, and then disappeared as I briefly closed my eyes. As we drank that last bottle, Ferne asked me more about O'Neil and Edith and what Vegas was really like. By then I was tired of confessions, tired of my own voice. It was only her thirst for information and her luminous eyes that made me continue.

There was a moment. On the landing, with the two of

us standing outside room 11. Ferne cocked her head to one side and put her hand on my shoulder. 'I'm sorry,' she said.

'What for?'

'For everything. No one should have to go through those things.'

'People do every day, though. And they cope with it better than I ever did.'

She shook her head. 'You did what you needed to do. You shouldn't be ashamed.'

She placed a kiss on my cheek and I wanted to kiss her back, wanted so much to hold her and tell her the whole true story, not just the edited version I'd presented. But I paused. I didn't want this, whatever it had become, to be coloured by the past; my partial truths leading from here to the bedroom. For all intimacy to be predicated on the intimacy of my half-confession.

*

Her reaction to the stories of my past had been balanced incredulity, pity and sympathy. She bit her lip and restrained herself from interrupting, only occasionally telling me to go on when I reached a part that caused me to stumble. When I finished, ending on the fight with Brooks, she looked at me wistfully and said nothing for a time.

'You know in science-fiction films, there's always a scene where the time traveller or the alien or whatever has to explain to someone that they've come from a different world or time or something? And the person they're telling never believes them, right? I've always thought that was bullshit. If it were me, I'd believe them straight away. Why would they lie? What on earth is in it for them?'

'Are you saying you don't believe me?' I said, the plate of green curry going cold in front of me. Ferne laughed.

'No, you dope. What I mean is that there's only so much you can invent. The rest has to be true. I had this friend at university, Laurie. He was always involved in some kind of strange romantic liaison or other, and then he met this girl. Lovely girl, too, I met her a couple of times. They fell for each other, but she had a boyfriend back home . . . Am I boring you?'

'No,' I said. 'Not at all.'

'Good. Right. Anyway, she breaks it all off with the boyfriend and she moves in with Laurie. For a year or two, they're deliriously happy. Then all of a sudden, they break up. He stays with me for a while and he seems okay. Pretty soon, he goes back to his old ways and pretty soon he's forgotten about this girl. Then one night he's at this club. He sees this girl and bam. That's it. Eyes meet across a crowded room and all that bullshit. They go straight back to her place.

'The next morning, he wakes up and she's sitting on the edge of the bed, crying. He asks her what's wrong and she says she's sorry, but she has a boyfriend and she's really not like that, but she just couldn't help herself. Laurie's disappointed and a bit pissed off, but they hug and she tells him that he'd like her boyfriend. He's a nice bloke. He deserves better than her. She tells him this, then says that just last week her boyfriend came home from business with a bunch of presents for her. He'd bought her three books. His favourite books in the whole world.'

Ferne pushed away her plate and lit a cigarette.

'Laurie just looks at her and says, "*Steppenwolf, The Unbearable Lightness of Being* and *The World According to Garp*?" She looks at him at first in amazement and then in horror. "Oh Holy Living Fuck," she says. "It's *you*. He told me all about *you*!"

'Her boyfriend was the guy Laurie had stolen his previous girlfriend from. The bloke had bought that girl the exact same books for her birthday. Laurie knew because they were the only novels his girlfriend owned when they moved in together.'

I had my mouth open, then shut it. Ferne tapped her cigarette in the ashtray.

'That's like Laurie's party piece story. He tells everyone that. Most people think it's kind of funny, some people think it's a bit sick. But no one thinks he's made it up: it's too stupid. I love that story, though. I love it because it shows you that even when you least expect it, life has something special up its sleeve; something to take your breath away.'

*

But there was the pause outside her hotel room. I said goodnight and thanked her for a lovely evening. Her hand was on the door. 'See you tomorrow,' she said. 'If you fancy lunch, just let me know.' She went inside without telling me how to contact her.

Bethany came back to talk for some time in the night. Mainly she talked about her father. She told me stories I already knew, asked me if I really thought it was right to be visiting like this. She stood by the window looking through the curtains and out onto the darkened town, glancing back at me whenever she wanted to emphasize something. I drifted off to sleep as she told me about how he used to sing 'Ballad of the Teenage Queen' when she couldn't sleep, his hand stroking her long hair and his voice getting quieter as she slowly settled down.

*

The breakfast room was deserted, silver dishes filled with meat and eggs under hot lamps, a fruit and cheese station, the same kind of juice dispensers we'd had at the canteen at school. *You should eat,* Bethany said, *it'll do you good.* I poured some coffee and drank it black, chewed on a croissant and looked at my notes. I wrote down the questions I needed answering, as I should have done before meeting with Parks. I read them back and they seemed stupidly formal, as if for a job interview. I crossed them all out and ripped out the page.

Out in the sunshine, an old man passed me by dressed in a crisp suit and a tie, a flat cap on his head. He nodded at me as we crossed paths, perhaps impressed that someone else was in their Sunday best. For him, it was a conscious flourish, almost an act of defiance: *you may forget, but we shall not; the way I knot my tie before leaving the house keeps those times alive.*

The corner shop was open, the same sign – Senior Service Satisfies – on the window of the door. We thought for years that this was a reminder that service, real service, could only be delivered by the old. That the elderly shopkeeper was one of the rudest women anyone of us had ever encountered – she had called Hannah a trollop as she bought cigarettes one evening – made the sign all the more perplexing. The woman was no longer there, but the man behind the counter could only have been her son. He had the same pinched face, the same errant hair and a comparably brusque manner. I bought chewing gum and cigarettes and he conducted the transaction without speaking, the whole time keeping his eye on a small television.

'Papers?' he said, eventually looking up.

'No,' I said. 'Just these, thank you.'

'No. Not now, papers for last week. You still owe for last week's papers.'

'I don't take any papers from you.'

'Yes you do. Mr Arnold, right? Up on Terront Road.'

'No, I'm not Mr Arnold.'

'You're sure? You look like him.'

'I'm not Mr Arnold. I don't even live here. I'm just staying for a few nights at the Coach down the road.'

He looked back at the screen, then at me again. 'It's my eyes,' he said eventually. 'Everyone looks the same to me these days. Sorry. Now that I look, I can see.'

I picked up the cigarettes and the gum and left him to his television, wondering whether I did actually look like this Mr Arnold, whether a doppelgänger had already taken my place.

At the end of Mike Wilder's road I smoked a cigarette and watched a small congregation leave St Stephen's Church: more men in suits, some of the women in hats. The vicar shook their hands as they left; there were some young couples too, putting in their stint to prove worthy of being married inside. *They would not bury me there*, Bethany said. *Funny, isn't it? You'd have thought they'd want the publicity.*

There were two cars parked outside the house, a BMW and a smaller town car. One had a 'baby on board' sticker, a child's seat set up in the back. *Don't you think you might have called first?* Bethany said, sitting on the doorstep. *But I guess if you called, you wouldn't have come. You'd have played coward again. Sounds like people are in, though. Maybe you'll get lucky and they'll have moved away. You could go to church, pray that he's gone.*

I ignored her and rang the doorbell. I heard someone shout, 'I'll get it,' and feet padding down the stairs. The door had been kept well, the same stained glass above the frame. It opened and there was Mike Wilder, older but demonstrably himself. He was thinner in both body and hair, but did not look bad for it. He wore denims and a polo shirt that had various milky deposits on its shoulder. Bethany said nothing.

'Can I help you?' he said. The hallway was blocked by his outstretched arm. The floor was bare floorboards now, rather than the green carpet they'd once had; a pushchair was folded up next to the staircase.

'Mike? Mike Wilder?' I said.

He looked me up and down and nodded.

'Yes. I'm Mike Wilder.'

I had assumed that he would recognize me, that he would stand in horror, as though seeing a ghost. But he only saw someone prepared to sell him something, perhaps canvass his opinion on the Labour government. Bethany remained silent and I put my hand in my pocket.

'Do you not remember me?' I said. 'It's been a long time, but I thought . . .'

'I'm sorry, but I don't . . . Look I'm rather busy. Two kids playing havoc in the kitchen, you know.'

I should have left. Made some apology and told him I'd made a mistake. He could go back to his children and later tell his wife that something odd had happened that afternoon. They could have spent the evening wondering who I was and what it was I could have wanted.

'Mr Wilder, It's Mark. Mark Wilkinson.'

He looked me up and down and scrunched up his face.

'If this is some kind of joke, it isn't funny. Has someone put you up to this? If—'

I shook my head. 'I'm sorry for coming over unannounced but I'm only in town for a few days and I really wanted to see you. To talk to you.'

He looked into the house and shut the door behind him. He leant in close to me and pointed a long finger into my chest.

'You fucking stay away from me,' he said. 'You stay away from all of us.' He was shaking, like he was about to lose control. 'After all these years and you come back like this?'

He pushed me backwards.

'I don't have anything to say to you. Nothing. After all that you've done, and you come back like this? My daughter. My daughter! You stay away. You don't come to this house. You don't come anywhere near me or my family. You come near us and I swear to God I'll kill you. I'll fucking kill you.'

He turned and opened the door, fixed me with a look of absolute disgust. 'I'm warning you,' he said and slammed the door so hard it made me think of my father.

*

The Woodman smelled of roast dinners and cigarette smoke. A family were eating at a small table while some men played on the quiz machine.

'You all right there, love?' the woman behind the bar said. 'You look white as sheet.'

'I'll be fine,' I said.

'Not going to be sick, are you?'

'No. Honestly. Just had a bit . . . can I have a pint of Guinness?'

She started pouring. 'Hair of the dog, is it?'

'Something like that,' I said.

'Well, go easy, won't you.'

I nodded and handed her the money. I drank half the Guinness down in one go and lit a cigarette. I thought I might throw up right there on the sticky mahogany bar, but managed to keep it down. *Well, you got your answer*, Bethany said. *You wanted to know how he copes. He gets on with it, got on with it. He has a new family, a new life. I keep saying it, but what did you expect? What precisely did you think was going to happen?*

Anger was not what I expected. I didn't expect to feel like a threat to him.

But the past is always a threat. When it came for you, didn't you try to ignore it, honey? Didn't you try to pretend it wasn't really happening?

But I was never angry. Never aggressive.

Brooks might disagree with that. You've just punctured my dad's life, just taken him back years. Have you any idea how that feels?

I'm living it now, aren't I? Isn't this what's happening to me right now?

Interesting choice of word, living. Really? Are you?

I finished my drink and ordered another.

And that isn't going to help.

I should just go.

Yes, but where? Just where would you go?

*

I sat on the bed, my suitcase open beside me. The room was a mess, a wine glass smashed on the floor, the contents of the dressing table swept to the carpet, a Gideon's Bible thrown against the wall and lying next to a pile of clothes. There were marks on my hands from where I'd punched the walls and slight scuffs of blood by the light switch. I didn't notice the knocking at the door for some time. I could hear a voice, but not exactly what it was saying. 'Do not disturb,' I shouted. 'Can't you fucking read?'

The knocking continued and I eventually went to the door and opened it a crack. Ferne stood there, slightly breathlessly.

'Joe, let me in.'

'I can't. I haven't got any clothes on.'

'Wrap a towel around you or something. They've called the manager.'

'Just leave me alone, okay, Ferne. Just leave me alone.'

'Fuck's sake, Joe,' she said and barged past me and into the room. 'I've got my eyes closed. Now shut up and get something on.'

I went to the bathroom and wrapped a towel around my waist. There was more knocking at the door and then the sound of voices, then the door being shut. Ferne banged on the bathroom door.

'All clear,' she said. Then: 'Jesus.'

With her in the room the damage looked even more extensive.

'What the fuck have you been doing in here?' she said. 'Looks like Mötley Crüe's come to town.'

'I don't know . . . I just.'

'Go and sit in the bathroom,' she said. 'Let me get some of the glass up before you cut yourself.'

I locked the door and sat on the toilet seat. Bethany was crouched in the bath, smoking and talking, but whatever she was saying was muddy and unintelligible. I stood up, eventually, and looked at myself in the mirror, the redness around my eyes, the oddness of seeing myself in that moment. *You once said that you'd look into a mirror and find it hard to believe that it was actually you looking back, and as you were thinking that, you couldn't imagine that it was really you thinking that and looking at yourself. Do you remember that?* Bethany said.

Yes. You said that I was a weirdo. But that you liked that I thought about those kinds of things. And it was true, I used to do that all the time. Maybe I thought, eventually, I'd reach the end point, that there was no going back.

But you never did.

No. Never.

Ferne knocked and I opened the door.

'I've done as much as I can, Joe. The rest you'll have

to sort out yourself.' She sat down on the easy chair by the curtains.

'What happened?' she said eventually. 'Actually, you know, I don't want to know. Let's get out of here, okay? Get away from here for a while,' she said. 'Get dressed and meet me in the lobby. I'll be there for ten minutes. After that, I'm gone. You understand?'

I nodded. She had done a remarkable job on the room, the full wastepaper bin and the smudges of blood on the walls the only memory of the mess before.

'Ten minutes,' she said, and left without saying anything more.

*

She was parked at the back of a cobbled courtyard, a small red car with a long aerial. We got in and she turned the key, snapped off the radio.

'So?' she said. 'Where to?'

'I don't know. Where do you want to go to?'

'Anywhere but here. Anywhere.'

'Let's just drive. Take a right, then another and just keep driving.'

'You're okay, now, Joe. You are, aren't you?'

'I will be once we get moving.'

'Okay,' she said, 'I like to smoke when I drive, so you'll have to light them for me as we go, all right?'

We drove up a thin avenue of red-brick houses, the gradient of the road making our progress slow; we passed the primary school that Hannah had attended then dog-legged right, the squat terraces giving way to bungalows with sloped driveways and manicured lawns. They looked like displaced holiday chalets, the kind of places rented out to tourists who want a little home from home; then the terraces were back, and then the country-side: fields out to the left, yawning expanses of green and arable land.

'It's hard to imagine, isn't it?' I said. 'All these fields and no one yet to colonize them, put up those boxy houses.'

To the right was the flooded quarry, though the old signs warning of blue-green algae had been swapped for advertisements for windsurfing lessons and a new mere-side development of houses. Through a copse of trees I saw the tips of the masts and sails, the roofs of the hous-ing complex in the distance. Once Bethany and I had got stoned there, stayed the night in a borrowed tent that had been difficult to pitch. We'd made love and hugged tightly in our zipped-together sleeping bags, the sound of nocturnal life both intimidating and distracting. *We never were at one with nature,* Bethany said, *it was what made New York so inviting.*

At the end of the road we hit a junction and Ferne looked at the oncoming traffic. 'So where to now?'

'Right,' I said, 'then first left. We go the other way we end up in Stoke. Nothing good can happen in Stoke.'

Ferne laughed. 'Okay, navigator.'

It only struck me as I directed Ferne that I had a half-idea as to where we were going. She was an attentive driver, so long as she had cigarettes, and did not speak as she awaited instructions. The motion was soothing, the traffic light, and the crispness of the afternoon made everything somehow burnished and new. We were in the countryside proper now, bisected only by the M6 and the various small towns we passed through quickly, despite being told to drive carefully.

'I used to ask my dad where the countryside was,' I said as we passed a field stripped and dotted with black, tautened bales. 'I assumed that it was down in London somewhere. He'd tell me that the countryside was all around us, but I wouldn't believe him. I thought it would be somewhere like Little Moreton Hall.' She turned to look at me. 'It's a National Trust place not far from here. I thought you'd have to buy tickets and queue up.'

'I've never much liked the countryside,' Ferne said eventually. 'Despite my stupid name.' We slowed behind a farming vehicle, its back mud-splattered and rusted.

'It's actually short for Fernanda. A bloody stupid name to give a kid, if you ask me, but my mum was set on it, apparently. Her great-grandmother had been called that, or at least someone told her that was her name. My dad's not the kind of person to argue. He's that type, you know?'

'They're still together?'

She nodded and tapped the box of cigarettes. I lit one and passed it to her.

'My parents are nauseatingly in love even now. They're in their sixties and still act like teenagers.'

'Sounds lovely.'

'For them, maybe. For everyone else it's a bit of a tough act to follow, you know? My elder brother – you know the one who lives in Scotland? – he's been married twice already and he's only forty. He keeps trying to recreate it, replicate their relationship. Doomed to romance as my sister says, though she's no better. The way I see it, we're all sort of fated to try and improve on the life of our parents. You know, do better at school, earn more money, be better people. But if you set the bar that high it's impossible to compete. You end up failing, or you end up not trying.'

'So you don't try?' I said, as we finally saw Jodrell Bank in the distance.

'Not any more,' she said.

*

There were few recognizable landmarks in the county, few places anyone would consider visiting from afar, but the observatory at Jodrell Bank was undoubtedly the only one that contestants on a television quiz show would be able to name: its space-age dish, its incongruity with the vast swathes of fields surrounding it. Every school trip would find a reason to end there; every tourist brochure featured it prominently on the cover. Dad considered it a feat of engineering, the way it moved imperceptibly to reach ever further into the heavens, and would describe it as the ultimate example of man's progress. I had, however, always been terrified by it.

People forget, that's what you always say, right? Bethany said. *Forget about the Russians in Afghanistan.* She laughed, sitting in the back, kicking her legs against my seat.

People do forget, though. I can't remember who it was who told me about the threat, but probably it was Neil Jackson from school, a puny lad with asthma and a medical condition that made him smell ever so slightly of urine. He knew more about the military than anyone, and during the Falklands War drew ever more startlingly realistic sketches of destroyers, tanks, aircraft carriers and Harrier jump jets. If it was him, then he no doubt would have explained in simple, nightmarish terms – probably cribbed from his VHS of *Threads*, which he often asked to be shown in history class – the effect of a close-by nuclear attack. Jodrell Bank would be the primary target, he or whoever else it was told me. The Russians would go after it immediately because the observatory was just a cover for an extensive satellite programme that was monitoring all known weapon silos in the world. We would be in the first wave after the blast: there would be a white light and then nothing. I can imagine Neil Jackson smiling then, perhaps wishing it would happen every night before school started again.

'Let's stop here,' I said. 'You ever seen Jodrell Bank before?'

Ferne looked at the huge structure and then back at me.

'Can't we just get some lunch instead? I'm starving. Unless you really want to go there.'

'No. You're right. Lunch is perfect.'

*

We ate steak sandwiches in a pub with a thatched roof and the remnants of a cycling club drinking in the back room, skinny men in skin-tight outfits, their legs muscular and shaved. Ferne was quiet and drank her one allotted glass of wine in careful sips. We did not talk about my hotel room, nor my confessions of the night before; instead we told humorous anecdotes as though we had known each other for years and were beginning to realize that we had little to talk about. I asked about her perfect parents, but she didn't want to discuss them, or indeed any of her family.

'What about yours?' she said. 'You always change the subject.'

'Like you just did.'

'That was different.'

'Why's that?'

'Because they're boring. Happy but boring. Yours are just like an absence. Like you're trying to pretend you came from a Petri dish or something.'

The story of Joe's parents came immediately; the car crash, my great-aunt, my longed-for sister. *You can't, though, can you?* Bethany said. *You've said too much. Already you've said too much.*

'My father and mother split up when I was about thirteen or so. They'd been childhood sweethearts, not so perfect as yours, but still pretty solid. My dad worked in aeroplanes and my mother worked as a secretary for a law firm.'

'So what happened?' she said, taking another carefully moderated sip of wine and lighting a cigarette.

'What always happens. He lost interest, worked all the time. She had an affair with her boss.'

So simple! And that's all that happened, isn't it? A mid-life crisis, an affair, the end of a relationship?

'Do you still see her?'

'I haven't seen either of them since Bethany died. Haven't seen my mum since she left.'

'You don't miss her?'

'I don't really remember her that well.'

Ferne put down her napkin and shook her head.

'I don't believe you. She's your mother, you can't not remember her! It's just not possible.'

I pushed away my plate. Bethany was sitting on the bar, her Dr Martens boots kicking at the wood below. *Tell her*, she mouthed.

'Mum got pregnant when I was eleven. It was an accident, one of those unplanned things. But the two of them were so happy about it. They couldn't believe it was real. My mother kept saying that we had been blessed, even though she wasn't religious. I told them they were sick for keeping it. I told them I hoped the baby would never be born.'

I looked over at Bethany. She had her eyes closed.

'And it wasn't,' I said, still looking at Bethany. 'She miscarried and that was that. One minute we were a family, the next we were just three people sharing a house, each of us blaming the others.'

Ferne put her hand on my arm, then her hand in mine. We stayed like that for a long time.

'Are you going to see him?' she said after a while.

'I want to, but . . . today I went to see Bethany's father. He told me to fuck off. To never go to his house again. He has kids now. A new family. Maybe my dad's the same. Maybe I'll turn up and he'll tell me to get lost, that it's just been too long.'

'He's your dad, Joe. He'll understand.'

'What if he doesn't?'

She stubbed out her cigarette, and drained the last of her wine.

'Let's go, okay? We can talk in the car.'

With Jodrell Bank behind us we got in the car and drove back to town. We listened to the Top 40 on Radio One as the fields roiled alongside the car. When she said, 'Did you ever?' I nodded and we did not talk for the remainder of the trip. I imagined the two of us, miles apart, both putting cassettes into ghetto-blasters, pausing the tape and recording the songs that we liked. Her younger than me. Her dealing with the same kind of boredoms and dreams of leaving. What was she like then? What was I like, in that silent house that should have rung with the sound of a baby howling, of a mother feeding her child, of a brother holding his sister in his arms and telling her he'd never let her down, always protect her?

We arrived back at the hotel and parked up in the same space. Ferne stayed there for a while; the radio still going, a song I didn't know by a pair of Russian girls that had, according to the DJ, been a number one.

'I can't imagine what you've been through,' Ferne said, taking her hands from the wheel. 'But if there's anything I can do. Anything at all, you've got to let me know, okay?'

'Thank you,' I said. 'For everything. For today.'

I moved to kiss her and connected with her cheek. She turned to face me.

'But I can't do that,' she said. 'I can feel her here with us now. You know what I mean? It's fucking creepy.'

Bethany was nowhere to be seen.

'I understand,' I said. 'I should never have, well you know. I just wanted. I don't know, something.'

'Joe. I can be here for you, but it can't be like that. Not with all of this stuff just hanging around. I called a friend of mine last night, Sara. I told her about you and she said that nothing good can come of any of this.'

I opened the door.

'I understand,' I said.

'Well, I'm glad you do,' she replied. 'Because I'm struggling here.'

Inside the van it is musty and warm. Bethany lies down on the mattress and Daniel half stands, half crouches. He takes off his T-shirt, his torso is thin and honed, almost hairless. He has a smattering of freckles on his chest and too-small nipples. He lies down next to her and kicks off his boots and socks. He unlaces her Dr Martens and removes them. Bethany thinks of the times her father has told her to take her shoes off when lying on her bed. It makes her laugh a little; perhaps it's the pot. He puts his hands on her stomach.

'What's funny, baby girl?'

'Nothing,' she says. 'And don't call me baby girl.'

He rakes his fingers up her stomach and onto her breasts. He squeezes them and tries to take off the Big Black T-shirt.

'I'm keeping it on, okay?' she says.

They kiss finally, his hands fumbling with her bra, finally unclasping it without her help. He starts then on her jeans, rolling them down her legs. She feels exposed.

She has bought new underwear for Daniel. She did not want to see her bra and think of Mark taking it off, her knickers having once had Mark so close to them. In Ethel Austin, she had felt somehow clandestine, as though anyone would be able to detect her intentions. Still, she had spent a while deliberating before settling on something black and indistinct. He pulls the knickers down without even looking at them, instead looking at where they have so recently been.

She has a small birthmark on the right of her groin. He kisses it. He puts his head between her legs, his tongue is inside her and then his fingers. She feels she should not be surprised, but nonetheless she is. His nails are too long and his stubble scratches at her skin. She will not tell him what to do. With Mark, she had given helpful tutorials. He seemed to have enjoyed them, Bethany's voice explaining what was pleasurable and what was not. It had not taken him long to understand. She understands, as Daniel's tongue plays along her, his fingers moving in and out, that this is not really for her benefit.

*

There are so many things that could have come to mind. The first time he made her come, or the night by the quarry where they talked about their wildest fantasies, or the sex they had on a Sunday morning while her father was out walking. It could have been the post-revision, post-sex conversations, the late-night whispers about their mothers, the increased speculation about her father and Hannah. It could have been any number of telephone calls, or random moments when one had told the other that they loved them. It could have been handing over all that money to the travel agent, the woman dabbing at her fingers as she counted out the notes. It could easily have been them imagining the brownstone in which they would live, the coffee shop they would go to on Sunday mornings and the bars they'd drink dry.

When it comes to it, though, Bethany does not think of anything specific. There is just a dull ache in her stomach; a reminder, like the Sunday evening feeling of not having completed her homework. Daniel is still between her legs, but he might as well be eating ice cream for all the sensation she feels.

She looks up to the roof of the van, the corrugated metal, the dirt that clings there. She knows exactly how she got here, but it still feels utterly alien. She watches his head bob up and down. He does not look up like Mark, checking that what he is doing is right. And it's not that she misses Mark, or that she feels that she is letting him down. It is simply that this is not working for her. When Mark finishes, he always asks her if it was good. Sometimes it irritates her, but mostly she thinks it's sweet.

'Enough. Stop,' she says. He looks up, his mouth moist and his eyes wide. He hitches himself up, unzips his trousers. His cock is straining and silverishly tipped. It revolts her. His smile revolts her.

'No,' she says. 'No. I can't do this. Not here. Not now.'

'Oh come on,' he says. 'I can't stop now.'

She kneels and starts to fumble around for her under-wear. She is in front of him now and he tries to slip a finger inside her from behind. She slaps him away.

'I said no, okay. Just fuck off will you.'

She feels arms around her. He twists her around and throws her down on the mattress. He holds her arms and she kicks her legs, kicks them hard. He is powerful though and uses his thighs to quieten her.

'What's wrong,' he says. 'I don't get it.'

'Get off me, Daniel. Get off me right now, okay?'

She can feel his penis. She can see the burn in his eyes. She closes her eyes. She has been told about this. At school. By her mother. It can happen anywhere, any time. Be vigilant. Be sensible. Do not put yourself at undue risk.

He relaxes his grip, then rolls off her body. He buttons up his jeans and pulls on his T-shirt. Bethany wants to get up, to hit him, to kick him, but she is immobile. He picks up her knickers and bra and offers them to her.

His breaths are shallow. She sees sweat at the corner of his brow, little beads.

'I'm sorry,' he says. 'I didn't mean to . . . if I scared you, then I'm sorry, I didn't mean . . .'

He looks pathetic and lost, nothing like the man in the pub, the lad with his mates. Is it shame? Or is it that he didn't have the bottle to actually do it? Hurriedly she puts on her underwear. He opens the door and jumps down to the ground. From the cab of the van he takes a pre-rolled spliff and lights it.

As Bethany gets out, Daniel apologizes again. She shakes her head.

'I just couldn't, you know? It's . . . I have a boyfriend and I thought I could do this. Wanted to do this, but I just couldn't. It's hard to explain.'

Daniel passes her the spliff and takes a can from a bag on the seat. He pops it open and drinks, then picks up a stone and skims it on the water.

'Had a feeling it were all too good to be true,' he says smiling sadly. 'Still . . .'

She smokes the joint and passes it back. He hands her the can. Her mouth is dry and the lager is cool and refreshing.

'So what now?' he says. 'What are you up to?'

'New York,' she says. 'Mark and I are going to New York.'

'I've never been,' he says. 'One day, you know? I wanna play a gig there before I die. Something small, anything really.'

'I'm sorry,' she says again.

'Don't be,' he says. 'No harm done.'

He takes the can of beer from her and drains it. He crushes the can and throws it into the river. It floats for a time, then sinks.

'I need to get off,' he says looking at his watch. 'You need a lift somewhere?'

Bethany shakes her head. 'I think I'll hang around here for a while. I don't feel like going back, you know? You got a can you can spare?'

He nods and throws her one from the cab. He gets in the driver's side and the engine takes on the third attempt. She waves goodbye. He toots the horn. There is silence. She stands there holding the beer. Around her everything is still. On the breeze she can hear the fairground. She feels relieved, lightheaded; her watch tells her that she has time enough to make it to the pub, perhaps enough to have a drink. But she wants to take stock, to pause for once. Her mother would be proud, she realizes. The relief turns into a sense of freedom, of being let loose. The van is gone, and so is Daniel. She can never return and she has not betrayed anyone, not really. She opens the beer and tries not to think of the moment he was on top of her, but instead the look of contrition that he shot her afterwards. The apology. She is grateful to him. She feels, at last, that she is truly ready to leave.

She takes her cigarettes from her bag and walks down to the river. She sits on the bank and puts her feet in the cool water. She lights a cigarette and closes her eyes. She has an hour or so before she needs to get back. An hour, just for herself.

NINETEEN

The taxi dropped me near what had once been my primary school. More houses, the same poky boxes, spread out over the playground and playing field. Somewhere they must have built new schools more technologically advanced than the shabby places Bethany and I had attended. More houses, more kids, bigger schools; buses to ferry the children there, assemblies of hundreds in their brightly painted school halls.

'When did this stop being the school?' I asked.

'Oh, must be ten year or so, I think,' the cab driver said. 'Long time. Place were falling apart anyway.'

I handed him the fare and watched him pull away. The streets where I'd grown up looked windswept and ill-kempt. I walked past the house with the bushes, as my father used to call it, and saw that they had become as tall as trees and now guarded the small bungalow like a prison wall. It was where I went when my parents went out. A comfortable house that smelled of tea and baking, owned by an older woman called Josie, who made Radio Four a permanent soundtrack until 8 pm when I was permitted to watch television. Josie's husband had died sometime in the seventies and she had made herself a cosy, protected life halfway up a hill in a small suburb of a small suburb.

The bicycle tied to the back gate and the two cars suggested she was no longer there, perhaps retired now to Southwold as she'd always intended. Bracketed to the garage roof was an enormous satellite dish, a baby Jodrell. Every light in the house was burning, tennis balls and other kids' ephemera littered the greasy lawns. Through the window of the kitchen extension, I saw a woman washing dishes. I thought of Ferne and what she'd said about people's lives going on without you. It was the first time I had seriously considered the possibility of my father no longer being at the same address.

The evening was slowly darkening, the clouds bunched and sprayed. On summer nights my father and I would watch the sun go down sitting in deckchairs, neither of us speaking, the rugged fields out the back sticky with cow dung and fronded with nettles. We would read, and occasionally one of us would say that it was beautiful, wasn't it? and the other would agree and then we'd go back to our books, sitting there until it was too dark to make out the text on the page.

As I walked down the hill, the fields were still visible, still just resistant to the march of the housing. The cows had been herded up to the top. To their right was a wooded area that we kids had called Bluebell Forest, a boggy clearing where a rope swing swung on warm evenings. It was the kind of image that people cling to: that summery abandon, the freedom of childhood; but like adolescence, I couldn't imagine wanting to go back. Even as a child it seemed that it was tinged with nostalgia. My father used to say, 'Get your time now, lad, those fields won't be here for ever.' And he believed it with grim inevitability. Seeing them still there was an argument he could not claim to have won.

There was a car in the driveway, a newish model, rust-free and clean. Dad had never had much luck with his cars; he spent more time underneath them than driving them. There had been an oil patch on the paving slabs for years, a remnant of a particularly truculent Vauxhall Cavalier, but the slabs had been replaced by tarmac, smooth and comfortingly grey. The curtains were open in the front room of the bungalow, a television light visible, the outside barge boards now painted red. It was only the garden that made it clear that Dad was still around. If he'd had bad luck with cars, it went double with plants. Dad had never managed to get anything to flourish, or even grow. The beds of the small lawn were lined with withered stumps, dying buds, falling flowers: the grass patchy and erratically mowed.

Are you going to do it, then? Really? Bethany said, sitting on the boot of the car. *Are you man enough?* She laughed. *What would Ferne say you should do, eh? You seem to listen to her little pearls of wisdom.*

The garage was joined to next door's: Dad's painted the new red, theirs green. I stood at the front door, the whorls in the glass distorting the hallway. I rang the doorbell and took a step backwards. I did not want to hear, 'I'll get it,' nor the sound of children or a woman's voice. It needed to be as though I had never taken the taxi, had never put my bag in the boot and headed to the airport without even saying goodbye.

The door opened. Dad had got fat, his face full, his torso three plump tubes inside a too-tight shirt. He was wearing his glasses and his hair had almost all gone.

'Yes?' he said.

'Oh, tell me you recognize me. Please.'

He took off his glasses and closed his eyes. He opened them and replaced the spectacles.

'You'd better come in,' he said.

*

The L-shaped lounge had been redecorated. There was still wallpaper – Dad was fastidious about wallpaper – but it was muted; the old sofa with the fleur-de-lis pattern replaced by something in dark fawn with thick cushions.

The carpet was deep and there was a glass coffee table and a massive television alongside two floor-standing speakers. He pointed for me to sit, but he remained standing. He was wearing slippers that had seen better days.

My father put his hands on the chimney breast and then leant his head against it. He'd done the same thing when my mother had left. Then he had been crying, but he didn't look like he was crying now. More like he was steeling himself.

'I knew it,' he said, calmly. 'I knew this would happen. You spend all that time thinking about it, but then the time comes . . .'

He turned to face me. He looked blank.

'Well, aren't you going to say something?'

I looked at him and half got up. He took a pace backwards. I sat back down and he shook his head.

'No. Thought not.'

He went through the dining area into the small kitchen and came back with two cans of beer. He put one in front of me.

'Thank you,' I said.

'So it does speak! After thirteen years I was beginning to bloody wonder.'

He opened his can and took a long pull on it. McEwan's Export, same as always.

'You've done the place up nicely—'

'Don't you speak. Don't you dare speak to me. "Done the place up nicely"? What the bloody hell are you talking about, boy? Couldn't you have written? Couldn't you have called?'

I made to answer, but he cut me off.

'I told you, don't you speak. Don't you say a bloody word.'

He put his can down on the coffee table. On the mantelpiece was a framed photograph of the two of us, him in a party hat and a seventeen-year-old Mark wearing a sulky smile. He picked it up and passed it to me.

'You know that's the only photograph of us?' he said. 'I know. I've been all over this house trying to find one. I even wrote to your mother. Called her too. She couldn't find any either. Just that one photograph to prove that you were ever here. Of all the things to do, of it all, to burn everything you couldn't carry? That was the thing that cut me. That was the thing I kept thinking about. To burn it all in the garden, every last thing. You heartless bastard. You unfeeling, uncaring bastard.'

I hadn't thought about the burning for a long time. I had been meticulous about it, filled up Dad's barbecue with everything not in my suitcase and covered it in lighter fuel. I'd thrown on a box of matches and lit the corner, the matches inside suddenly catching. It was something I used to do as a child. We used to call it a genie.

I'd watched everything turn to ash and flame; posters, cassettes, photos. It had looked spectacular against the night sky. I'd warmed my hands on the flames, imagining it was my own cremation.

'I was grieving,' I said. 'I didn't know what I was doing.'

'Grieving? To grieve you have to care, Mark! To grieve you need to feel something for someone else and you never cared for anyone but yourself. For what affected *you*. Your mum and I hoped you'd change, but we knew. We knew really. When I told her you'd gone, she wasn't surprised. She even said, "Perhaps it's for the best, all things considered." Do you have any idea how much a mother has to be broken to say that: to give up on her only son? You don't understand. You never did. These days they'd give you a fancy bloody name, but to me you're just cold. Cold and vacant and heartless. And now you're back.'

'I shouldn't have come,' I said. 'I'm sorry, I should have—'

'What you should and shouldn't have done doesn't matter now,' he said, still standing by the fake gas fire. 'You can't fix it, even if you were capable of such a thing, which you aren't. You're a spoiler. You broke down my marriage; you destroyed everything. And then you left. Just like that. Just like your work here was done. Did you ever think of me? Did you ever once consider what this was doing to me?'

'I was angry. What you said about Bethany, about how things weren't what I thought—'

He laughed dismissively.

'I was protecting *her*, not you, Mark. Mike came to me and said he was concerned about you and her. That she was throwing her life away on the dreams you were filling her head with. That girl! That beautiful girl! We could all see what was going to happen. We all knew it. You'd do for her what you always did for everyone. Part of me thinks she had a lucky escape dying when she did. I mean it. I honestly fucking mean it.'

Bethany sat at the head of the dining table dressed in her carnival-queen outfit, her make-up smudged with tears. *Don't listen to him, honey, he's just angry. He doesn't mean those things. Honestly, he doesn't mean them.*

'Don't talk about Bethany that way,' I said quietly. 'You don't know anything about it.'

'Really,' he said. 'Really?'

He picked up his can and sat down in the armchair. His face was red and small, patches of sweat had crept beneath the armpits of his shirt. I could hear the clock ticking in the hallway, a grandmother clock that he wound each night before bed.

'You're angry,' I said. 'You don't mean what you say. I understand that.'

'You understand nothing, Mark. You only see what you want to see.'

'I've changed,' I said. 'That's why I'm here.'

Is it? Bethany said. *I thought this was about me. About what happened.*

'I've been having, I don't know . . . episodes. I can't stop thinking about what happened. About leaving you here, about Bethany, about everything. It's like it's consuming me. Taking more of me every day.'

He shifted in his seat, his breath and body odour close and pungent.

'Welcome to my life, Mark. Welcome to every day for the last thirteen years. This is what it feels like to feel. And if it hurts, then so much the better.' He smiled. 'You think I'm joking? I'm not. I want you to understand the bloody dread of it all. They say that you only take your troubles with you when you run away, but I bet you didn't. I bet you just started out like nothing had ever happened. Scorched earth in the past, green pastures in the future. Even as a child you were like that. You say I don't know about you and Bethany? I know that you told her your mother was dead and that's why you never spoke about her. I know that you bought her books about New York and told her all the great things you'd do. That you'd go there and then stay, live in a small apartment and read books and live the lives you'd always dreamed of and—'

'They were just dreams,' I said. 'Fantasies. All teen-agers have them.'

'Except they never were fantasies for you, were they? You believed them all. And you went and lived them. And sod the consequences.'

He's jealous, honey, he's jealous and angry and sad. Bethany's tears lined her face, she looked clownish, bedraggled.

'I'm sorry,' I said. 'I did what I needed to do. What I thought was right.'

He started to cry, his body heaved and his fat pumped and his spectacles fell to the floor. I got up and went to him, placed a tentative arm on his shoulders. His arms extended and he grabbed me. He held me for a long time, his tears dampening my jacket.

'Oh my boy,' he kept saying, 'oh my boy, what did you do?'

*

We went outside to smoke. We sat on a picnic bench underneath a faded parasol, both on to our second beer. It was warm still and the light was dim and orange.

'Don't think I didn't mean what I said,' he told me as he flicked ash into a plant pot. 'I won't take it back.'

He loves you. He always loved you. You just saved all your love for me. You didn't have enough to share around. Things are different now, aren't they, honey? Aren't they?

Bethany was wearing the clothes she was wearing when she was found. There was mud on her jeans, bite-size rips on her calves. Her hair was a mess.

'I can't take anything back either.'

And neither would you want to, right? Who'd want to be stuck here? Who'd want that for a future?

'But you came back.'

'Tell me,' I said. 'Tell me about you.'

He looked at me quizzically and stubbed out his smoke.

'What's to tell, Mark? Years slip by, the days get easier. I retired two years ago. Early. I play some golf, go up to Ringway every now and again. See old work friends. There's a woman I know. Nothing serious.'

He smiled. It exposed his crooked teeth and a green-grey tongue.

'Not much for thirteen years,' he said and shook his head, smoke wreathing his fingers.

'You don't have kids, do you?' he said. 'Please tell me you don't have kids.'

'No. No kids.'

'Wife?'

'No.'

'Girlfriend?'

'No.'

'Gay?'

'No.'

He looked relieved, then partly ashamed.

'And you've been in New York all this time?'

'Mostly. I've been in Las Vegas the last six months, selling apartments.'

'Estate agent, eh? Might have preferred it if you were gay.'

He laughed and swigged down his beer, picked up his can and went back inside for more. In the distance there was the mazy sound of a tractor. Time felt oddly out of rhythm, bits of different years tessellating. The bench belonged to now, the sky to the summers we spent reading, the barbed-wire fence to childhood, the beer and the cigarettes to all points in between. Dad returned with two cans and sat back down.

'What do they call you now?' he said. 'I looked up the easiest way to get papers. If you're not married then . . .'

'They call me Joe. Joe Novak.'

'Sounds like a no-nonsense cop to me.' He opened his beer and held it up.

'Nice to meet you, Joe Novak.'

*

It got dark quickly and we ran out of conversation. We had exhausted old comedy routines, exhausted the little we were prepared to reveal about our lives, exhausted each other. I told him all about O'Neil and Edith and we sat in silence for a short time.

'I went to see Mike,' I said eventually. 'I went round this morning.'

He looked up from his drink, his face carrying all that extra weight.

'Pleased to see you, was he?'

'He told me to fuck off.'

'Let's go inside,' he said. 'It's getting cold.'

We sat at the dining table, the bookcases stacked with hardback books, the military history he had always read. There was a picture of my mother there too, when she was younger, her hair big and her dress short.

'I don't see Mike any more,' he said. 'Did you meet his wife? No of course not, you'd have mentioned it if you had.'

'He's got two kids, he said.'

'Five and three. Both girls.'

'Did you ever—'

'Don't be bloody stupid. At my age? I don't know where he finds the energy. I really don't.'

Something flashed before me for a second. Bethany was standing behind my father. She had her hands on his

282

shoulders. *Don't ask*, she said. *This is bad. I know this is bad. Don't ask. It'll be better that way.*

'You said something . . . what did you mean, you said something like I'd have mentioned his wife.'

'Oh, come on, soft lad, do I need to spell it out?'

'Oh, I see,' I said.

'It can't be much of a shock. We all suspected it. Even me.'

'I don't know, I just sort of thought it was rumours, you know. Bethany joked about it, but . . .'

'Been married about eight years or so now, I'd say. I wasn't invited.'

I had always known. That's why I joked about it. It had to be a joke; it couldn't be real. If I made light of it then they couldn't be.

'It explains a lot.'

'It explains nothing,' Dad said. 'Look I'm going to have to get to bed. It's late. You have somewhere to stay? You can stay here if you want, but . . .'

'I'm staying at the Coach House.'

He nodded. I stood and he grabbed me again. We embraced, but all I could think about was Hannah. Dad held me like I might never see him again, then when he released me we were back to the same two people, the same strangers in a room both of the past and of the present. I kissed him on the cheek.

'Thanks.'

'I can't ever forgive you, you know that.'

'I know.'

I walked to the door. I opened it and he called out.

'You still follow the football?'

'Sometimes,' I said. 'When I can.'

'Still Red?'

'Still Red.'

'Good lad,' he said and waved goodbye. I waved too and closed the door.

*

I decided to walk back to the hotel, Bethany shuffling alongside. *He had no right,* she said, *to say those things. I know why you said your mother was dead. I knew what I was doing, I wasn't an idiot. The arrogance of that man! You didn't persuade me to do anything, you didn't force dreams onto me; they were my decision and my decisions alone.*

He could have been right. I haven't thought about it for so long, maybe he's telling the truth. He seemed so certain.

He would, though, wouldn't he? He's spent years chewing it over, stewing in it all. Fuck what he thinks; he was never there for you anyway. Not like I was.

I never gave him the chance. And wouldn't you have

been angry if I'd have told you how I reacted with the baby? How I ruined everything for them?

An eleven-year-old does not break up a marriage, honey. Even you must realize that. You're the easiest to blame. The one who's not around to take account. He knows he's wrong.

I can't believe it about Hannah and your dad.

Yes, you can. Of course you can. We never trusted her, did we?

She was our friend.

But now she's married to my father, what kind of friend is that?

One who's alone and frightened.

Are you excusing her?

Has she done anything wrong?

Bethany stopped by the gates of a small paper factory that had been there for as long as I had been alive. She kicked at an errant piece of cardboard and sat down by the railings.

Honey, I don't know. I don't know anything any more. I blame myself for dragging you back.

I made the decision: not you. I should have expected all this.

But you didn't, she said, getting up and dusting herself off, though she was still dirty all up her back and down her arms. *You're as lost now as you ever were.*

'What do you want from me!' I shouted, the words echoing down the road. I put my head in my hands and squatted down. 'Just leave me alone, okay? I need to do this by myself. Just please, please, leave me alone.'

A man was walking his dog, a dirty-coated collie. He was smoking a thin cigar and watching me with his weasel face. He threw a stick for the dog and kept his eyes on me.

'What are you looking at?' I said. 'Fuck off.'

He increased his speed and looked back over his shoulder once with hurried, angry eyes. 'That's it, fuck off,' I shouted as they disappeared into the gloom.

It took over half an hour to get back to the Coach, the town listless and quiet. It was past eleven and the pubs were shut. I decided to walk past Mike and Hannah's home and was surprised to see the living-room lights still on and the shape of two people arguing. Hannah came to the window to draw the curtains and I saw her for a moment, illuminated. She seemed wiry, her hair closely cropped to her head, her lips still in that cupid's bow that so many had found attractive. She pulled the curtains with irritated tugs. I ducked behind the wall of the church to make sure she couldn't see me. Then she was gone.

I sat there for some time. It seemed unlikely that I would get to speak to her now. *So?* Bethany said. *What happens now?*

Down the road and through the town she kept on with

her questioning. *Answer me. What are you going to do? What happens next? Are you going back to O'Neil? Are you going back to New York? Tell me, what the hell are you going to do with yourself?*

O'Neil had asked the same question when my papers had come through. He was concerned about me, about my plans.

'Son, you've got to have a plan. This is America. People have plans. They don't have a plan, how they going to see it fail?' He'd smiled about that, but he was deadly serious.

'I'm going to make a shit load of money, then spend it,' I said. It was what he wanted to hear.

'I'll help you with that, Josef Novak,' he said. 'Believe me, you've got a friend for life.'

*

He picked up on the fourth ring. I had no idea what time it was there, or whether he was alone or with Edith.

'It's me,' I said.

'Thank God. Jesus, son, you've had me fucking all ends up here. Where the hell are you?'

'Home,' I said. 'Been here a little while.'

'We almost called the cops, you know. You know that, you dumb fuck? Why didn't you tell me what was going on?'

'I just needed to get away, sort some things out.'

'After you knocked out Brooks, you mean? You know what we've been through with that cock-sucker? We sorted it out, though. You don't have to worry, it's all sorted out. Taken care of.'

'He's not swimming with the fishes, is he?'

'Don't fuck with me, Joe, it was serious. We had to get Mac involved. I smoothed it over with him, but I don't think you should show your face for a while. Maybe it's best that you took a holiday.'

'I saw my dad.'

There was a buzzing silence on the line. I heard him switch the phone to his other ear.

'Was it okay?'

'I don't know. I really don't know.'

There was a noise in the background, the play of sheets over a body.

'So what you going to do now. You staying for a while?'

'There's nothing for me here.' It sounded like a lie.

'You need help? Money, whatever?'

'No, I'm good. Just need some time, that's all.'

'You want me to come over? I will you know. I'll get the next flight.'

I smiled.

'No. You stay where you are, I'll be back soon enough.'

'You know I'm here, right. You know where I am.'

'I know, O'Neil.'

'And I want you to call me every day. Doesn't matter when, okay?'

I reached for the cigarettes and lit one.

'Why do you care, O'Neil?' I said. 'Why do you care so much about me? Why is it that you see me so differently?'

'What's this shit? You high or something? I don't have to answer that.'

'I'm interested. It's just something my father said earlier on.'

'Why do I care?' he said after a time. 'I care because sometimes two people need each other at a point in time, and if you find that person, you'd best take care of them.'

'Like you and Edith?'

There was a long silence.

'Yeah, Joe, like me and Edith.'

*

I called room service just before midnight and ordered a hamburger and fries and a bottle of red wine. I took a bath and washed my hair. Bethany looked more bruised, sitting in the easy chair flicking through my notes. I looked at my suitcase.

You're giving up, Bethany said, *just when you're so close?*

There's nothing to see, nothing more to find out, Beth. You're dead. He's dead. Nothing's changed.

You need to see Hannah. You need to talk to her.

She isn't going to talk to me. Why would she? I've done what I need to do, I've done what I came here for. Can't I just go now?

Just go and see her. You can scope out the place like in those shitty movies you used to watch with O'Neil. You can play detective. She stood and took a step towards me. There was a knock at the door.

Go eat. You need the energy.

I got the tray and poured the wine. The burger was surprisingly good. I'd had a couple of mouthfuls when the door went again. It was Ferne. She looked a little drunk, her hair up and her sloppy Joe clothes on.

'I heard the trolley. Was hoping you had some wine.'

I nodded and let her in. She had been crying and had spilled something on the front of her T-shirt. Her toenails were painted and her sweatpants hung low on her hips. She sat on the easy chair and I offered her a glass of wine and a bite of the burger. She took both, cheese and sauce bunching at the corner of her mouth.

'I called my ex,' she said eventually. 'I haven't done that in months. He's seeing someone else. He thought I knew. A friend of mine saw them together about a month ago and he assumed that she'd told me. I don't know her. I don't know if that's better or worse.'

'I'm sorry,' I said. 'I really am.'

We stayed like that, quietly drinking and smoking. I wanted to tell her about my dad, but it was already late and the thought of us talking long into the night made me nauseous. I looked at the clock on the television.

'I know it's late,' Ferne said, 'but I'm not sleepy. Not at all. Can we just watch television for a while? Just for an hour or so. You don't have to talk if you don't want to.'

I handed her the remote and we both lay on the bed. She flicked through the channels until she came to an old movie O'Neil and I had watched once on cable. She propped the pillows behind her. 'Jane Fonda is incredible in this film. I saw it at college for a course I was on. I wanted to be her so much.'

By the time the dance marathon MC told us that it just keeps going, no one ever knowing when it will ever end, Ferne was asleep on my arm, her shallow breaths on my shoulder. I kissed her on the forehead and then on the cheek. On and on it goes, the man said, when will it ever end?

Bethany feels him approaching at the very last moment before he grabs her by the hair. He has her caught with her neck turned slightly. She can see his face. He is a normal-looking man in a jumper and jeans and dirty trainers. She doesn't know him. He drags her up the bank by her hair, cursing and muttering to himself. She catches the odd word – bitch, slag, whore – and then he punches her with his right fist. Her feet are cold from the water. She cannot feel them. She is numb. He kneels on her arms and she tries to thrash away from under him, but he punches her again and then she really can feel nothing at all. She is half awake, looking at the sky. She does not feel him enter her. She does not feel the punches alternating with the thrusts. She does not hear him call her those names. She feels nothing. Bethany feels nothing at all.

In the sky she sees clouds from above, the view from an aeroplane cabin window. She is slightly drunk and the clouds are below her and they are descending. Mark is beside her and they are both craning to see their first glimpse of New York City. They see Liberty, swathed in scaffolding, her lamp covered and her gold shrouded. They see the skyline and the pilot says that they need to buckle up. They land perfectly. The captain welcomes them to America. Outside there is heat haze on the runways, the sky blue and smoggy. Mark and Bethany kiss for a long time and take their bags from the overhead lockers when almost everyone has disembarked. They kiss again as they queue through immigration.

In the sky she sees the clouds from below, looking out of a car window. They are in a yellow cab and they are driving across Newark to The Knight's Inn Motel. The traffic is slow and it takes a time to get there. It is perfect. It is God's own American motel. They check in and the man behind the counter asks them if they have quarters for the television and Bethany changes a ten-dollar bill into shiny coins from a roll. The room is cool and smells of lighter fluid. It is perfect. They flick through the channels, eventually falling asleep while watching a base-ball game. When they wake they will have pancakes and sausage and proper coffee.

In the sky she sees the clouds so close she can touch them. They are at the top of the Empire State Building looking out over Manhattan Island. The buildings are bigger than they'd both expected, yet after a few minutes they seem to settle. Looking down they see the gridline and the traffic, the stink and hunger of the place. They hold each other, amazed that this has happened, that this is happening.

In the sky, she sees a darkening, the neon lights of Times Square. It is as dirty and corrupt as she had ever hoped. She tells Mark she loves him.

In the sky it is getting hard to see anything at all. They are walking on the Bowery. They have a drink at CBGBs and tell each other jokes. There's a joke she remembers from school, she tells it to Mark: there's a little girl lost in the woods. She's petrified of wolves and all those other creatures. Then she sees a little cottage. She knocks on the door. An old man answers. She tells him that she has lost her parents and she is cold and alone and scared. The man opens the door fully. He unzips his fly. 'Well, I guess today isn't your lucky day, is it?' Mark does not laugh, but she does. He tells her that he thinks the joke is sick.

In the sky she can see nothing. She is on the Brooklyn Bridge, she knows that. She can't see anything, but she can feel the wind and the sound of the East River below her. Bethany's hand is in Mark's. They are standing still.

'Is this where we say goodbye?' she says.

Mark is crying. She can no longer feel his hand. She calls for him, but she can no longer hear what he is saying, just the rush of the East River and the sound of the wind.

The man picks up a rock and hits her hard on the

temple. He smears his mess on her now exposed breasts. He lies next to her, looking up at the same sky. He waits for them to come. He knows that they will. He looks at Bethany and holds her in his arms. He has her blood on his face.

The man is still holding her when they find them. He is rocking her back and forth, saying over and over: 'What have I done? What have I done?'

TWENTY-ONE

Ferne had gone by the time I woke. She'd left a note on the dresser apologizing for falling asleep. She had attractive handwriting, the kind that looks better in ink, but still retains a flourish when using a biro. For a moment I had a stark image of waking late to find a note like that on the fridge, a magnet holding it in place. 'Gone to the gym, back in an hour', two kisses below.

Give the girl a break, Bethany said. *You've not even fucked her yet.*

You have a delightful way with words.

It's the truth, honey. You know it and so does the whole world. She smiled weakly and pointed at the notes. *So, detective, are we heading out?*

No. I need. No.

He'll be out all day. You know that. At least you'll have tried. Isn't that what you want?

I want some coffee, is what I want. And then I want to be out of here. Out of this place. It's driving me crazy.

And it's this place that's sending you crazy? Nice theory.

It's mine and I'm sticking to it.

Fine. Have your coffee. You just need to make a move. Sooner you see her, sooner you can go. Unless . . .

What?

You know.

As you so eloquently put it, we haven't even fucked yet.

Drink your coffee. Then we can go and play sleuth.

Did you ever love me?

What kind of a question is that?

I slammed the door to the bathroom and showered. I couldn't remember a time when I'd fantasized about something real and tangible: usually my mind wandered over all kinds of different subjects and positions, situations and sensations; but the previous night's glimpse of Ferne's pubic hair, her breasts against my chest, was enough. I washed myself thoroughly, then sat at the desk and looked at the notebook. I started at the front and ripped out every page, every last line of Joe Novak's life, then put them in the wastepaper bin. It did not feel cathartic, simply destructive. I could have burnt the pages too, but that would only have set off the fire alarms. It was not that kind of symbolic gesture; it was just a whim.

In the restaurant, I read a newspaper properly for the first time in many years, endless pages devoted to the Iraq

War. I looked at the detailed maps and graphics, the photos of the military and the dusty desert backdrop. Four days it had been going on. I flicked to the sports pages. Liverpool had beaten Leeds. I read the match report having little idea who any of the players were.

'Excuse me, sir.' A man I'd not seen before stood beside me dressed in the hotel uniform.

'Sorry to interrupt your breakfast, sir, but you have a telephone message.' He passed me a folded piece of paper.

'Thanks,' I said. 'When—'

'About ten minutes ago.'

I opened out the note. It said: '12.30. Horse and Groom. I'll be out the back. Hannah.'

*

In the beer garden, two children were playing on a brightly painted milk float. One turned the wheel as the other stood on the back, pretending to give out milk to customers. Hannah was sitting at a nearby picnic bench. She had a cup of coffee steaming in front of her and was checking her make-up in a mirror. I sat down and she continued looking in the compact then snapped it shut.

Her clothes were well cut, her jewellery expensive yet subtle. She wore a wedding and an engagement ring. They were similarly subtle.

'You got the message, then,' she said not quite looking

at me. 'For someone who's disappeared for so long, you were pretty easy to track down.'

'Yes. Thank you. Mike said that—'

'Mike doesn't know I'm here,' she said and sipped at her coffee. She looked over her shoulder at the girls and was about to shout something to them, then looked away.

'Are they yours?'

'One of them. The other's a friend's. The eldest is at school.'

I nodded. We sat there in silence.

'You haven't changed,' I said. 'You look just the same.'

'You have,' she said. 'It's to be expected, I suppose.'

I went to touch her hand. We should have hugged. We should have been relieved to see each other. It should have been more of a reunion.

'Why did you have to come back, Mark?' she said eventually. 'Why didn't you just leave it?'

She seemed almost reasonable, resigned almost. Bethany was sitting next to her. She said nothing.

'Because it was the right time,' I said eventually.

'For you, you mean? You left me, remember? You left me all on my own. You never even said goodbye.'

'I wanted to, but . . .'

She shook her head and smiled. 'Yes, I'm sure you wanted to. Wanting to isn't the same. Wanting to didn't help me much, I can tell you.'

'You had Mike.'

'Fuck you, Mark. I had Mike? You have any idea how it was after you left? Do you have any clue?'

'I can imagine.'

'That's all you were ever good for,' she said and shook her head. The children were screaming and she told them to quieten down. I asked her if she wanted another drink, but she ignored me. I got up and went inside, ordered a coffee.

She was still there when I got back, checking messages on her phone. The kids ran towards her and she pointed to the slides at the far edge of the beer garden. They trooped off, their Wellington boots gummy and bright.

'How was New York after all?' she asked. 'Everything you ever dreamed of?'

She didn't wait for a reply.

'We went before the kids were born. Every road I walked down I thought I saw you. Every restaurant we ate in, all I could think was that you would be there. Mike just looked around saying that Bethany would have loved it here. He couldn't help it. At the top of the Empire State he cried. At the foot of the Statue of Liberty he left her a flower. I had to watch him go through that. It burned me to see it.'

'Dad said he blames me. For New York, for all of that.'

'Mike doesn't know who to blame.'

She blew on her coffee and looked at my cigarettes. 'Can I sneak a drag?' she said. 'It's been years, but I still miss them.'

I lit one and passed it to her. She took a long suck on the filter then passed it back. She had grown into a sophisticated-looking woman, well-heeled, well-spoken. She wore her make-up well and she carried none of the nervous energy she'd had as a teenager.

'Did you know?' she said. 'About Mike and me?'

I nodded. Bethany looked away, over towards the kids.

'Bethany suspected. It was the way you clammed up when he was mentioned, or something.'

She faltered: 'Hold me, Mark. Please hold me.'

She sobbed against me. 'It's all my fault,' she said. 'All my fault.'

*

Bethany and I sat at our usual bench beside the jukebox; Hannah was feeding ten-pence pieces into the slot. The Coach was empty, it was late and the regulars had gone. While she punched numbers into the keypad, I took out a guidebook I'd bought that morning and set it down on the table. We'd just reserved the airline tickets and all I wanted to do was plan.

'I was thinking we should book somewhere for our first night,' I said, flicking to the hotels section.

'What you should do is get a cab straight to Manhattan,' Hannah said, turning away from the umber glow of the jukebox. 'Then stay at somewhere really opulent and glamorous. Y'know, pretend that you're rich, uptown sophisticates, just breezing through to paint the town red.'

She was sick of the talk, she'd made it quite clear, but that had just made it all the more fun. We had, at one point, invited her along; but she saw the hope in our eyes that she'd say no. No doubt, she also saw the possibilities.

The jukebox clunked and Bethany lit a cigarette. 'That's such a cliché,' she said.

'I was just saying what I'd do,' Hannah said as she came back. 'You two do what you want.'

'What I meant to say,' Bethany said, by way of apology, 'is that everyone just goes straight to Manhattan. And the first time they see the place, they're all tired and jet-lagged.'

'We should get ourselves a cheap place. You know, a proper motel,' I said.

'Like I said, knock yourselves out.'

My idea of a proper motel was one plucked straight from the road-movies and television shows we loved. Roaches on the walls, odd stains on the carpeting, a coin meter on the side of the television, thin plasterboard walls that shivered under strong winds. The kind of place alcoholics go to die, or swindlers rendezvous to count their bounty. So the three of us pored over the budget brochures and tried to find the perfect place. Eventually I hit upon The Knight's Inn, a mile from Newark Airport. Bethany read the description and looked at the photo.

'It's God's own American motel,' I said.

'It looks weird,' Bethany said. 'And dangerous.'

I sniffed and finished my drink. 'Don't be stupid. It's perfect, isn't it, Hannah?'

'It looks really authentic,' she said. The motel was a squared-off 'C' with fifteen rooms on each side. It was set on stilts – you parked your car under your room – and was exactly what I'd wanted. Bethany lit a cigarette and looked out of the window. It was raining again.

'And you've got to say it looks cool, doesn't it?' I said.

Hannah looked straight at me and then shook her head.

'You poor deluded creature,' she muttered. 'It's a shit house. You'll be dead or have AIDS in minutes.'

I went to get more drinks and Hannah joined me at the bar.

'You need to live in the real world. You know that?'

'It's just a holiday, Han.'

'You should try and remember that sometimes. Seriously.'

I looked at her then, expecting her to be laughing, shooting the breeze. But all I saw was the first of several goodbyes. She was the one who wanted to escape the most: she had something that was tenable, not couched in dreams and late-night what-ifs. At that moment, did she think that she'd end up with what she wanted? That Bethany would be out of the picture and all these childish things would be behind us? She was always more practical, more real, than either of us.

'Frankly I'll be glad when you're both gone,' she said eventually.

*

One of the kids had fallen over and was crying; the other was shouting, 'Mummy!' at the top of her voice. Hannah ran to them. Bethany and I stayed where we were. The girl had a scuffed knee and Hannah brought the two of them to join us at the table. Hannah hugged the injured child close to her and told her it was okay, that she was fine and she should probably go and apologize to the slide. Hannah's child, Bethany's sister, sat beside me. Bethany wandered off, kicking at the turf.

'Who are you?' the child said.

'I'm a friend of your mummy,' I said.

'Like Aunty Beck?'

'A bit, yes.'

'What's your name?'

'Joe.' It was instant. I couldn't take it back.

'My name is Molly.'

'Nice to meet you, Molly.'

'Do you know my daddy too?'

'Yes, I know your daddy.'

Bethany was nowhere to be found.

'Do you know this song? "There's a story in our town",' I sang.

'"Of the prettiest girl around",' she sang back. 'That's what Daddy sings when we can't sleep.'

The other child quietened and Hannah looked over at Molly and me. 'Molls, take Sara over to the swings, please.'

'I want to stay with Joe.'

'Well, Joe and I need to talk. So do as Mummy says, okay?'

Hannah and I were alone again.

'She's gorgeous,' I said.

'None of your own, I take it.'

'No.'

'They change you,' she said. 'But not enough.'

Bethany was back, suddenly. She wouldn't look me in the eye.

*

Bethany had always said that she wanted kids one day. It was at odds with everything else she used to talk about.

She said she wanted to feel the same way her mother had, the way her father used to talk to her as though she was the only person on earth.

'When I fell pregnant the first time, I had the most incredible pains,' Hannah said. 'Even the midwives said that I had it worse than most. I used to think it was retribution. Karma or something' – she waved her hand – 'just bad luck, I suppose. When Ada arrived, I was beyond myself, but all I saw was Bethany. That was all. I looked down at my baby and I saw her face. Mike couldn't see it, thankfully, but I could. Every time I fed her, every time I changed her, it was Beth looking back.'

She finished her coffee and asked for a cigarette. I passed her the pack.

'You really didn't know, did you?' she said as she was lighting the cigarette. 'You really had no idea?'

'I told you,' I said. 'We both knew.'

'Not about that,' she said. 'About Beth.'

Bethany had been standing by the kids but stopped and straightened up. She sat next to Hannah, cross-legged, and shaking her head. Hannah lit her cigarette and smiled. She knew what she was doing, and there was a sort of relish to it. Retribution. Bethany kept her eyes on her. I couldn't work out whether she was asking her to stop, or giving her permission to continue. Bethany seemed to have lost the ability to speak.

'She wasn't going to New York, Mark,' she said. 'You knew that really, didn't you? You knew that she loved you, but you were unnerving her. You were there all the time, like you were trying to actually *be* her. To live her life *for* her. Mike had cancelled her ticket. He booked us tickets to go away, me and Beth, for a holiday.'

I smiled, thin-lipped, there was a howling wind, there was Bethany Wilder, still avoiding my gaze.

'Look, Hannah, whatever Mike has said to you—'

'This isn't about my husband, Mark, this is about *Beth*. Don't you remember? You'd made everything so difficult. All that talk! All she wanted to do was go to university. Have a normal life. Kids. And all you wanted was for her to do what you wanted. Your stupid bloody dreams of leaving.'

The kids were shrieking and Hannah looked around to check on them. Bethany was standing next to them. The pale pastel colours of their clothes made them look almost edible.

'This *was* what you're here for, right. The truth?'

Bethany stood. She didn't say anything.

*

The Brooklyn Bridge is cold and the wind chills. I look over to Manhattan, tourists streaming past me. I'm wearing a warm coat with a fur collar that I've borrowed from

O'Neil. I have the baggie in my hand, the last remaining things of Bethany Wilder. Of us together. Horns honk, and the wind fingers my hair. I open the baggie and send the ashes down onto the East River. They float on the air. They disappear too quickly, catching on the breeze.

*

The two children came running back. They wanted Coca-Cola. I went inside to get them the drinks. Bethany was sitting on a bar stool.

So you know.

I ordered the Cokes and a whisky for myself. I drank the whisky.

I always loved you, Bethany Wilder.

And now that you know? Now that you've got the truth?

I think the truth is whatever you make it.

Bethany smiled. *That's what you always thought, not me.*

I took the Cokes outside, but the kids and Hannah were gone. I threw the still-full cans in the bin and sat down at the picnic table. I stayed there for a long time, but they did not come back. Bethany did not follow me out from the bar, and she was not in there when I ordered another drink.

*

There was a wedding at the Coach; pale linen draping the steps, the fabric held in place by lumps of coal. I passed a man in a kilt and a couple of women wearing hats. They were drunk though it was no later than three. I went to my room and sat on the edge of my bed, picked the ripped notebook pages from the waste bin. They came out in a random order, like a puzzle. It took me hours to put them right, and then I read again what I had written. I read it three times, then put a call through to reception. They said that they were very busy.

I went out into the town. There were a lot of school children in blazers. I saw myself and Hannah and Bethany, cigarettes burning in our hands and no idea of what was to come. I went into the newsagent's and bought an ink pen and a new notebook. I imagined my father browsing the racks, Hannah telling her kids that they couldn't have the magazines they were waving in her face.

The hotel bar was too busy so I bought some wine from the off-licence up the road and carried it back to my room. I poured a glass and looked at the empty pages, the pen heavy in my hand. Bethany wasn't by the window, she wasn't in the bath. There was just the notebook, the pen and the bottle of wine.

The page was white and lined and I hovered over it. Eventually, after a long time, I wrote something. 'In moments of crisis, Bethany Wilder always thinks of America. Or more accurately, she thinks of New York City.' I put down the pen and finished my glass of wine. I wrote for several hours straight.

Just after seven there was a loud knock on the door. I looked through the spy hole and opened the door.

'There was a message for me,' Ferne said after I let her in. She looked around the room. 'What's up?'

I looked down at the notebook. 'Nothing,' I said. 'Nothing at all. I'm writing . . . Doing some work.'

'So . . . ?'

Her eyes lifted. I saw Post-it notes held by fridge magnets; her handwriting on them all.

'Let's go out tonight,' I said. 'I mean properly.'

Ferne paused and looked at the desk.

'Okay,' she said. 'Where do you want to go?'

'Anywhere,' I said, 'anywhere at all.'

Acknowledgements

Thank you:

Andrew Kidd for unwavering support. Kate Harvey for sensitive and inspired editing. Nicholas Blake for the copy edit. Sally Riley, Anna Stein, Imogen Pelham and all at Aitken Alexander; Sandra Taylor, Alison Menzies, Paul Baggaley and all at Picador.

William Atkins, Simon Baker, Barbara Baker, Matthew Baker, Gavin Bower, Lee Brackstone, Rebecca Bream, Gareth Evers, Jen Field, Daniel Fordham, Niven Govinden, Guy Griffiths, Aidan Jackson, Helen Knowles, Jude Rogers, Lee Rourke, Victoria Seal, Nikesh Shukla, Oliver Shepherd, Hyun Sook Shin, David Stewart, Sarah Taylor-Wilcox.

My parents – John and Joyce Evers – for love, inspiration and understanding.

Lisa Baker – for green leaves and Light Years.

picador.com

blog
videos
interviews
extracts